14 Nov '92

Dear Samantha,

Since you've refused my calls, please accept this letter. Honey, I'm sorry I came down on you again. You're right, I can be an overbearing ass. It's just...you're so damned trusting. It's one of the reasons I love you, yes. But, sweetheart, I've seen things—life—and I'm not just talking about the war. There's so much I want to spare you, mistakes and pain I'd give anything to help you avoid. But you're right, I can't. It is your life and I don't want to live it for you. I want to live it *with* you. I know there's a balance. Help me find it, Sam. Help me find my way back to us. The air force can't do anything about my orders, I tried. I'm stuck in Alaska for the next year. Please accept this ticket, and visit so we can talk about it, about us. The dates are open-ended. I'll be waiting. For as long as it takes.

Lost without you,

Griff

Dear Reader,

What better way to start off a new year than with six terrific new Silhouette Intimate Moments novels? We've got miniseries galore, starting with Karen Templeton's *Staking His Claim*, part of THE MEN OF MAYES COUNTY. These three brothers are destined to find love, and in this story, hero Cal Logan is also destined to be a father—but first he has to convince heroine Dawn Gardner that in his arms is where she wants to stay.

For a taste of royal romance, check out Valerie Parv's *Operation: Monarch*, part of THE CARRAMER TRUST, crossing over from Silhouette Romance. Policemen more your style? Then check out Maggie Price's *Hidden Agenda*, the latest in her LINE OF DUTY miniseries, set in the Oklahoma City Police Department. Prefer military stories? Don't even try to resist *Irresistible Forces*, Candace Irvin's newest SISTERS IN ARMS novel. We've got a couple of great stand-alone books for you, too. Lauren Nichols returns with a single mom and her protective hero, in *Run to Me*. Finally, Australian sensation Melissa James asks *Can You Forget?* Trust me, this undercover marriage of convenience will stick in your memory long after you've turned the final page.

Enjoy them all—and come back next month for more of the best and most exciting romance reading around, only in Silhouette Intimate Moments.

Yours,

Leslie J. Wainger
Executive Editor

Please address questions and book requests to:
Silhouette Reader Service
U.S.: 3010 Walden Ave., P.O. Box 1325, Buffalo, NY 14269
Canadian: P.O. Box 609, Fort Erie, Ont. L2A 5X3

Irresistible
Forces
CANDACE IRVIN

Silhouette®

INTIMATE MOMENTS™

Published by Silhouette Books

America's Publisher of Contemporary Romance

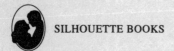

SILHOUETTE BOOKS

ISBN 0-373-27340-1

IRRESISTIBLE FORCES

Copyright © 2004 by Candace Phillips Irvin

This edition published by arrangement with Harlequin Books S.A.

® and TM are trademarks of Harlequin Books S.A., used under license.
Trademarks indicated with ® are registered in the United States Patent
and Trademark Office, the Canadian Trade Marks Office and in other
countries.

Visit Silhouette at www.eHarlequin.com

Printed in U.S.A.

Books by Candace Irvin

Silhouette Intimate Moments

For His Eyes Only #936
In Close Quarters #1078
*Crossing the Line #1179
The Impossible Alliance #1214
*A Dangerous Engagement #1252
*Irresistible Forces #1270

Silhouette Books

In Love and War
"An Unconditional Surrender"

*Sisters in Arms

CANDACE IRVIN

As the daughter of a librarian and a sailor, it's no wonder Candace's two greatest loves are reading and the sea. After spending several exciting years as a U.S. naval officer sailing around the world, she decided it was time to put down roots and give her other love a chance. To her delight, she soon learned that writing romance was as much fun as reading it. A finalist for both the coveted RITA® Award and the Holt Medallion, as well as a two-time *Romantic Times* Reviewers' Choice Award nominee, Candace believes her luckiest moment was the day she married her own dashing hero, a former U.S. Army combat engineer with dimples to die for. The two now reside in the South, happily raising three future heroes and one adorable heroine—who won't be allowed to date until she's forty, at least.

Candace loves to hear from readers. You can e-mail her at candace@candaceirvin.com or snail mail her c/o Silhouette Books, 233 Broadway, Suite 1001, New York, NY 10279.

For Tony Newcomb,
the coolest Special Forces dude ever!

A special thanks to fellow military veteran Cindy Dees
for her awesome help with all things U.S. Air Force.

And as always, my eternal gratitude to CJ Chase
for her vigilant eye and razor pen.

Chapter 1

The truth is rarely pure, and never simple.

—*Oscar Wilde*

The rules of the game were about to change.

United States Air Force Captain Samantha Hall knew it the moment she spied the crisp envelope amid the stack of manila folders she'd grabbed from her overflowing in-box. The envelope wouldn't have given her pause were it not for the tastefully embossed medical insignia in the upper left corner—and the tiny, inked script at the lower edge.

Personal.

That single word was enough to put the fear of God into her. Or at the very least, the fear of man-made medicine.

Why had she decided to bring the files, anyway? She had enough to worry about. She should stuff the letter back into her briefcase and forget about it. In less than two hours their C-130 Air Force transport would be touching down in

Moscow and she'd yet to polish her presentation. A presentation she'd scripted while mourning her boss of four years, no less. If she opened that envelope, she'd have to read the reprimand that was undoubtedly inside. Where would her hard-earned concentration be then?

Damn it, she didn't need this, especially now. Frankly, there were times when dealing with possibilities and conjecture were easier than dealing with reality.

Pretty scary admission for a scientist, Sam.

She frowned. The heck with it. It wasn't as if she'd been able to keep her mind on her work anyway. Sitting in the cargo hold of a C-130 Hercules wasn't conducive to concentration of any kind. The Herc crews were right, the cargo compartment *had* been designed to keep noise in. Even with foam plugs and a set of rabbit ears layered on top, she could still make out the distinctive drone of the Herc's four turboprop engines, muffled though they were. Might as well get it over with. She wouldn't be concentrating on anything until they landed.

Sam flipped the envelope over, slipping her index finger beneath the seal to tear it open. Her hands shook as she retrieved the sheet of paper within. She took a deep breath and unfolded the sheet, quickly skimming the Kirtland Hospital letterhead and the brief note that followed. As expected, the reprimand was there. But what followed was worse.

Second opinion jumped out immediately.

When she reached *as we suspected*, the bottom of her stomach dropped out. Nausea sloshed into its place as the worst-case scenario she'd discussed with her doctor slammed in like she'd never anticipated. She had to force herself to read the rest, until she finally reached her doctor's heartfelt apology. He hated informing her like this. Unfortunately, she'd left him no choice.

Stan was wrong. She wasn't ducking him. At least, not completely. Yes, she'd missed her last two appointments. But she'd intended on keeping them.

Life just kept intervening.

She'd called the lab the morning of her first appointment to remind her secretary she'd be late, only to end up taking the entire day off. She'd opened the front door to her house to discover one of her closest college sorority sisters pulling into her driveway. Even before she'd succeeded in prying Anna's death grip from the rental car's steering wheel, she'd known Anna had been in no condition to leave alone. Not with her sanity hanging by a thread and her once-illustrious naval career all but torpedoed by one of the more nebulous elements within their own government. Instead of heading for the hospital, Sam had spent the day listening to the trap an ethically-stunted special agent had set for her sister amid the Panamanian underworld. The following night had been spent planning or rather, plotting, the best way to salvage her Sister's career—and life. She'd rescheduled the appointment for as soon as she could. The three days after Anna had been summoned back to Panama, in fact. But fate stepped in again. This time during a noon meeting at the lab.

One minute, she was helping her boss with his last-minute preparations for a scientific conference in Moscow and the next, she was being tasked with taking Phil's place while the man lay on a cold slab at the morgue, dead of a heart attack at the ripe old age of fifty-eight. Just went to show, once again, that even when you thought you'd figured out which piece the Grim Reaper had chosen to checkmate you with, he selected another. Sweat slicked her palms as she carefully re-folded the letter and slid it back into the envelope.

The rules had changed for her, too. Her mind and her heart no longer had a choice in the matter.

Her body had made it for her.

She rubbed the corners of her eyes in an effort to ease the inexplicable burning, staring in shock at the tips of her fingers as she pulled them down to her lap.

Tears?

But she didn't even want children. She hadn't for years. Not since a cocky chopper pilot by the name—

She slammed the name back out of her brain before it could settle in, automatically using the pain-control biofeedback techniques she'd gotten too darned good at these past few years to ease the inevitable ache that followed, this one in her heart. The throb was almost—*he* was almost gone—when a hand tapped her left shoulder, jolting her back to the here and now.

Dimitri. He'd returned.

The letter! She folded the envelope discreetly before slipping it off her lap to tuck it down between the steel frame of the webbed seat and the trousers of her Air Force Blues. Yes, Dimitri knew and, yes, he'd been nothing but supportive. It didn't matter. She was not in the mood to talk about it. And he'd only be hurt. She'd discovered that two weeks earlier when she'd declined to discuss much less introduce Dimitri to her "mysterious houseguest" as he'd dubbed her sorority sister. Sam swiped her eyes and pushed a smile to her lips as she tugged the rabbit ears from her head. Without the second degree of ear protection, the roar from the Herc's turboprops reverberated straight into her. She turned to meet her friend and fellow scientist of three years, raising her voice to compete with the engines.

"I thought you wanted to check out the scenery. You know, gaze upon the land of your parents' birth."

His brow furrowed at her teasing. "I did. Samantha, I've been chatting with the pilots for twenty minutes."

Really?

She pushed a shrug out after the smile. "I didn't realize it had been that long." She tapped the stack of files on her lap. "I guess I got caught up in these, after all."

Guilt flooded her as the concern in Dimitri's warm brown eyes deepened. It intensified as he removed the jacket to his dark gray suit and laid it across two of the empty webbed cargo seats further down before claiming the one beside her.

"What's wrong?"

"What makes you think there's something wrong?" The

second the words came out, she regretted them because he studied her face. Her eyes weren't red, were they?

"You seem upset."

"Nonsense. I'm just tired, that's all. Ten hours in the air is my limit and we passed that four hours ago."

Dimitri chuckled as he slipped his hands over hers and squeezed lightly. "You are the only aerospace engineer I know who dislikes flying."

She managed a real smile at that. "I don't dislike it. I just get bored. Especially when I've been jammed into the side of a cargo bay like an afterthought." Like they were now.

There were so many pallets and crates tied down in the Herc, she couldn't see around them—much less deduce which crew member had just slipped around the corner of the pallets to sneak a smoke. She knew someone had, because she'd just caught a whiff of the match. Evidently she wasn't the only one who wasn't pleased with the length of the flight.

"Besides." She squeezed Dimitri's hand. "You know as well as I do that designing an aircraft is a heck of a lot more fun than flying in one." At least, that's what she'd been telling herself since her rotten eye-hand coordination had knocked her out of the running for flight school before she'd even graduated college.

As usual, Dimitri took her seriously.

"True." Despite her attempts to prevent it, her smile bled off as he tugged her hand to his mouth and pressed his lips to her knuckles. "Naturally, this only adds to my arguments on why we make a perfect pair."

"Dimitri, I—"

He shook his head, saving her from the embarrassment of voicing it out loud. He really was a good friend.

It should have been enough.

It had been enough. Until a couple of months ago. The day the twinges in her abdomen had started up again, she'd started thinking about the past. Children. She shoved both out of her mind now.

Tried to shove *him* out.

But this time, he wouldn't go.

Dammit, Griff Towers had no bearing on her future. He hadn't for a very long time. So what if she'd been fighting this insidious urge to look him up? The fact that it had been so easy to find him only made it worse. What if she did call him? What would she say? Would she really have the nerve to look into those dark gray eyes and demand to know why?

As if his absence hadn't been answer enough.

Besides, a man like Griff was bound to be married by now. She knew that better than anyone.

"Samantha?"

As Dimitri touched her cheek, she flinched. Regret bit in as hurt flared in his eyes. He released her hand to busy himself with retrieving the briefcase he'd stowed beneath the green webbing of his seat hours earlier. She reached out and squeezed his arm. "Dimitri, I'm sorry. I've got a lot on my mind with the conference—"

He nodded stiffly. "I understand."

But he didn't.

The envelope burned into her thigh. Still, she couldn't bring herself to discuss it. Maybe that was the problem. Dimitri was right. They were alike. Perhaps too much. When he'd hinted at taking their friendship to another level six months ago, she'd balked. She knew Dimitri was lonely but, frankly, she'd been holding out for more. She'd been holding out for another Griff. Deep down she'd always suspected there might never be another man who fired her blood as quickly and as thoroughly as Griff Towers had. But she always hoped she'd have time to look, to make sure. Evidently not. She'd known that from the moment the twinges had begun.

Again.

"Hey, Towers, that you?"

Griff tossed his flight helmet on the seat of his Pave Hawk and spun around, his curiosity fired by the familiar shout that rang out from two choppers away. Three Secret Service suits were striding across the tarmac but none looked familiar. As they drew closer, he caught a glimpse of red hair pulled into a thick braid and smooth skin beneath the splatter of freckles.

"Meg!"

The same wide grin he'd first seen his freshman year at Texas A&M University on a slip of a kid tagging after her Marine officer instructor of a father broke out as Meg Gallagher reached his chopper. As fate would have it, the same grin that'd teased him years later as Meg watched him fall head-over-heels in love with her best friend at the University of Texas at Austin. Bright blue eyes winked up at him as she whipped off her sunglasses. "Fancy meeting you here, Zoomie. Been a while."

Griff laughed, bypassing the faint disapproval in her companions' matching aloof frowns as he reached out to grab Meg by her shoulders and haul her in close. "That, it has."

Eleven years, one week and three days to be exact.

He had one heck of a marker.

He kept that to himself as he pulled away, focusing instead on the irony of running into two Gallaghers in as many days. "It's good to see you. Though I have to admit, I had a heads up. Ran into your old man out on the tarmac yesterday. His chopper landed a few minutes before I did." Griff flicked his gaze over Meg's conservative navy blue suit. "Your dad didn't mention a career change, though. What did you do with the uniform, Jar Head? You trade it in for a pair of mirrored shades and that cool earpiece?"

She shook her head. "Nah, I've got it crammed in my sea bag, just in case." Meg's throaty voice lowered to a whisper as her companions nodded stiffly before heading off toward the aircraft hangar beyond. "The brass thought I'd blend in better if I slipped into a monkey suit with all the trappings before teaming up with Tweedledee and Tweedledum."

"In other words, Secret Service doesn't like taking orders from Marines, much less on Russian soil."

"Give that man a medal, or in your case a silver eagle." Her grin broke out again, this time wider. "Congratulations, by the way. I saw the promotion list, *Colonel*. How long are they gonna let you continue to fly?"

"Until my orders come through."

"Bummer."

"Yeah." He turned slightly and slapped the side of his bird. This time next year, he'd probably be begging to fire this baby up and take off to hang out up in the wild blue yonder for longer than a thirty minute check ride. "But command should make up for it."

He hoped.

"Any idea which one, or where?"

"Nope." With his ticket already punched in both Afghanistan and Iraq, there was no telling where he was headed. But, then, that was the beauty of the life wasn't it? And the addiction. One minute you were dodging anti-aircraft rockets over Baghdad and the next, you were playing taxi, ferrying the military and political brass around Moscow during the upcoming Anti-ballistic Missile Treaty Summit. Best job in the world if you could get it, though it did tend to wreck havoc on a man's personal life. Not that he'd ever bring that up with this woman. Her father might've been more mentor than instructor his first year at A&M, and Meg might still greet him like an older brother of sorts, but her allegiance had shifted once she'd formed that cross-branch ROTC sorority at UT. Sisterhood had quickly taken priority.

With one Sister in particular.

Griff deliberately shifted to a safer topic. "So, you had a chance to link up with your dad?"

The glint in that razor gaze told him Meg had recognized the evasive maneuver for what it was.

Fortunately, she let it slide.

She shook her head. "Nope, haven't seen him yet. He'll have his aide call when he gets settled. He always does. Then I'll end up trying to sanitize my own silverware under the table at some local dive he just heard about because it has the *best* food." She didn't bother suppressing her shudder.

Griff couldn't blame her.

Then, Major Bud Gallagher's culinary finds in and around College Station, Texas, had been legendary—and at times, emergency-room worthy. He ought to know. He'd spent a night in the cadet barracks worshiping the porcelain god himself. Not that it had stopped him from accepting another invite. Two decades ago or this morning. Griff leaned back against the steel skin of his dormant bird. "I've got bad news, Meg. Your dad's translator has already hooked him up. I know 'cause I got suckered in. We'll be rehashing old Aggie times tonight over Chicken Kiev and borscht. Ten-to-one you've got an invite already waiting for you at your quarters. Who knows, we hit the right joint, you might be dodging fire outside your stomach for a change." Something odd flickered in her gaze and he didn't think it had to do with his reference to the recent rise in Chechen terrorist bombings in and around the city. He was about to ask if something was wrong, but it was gone.

She smiled brightly. A bit too brightly. "Sorry, I'm off the hook this time. You'll have to suffer through alone. I've already got a dinner date."

"So bring him along."

He wasn't worried she'd get the wrong impression. Meg Gallagher might be an attractive woman, but she was not his type, nor he hers. Or was that it? Had he inadvertently hit on the source of that odd expression, as well as her brief, uncharacteristic, hesitation?

He shot her a teasing grin. "What's the matter? You got some knee-knocking Marine captain on the string who's too scared to meet the mighty General Gallagher?"

But instead of shooting back a retort, her smile faltered. The odd glint had returned, too. She shook her head slowly. "You really don't know, do you? I mean, I thought you were just avoiding talking about her, but—"

His stomach fisted as she broke off, sighed.

No. It was not possible. Meg was *not* trying to tell him what he suspected she was. He'd have known. The moment he'd learned he'd been assigned to ferry scientists from Jarco Labs out of Kirtland during the coming week, he'd checked the names on the security manifest. Then he'd double-checked.

Five times.

It wasn't there.

But the apology in Meg's shrug claimed otherwise. "Griff, Samantha's a last minute substitute for Jarco Labs. Her boss had a heart attack yesterday. Her C-130 is due to land about an hour and a half from now. That's why I'm here. That's why you're here. You're *her* escort now."

Griff stiffened against the side of his chopper as the confirmation punched through his gut with more force than one of those damned ballistic missiles this entire summit was centered around. Against his will, his gaze shot out over the acrid, oil-stained concrete aircraft apron, past the half-dozen choppers lined up behind his own, out toward a distant runway where a KC-130 refueler was touching down. Where Sam's C-130 would be touching down. Today. The images slipped in before he could shutter his mind against them. Long blond hair, straight and thick with the barest hint of a wave at the ends. Dark, whiskey eyes. Soft, clear skin with just a hint of the fresh peaches she'd smelled so much like. Smooth cheeks and a gently curved jaw. Full, sinfully perfect lips.

Perfect everything.

For a moment, he allowed himself to wonder how much she'd changed during the intervening years. He knew she had. To be honest, he'd never been completely comfortable with their eleven-year age difference. He'd actually looked forward to Sam's lithe, nineteen-year-old body blossoming into the fuller curves of womanhood. To watch time gradually etch the proof of her quick wit and ready laugh about those mesmerizing eyes. Of course, he was supposed to have been by her side while it happened. He purged the memories from his brain. The fantasy.

Reality was, Samantha had wanted someone else.

Someone her own age. Someone *there*.

He pushed past the unwelcome tightening lingering in his chest as Meg began tentatively, "I don't suppose you'd like to join—"

"*No.*" He might be a crate short on Maalox, but he would not be blowing off dinner with her father to dine with Samantha Hall. How the hell could Meg even ask?

Still, the rebuke had come out sharper than he'd intended. Ruder. It had also drawn the attention of the twin Suits twenty yards away at the entrance to the chopper maintenance hangar. As far as Tweedledee and Tweedledum knew, Meg was a Marine Corps captain, he an Air Force colonel. From their smirks, the Suits had also evidently assumed Meg had just received the set-down they had to have been itching to give her since the moment she'd been ordered to invade their turf and usurp their authority.

"Sorry, Meg. Didn't mean to draw attention."

"S'okay. They'll get past the gloat. I didn't mean to intrude either. Sam never said why you guys broke up. The rest of us just assumed it was the distance. I wouldn't have even mentioned it except…well…Sam's taken a few knocks lately. We both have. One of our sorority sisters died recently and two others have ended up with their careers on the block."

Griff nodded. He'd heard. It'd been hard to miss. The Army Black Hawk crash that'd killed Carrie Evans and all but ended Eve Paris's career had led the nightly news six weeks ago not to mention the military flight communities' rumor mill. To make matters worse, a mere month earlier their Navy sorority sister, Anna Shale, had been accused of stealing and then selling classified information. Though the Navy Criminal Investigative Service had issued a follow-up statement claiming there was no evidence to support Anna's guilt, her commission had been terminated nonetheless. Griff had thought of Sam on both occasions. Despite her humiliating kiss-off eleven years ago, he'd felt for her. A college junior

to the remaining women's freshman status when Sisters-in-
Arms formed, Sam had been unofficial mother-hen of the
group. It was nice to know Samantha's loyalty had persevered
in one area of her life. It'd barely survived two months following his departure.

Meg sighed. "Anyway, I was just hoping—"

"What? We'd all sit down and have a good old-fashioned
friendly reunion?"

She frowned. "I guess it was a bad idea."

He didn't bother denying it. It was also time for him to ex-
tricate himself from *this* reunion and head for the ready room.
He didn't know which pilot he'd bribe into swapping flight
assignments with him or what he'd have to give up in return,
nor did he care. He might manage to be civil to Samantha if
he ran into her during the summit, but he'd be damned if he'd
shuttling her around for a week. He clipped a nod. "Well, it's
been great seeing you again. I'll let your dad know I ran into
you when I see him tonight."

He stuck out his hand.

To his surprise, she didn't take it.

Instead, she stiffened. A moment later, Meg's entire five-
foot-eleven-inch body flinched. Her color bled off as she
snapped her right hand up to cup the audio receiver in her ear.
An unconscious attempt to amplify the sound, he knew.

"What's wrong?"

She waved him off.

Griff caught sight of his copilot as Vince left the hangar
and skirted the twin Suits—who were also cupping their respective earpieces—to stroll across the tarmac to their bird.
Griff snapped his gaze back to Meg's, his earlier anger suddenly and completely purged. Apprehension had replaced it.
The daughter of the current Commandant of the Marine
Corps, Meg had been trained from an early age not to panic.

But she was panicking now.

He could see it in those wide blue eyes.

By the time she focused on his face, he could see the horror, too. "It's Sam's C-130. She's not going to be here in an hour and a half. The Herc is going down *now,* Griff. It's on fire. The pilot's trying to land in a remote ravine a hundred miles southeast of Kursk. But it's not looking good—"

He was in his bird, powering it up before she could finish, his heart pounding harder and faster than it had over Iraq and Afghanistan combined as he raced through his remaining pre-flight checks. "Vince, find Chief Kitterman and get the hell in here!" Something in his bellow must have stood out, because his copilot and best friend spun around and hauled-ass like Griff had never seen the man move before.

"Griff?"

He shook his head as he donned his helmet. Meg grabbed his hand the second he finished locking his harness into place. He forced a calm he didn't feel as he squeezed hers hard. "She'll be fine, Meg. We'll be there before those turboprops cool."

It was a lie and they both knew it.

Kursk might be an hour and a half away by C-130, but it was a good two and a half hours away by rescue chopper, *with* a decent tail wind. Unfortunately, they didn't have a choice. Neither did Sam. The next closest American air wing was over a thousand miles away in Turkey. To add to the gravity of the situation, there'd been a blitzkrieg of coordinated Chechen terrorist bombings from the northern steppes of the Caucasus Mountains, all the way up into the Russian interior during the preceding weeks in an attempt to draw the world's attention away from the Anti-Ballistic Missile Summit and focus it instead on the plight of the Chechen separatists. Their goal? To bring the decades-long struggle out of Chechnya and into the heart of Russia at a time when the entire world was watching. They'd succeeded. The Russian cities of Kursk and Voronezh had felt the deadly punch in a dozen separate car bombs just that morning. Russian troops were still spreading out into the surrounding fields and forests to retaliate. At a cruising altitude of twenty thousand feet, the roiling internal dispute hadn't mattered.

It did now. God help Sam and the rest of the Herc's crew if they got caught in the cross-fire.

If they even survived the landing.

Vince raced across the now scrambling tarmac, Chief Kitterman in tow as Meg finally released his hand. By the time his crew vaulted inside, Griff had already shoved Meg from his mind. God help him, all he could think about was Sam. The piercing irony of it. Two minutes ago, he'd have traded in his brand-new silver eagles to avoid the pain and, yes, humiliation of running into her during the coming week. In an instant, everything had changed. He'd changed. He'd sell his soul to see Samantha Hall one more time.

Alive.

Chapter 2

"Has he regained consciousness?"

Sam shifted her gaze from the pilot's pale skin. The navigator's drab green flight uniform was barely visible among the lengthening shadows of the forest beyond. "No, and he's not looking good." It had been two hours since the crash. Two hours closer to what even she could tell was certain death for the man lying on the ground in front of her if help didn't arrive soon. "He needs a hospital, a surgeon."

The navigator nodded. "I know. Captain Deavers and Dr. Alibek should be returning soon. If we're lucky, they've found someplace we can hole up until a rescue bird arrives. Getting him out of the elements might help."

Rescue.

Sam focused on her patient as the navigator waded into the freezing lake to rejoin the rest of the crew in their methodical efforts to destroy classified information and equipment before stripping the waterlogged plane of anything useful. With night moving in, rescue was looking less and less likely. The

C-130's communications equipment was down due to the scattering of partially submerged trees that had ripped through the nose and then the underbelly of the plane during landing. At least their emergency transponder functioned. A lot of good it would do if one of the pockets of Chechen separatists that had infiltrated the surrounding countryside located them first. The Chechen fight might be with Moscow, but a handful of American airmen would make an attractive bargaining chip in the separatists' bloody quest for sovereignty. If they weren't outright murdered to send yet another chilling statement of Chechen resolve.

Damn it, they would be rescued.

She, Dimitri, and the Herc's crew had not crawled out of that sinking bird and swum across a freezing lake with Major Sloane in tow, just to die now. Dimitri would find someone willing to hide the seven of them for the night and Major Sloane would regain consciousness. She pressed her palm to the pilot's clammy temple, wishing she could do more besides pray. Unfortunately, she was more qualified to doctor the plane.

Hell, she hadn't even been able to administer first aid to herself. The navigator had had to do that. Sam glanced at the makeshift sling on her left arm. Given the level of pain she'd been in before the navigator had injected her with morphine, it was broken in several places.

Just like the Herc.

Sam stared at the faint outline of the shattered fuselage in the rapidly receding light. Even if the sun hadn't already set, she wouldn't have been able to see much more. Major Sloane had managed to use a gully feeding into the swamp as a makeshift runway. While he'd succeeded, the Herc had come to rest a quarter of the way into the lake. The plane was buried up to its belly in sludge, rotting tree trunks and water.

At least the water had succeeded in putting the fire out.

She shifted her attention back to the man who'd saved their lives, more determined than ever to return the gift.

"*Samantha.*"

She jumped as Dimitri's whisper sliced through her. She couldn't help it. The eerie rustling coming from the shadowy trees beyond the bank had her on edge. "You startled me."

"Sorry. I didn't want to disturb your patient."

"I'm afraid you still can't." She adjusted the jacket to her uniform beneath the pilot's head as Dimitri joined her. It was still something of shock to look at him. Dimitri's meticulously clipped, silvering hair was caked with mud, his normally starched, creamy shirt torn, the right arm bloody from administering first aid to her—and, of course, the conservative tie she liked to tease him about was missing.

It was busy conserving Major Sloane's blood.

The navigator had used it as a tourniquet to slow the loss of blood from Sloane's right calf down to a trickle two hours earlier. But eventually, that trickle would cost him.

"Please tell me you and Deavers found help."

Dimitri shook his head. "But we did find—"

She stiffened as he broke off abruptly and stood, because she'd heard it too. The distant, approaching thunder. But not just any thunder. That beautiful, rhythmically whopping thunder came from a set of composite main rotor blades powered by twin General Electric turboshafts.

A UH-60G Pave Hawk.

Their *rescue* chopper.

She knew the crew had heard it too, because a split second later, a flare shot up into the air, leaving a searing trail of white phosphorous in its wake, marking their position. Moments later, the crew began wading out of the water toward them as quickly as they could. By the time the men reached their side, the Pave Hawk had skimmed over the tops of the trees of the steep rise that formed the opposite side of the lake. But instead of shouting for joy, Sam gasped as a second fiery trail lit up the sky.

This streak was *red*.

Someone had lit off a surface-to-air missile—and it had zeroed in on the chopper's heat signature with a vengeance. To her horror, a second SAM screamed up after the first.

The pilot banked the chopper sharply to the left, then the right, deliberately losing altitude in an attempt to throw off both SAMs. Decoy flares exploded in the chopper's wake, lighting up the sky as the pilot punched on the airspeed and followed up with an increasingly daring and desperate succession of maneuvers designed to break missile lock. Mercifully, the first SAM slammed into a flare and exploded well off the chopper's tail. But the second SAM remained on his tail—coldly determined, and now mere meters from its deadly kiss. The pilot banked the shuddering bird one last time. A split second later, the anti-aircraft missile ripped into the Pave Hawk's tail, the force of the subsequent explosion spinning the chopper a hundred and eighty degrees about. The half-mangled bird hung there for a brief, horrifying heartbeat before falling out of the sky with all the grace of a feather-less chick dumped from its nest.

Sam flinched as it slammed into the middle of the lake. And then she was running along with the crew. Then wading and, finally, swimming. Or rather, trying to.

Sam gasped as the icy water ripped through her uniform blouse to stab at her chest. A buried tree branch slashed at her thigh, gouging her flesh as she crawled past, but she kept going. Kept swimming along with the rest of the crew, her modified side stroke leaving her increasingly behind. Captain Deavers reached the sinking shell first, his thick, bulging arms peeling the copilot's swamped door open, half-assisting, half-dragging the man out by his flight vest before he passed the man, coughing and hacking, off to the navigator's waiting grip. Dimitri and the Herc's loadmaster pulled the chopper's crew chief out of the side door next.

Then Deavers reached in again.

But this time, those beefy arms came up empty.

"He's pinned! Can't get to his harness. My arms are too damned big!"

The navigator moved into position and tried. "Mine, too!"

Sam swam up. "Here, let me!"

Deavers grabbed her by the back of her blouse and bra, using the fabric to anchor her to him as he propelled her toward the opening. The chopper was sinking fast. Sam knew she'd find the pilot inside fighting for his breath, if not his very life. But of all the helicopter pilots in the entire Air Force, she never, ever, expected to recognize him.

"Griff?"

This was not the way it was supposed to go down.

Griff blinked, momentarily stunned, as he stared into the very pair of whiskey eyes he'd been unable to exorcise from his dreams during the past decade—and promptly choked as the level of the icy water rose enough to slosh over his mouth.

"Sam...you think you could reach my—"

Samantha jerked herself from her own daze before he could finish, her hand slipping neatly between the V of his harness and the section of steel that was currently jammed against his chest, damned near crushing his lungs whenever he dared to inhale. He could feel her slender fingers searching along the webbing at his torso, hear her praying until she finally found the buckle. He forced out his remaining breath and held fast against the searing need to replace it to give her more room to maneuver. A muffled click followed. He closed his eyes in relief, refilling his lungs as the latch gave way.

When he opened them, she was gone. He was still trapped...and the water was still rising.

He was dimly aware of her telling someone his torso was wedged beneath the chopper's warped instrument panel just before the icy water swallowed him completely. In the moments that followed, he swore he saw a massive human bear pushing his way into the flooded cockpit, displacing half the murky water that had rushed in. Huge paws ripped the steel panel away from his chest. He would have been able to breathe then...if he wasn't already drowning. But before he could truly panic, the paws were back, grabbing his flight vest and hauling him, hacking, choking and gasping, out of the bird.

Seconds later, his chopper sank beneath the surface.

Damn, but there went a mountain of paperwork.

As he coughed the last of the water from his lungs, Griff stared at the massive paw still locked to his flight vest as if its owner was afraid to let go. The opposite paw was fused to the back of Samantha's soaked and shredded uniform.

Apparently, he hadn't been dreaming.

Sam *was* here and a bear *had* just saved his life. A gigantic, Nordic bear of a man. And damned if that bear wasn't treading water for all three of them. Griff reached out instinctively to grab Sam and help her himself. He stopped himself in the nick of time.

Samantha was fine. Perceived favoritism was not.

Especially under these circumstances.

He forced his grin to encompass the lot of them. "Well, Airmen, it's been a pleasure rescuing your collective asses. But if you don't mind, it's time to get the hell out of here. Someone out there doesn't like us." The distant spatter of gunfire underscored his assessment.

They struck out as a group, crossing the lake in record time. Though it was difficult to make out Sam's face as the murky water dropped to chest level, he knew something was wrong. As she stood, he saw why. Her left arm was broken. Due to the water level in the cockpit and his desperation for air, he hadn't noticed. With the splint and sling someone had rigged saturated with water, he couldn't tell if the blood staining the dark green cravat was two hours old or fresh. But from the set of her jaw, that break hurt like the devil. He could see the uncharacteristic fear in her eyes, too.

Doubt.

The need to pull her into his arms to ease it slammed in. He smacked it back. A decade had passed, dammit. She was just another airman now. And he had a job to do. They all did. Fortunately, the situation was not as rotten as it looked. Despite her broken arm and the scrapes and bruises marring her face, Samantha was whole. Alive. And so were the six other airmen wading out of the lake alongside them.

It was up to him to keep it that way.

Sam stumbled as they reached the water's edge. He was about to hook a hand beneath her good elbow to steady her when another spat of gunfire filled the air, this one more vicious—and closer—than the last. Griff lashed his arm around Sam's torso, instead, and dragged her from the water before she could protest. He shoved her down on the grassy bank beside the bear's sheltering bulk as he, his crew, and half the Herc's contingent drew their 9 mm pistols. He winced as Sam landed on her left side, directly over the sling.

"Are you okay?"

"*Fine*, Colonel."

He didn't argue with the terse comment or the title, much less ask how she knew. At the moment, they had more to worry about. Like finding shelter from that testy welcoming party. As the current ranking officer of their combined crew, it was his job to assume command and find that shelter—and soon. Judging from yet another spat of gunfire, the pocket of Chechens who'd taken out his bird were at least a mile away. But they were bound to be on the move, searching for survivors—and bargaining fodder. As Griff studied the shadowy perimeter beyond the bank, a stiff breeze picked up, biting through the drenched fabric of his flight suit, straight into his bones. Given the way Sam and the others were shivering as they lay threaded among the marsh grass, they'd felt it, too. Great. A chilly early March night in Russia and they were already soaked to a man. Or just about.

Roughly ten feet beyond the grassy bank, Griff spotted the outline of a body on one of the Herc's first-aid stretchers. Another man had hunkered down on the far side.

"Who's the patient?"

"Major Sloane—the pilot." Sam's whisper had followed his. He could feel the chilled fingers of her good hand gripping his shoulder. "He's lost a lot of blood, Colonel—and he's probably still unconscious. If we don't get another chopper in here soon, he won't make it."

Griff caught the gaze of his crew chief's two airmen to his

right and nodded. A medic during Desert Storm, Sergeant Kitterman immediately cradled his 9 mm and high-crawled toward the major and his companion. From the flash of a shredded white shirt as Kitterman displaced the other man, Griff assumed the civilian was Samantha's esteemed colleague from Jarco Labs. Kitterman shot him a nod of agreement across the marsh grass. The major was unconscious. Worse, from the frown that followed, Kitterman didn't think the man would survive the night.

Damn.

The chances of another chopper arriving before dawn were slim to none and Kitterman knew it. Not with proven hostile activity in the area. Automatic rifles, anti-aircraft rockets, and God knew what else against ten men with half a dozen 9 mm pistols and a couple of signal flares? Frankly, their odds stunk. It was time to improve them.

"Who did the recon of the area?"

The Nordic bear beyond Sam inched forward, his rumbling whisper filling the dark. "I did. Captain Deavers, sir. Major Sloane's copilot." Deavers pointed toward the civilian hunkered down beside Sergeant Kitterman and the stretcher. "I brought Dr. Alibek in case I needed translation."

"Did you?"

"No, sir. But we did find shelter. A cabin." Deavers pointed thirty degrees to his left, off into the trees. "Two klicks that-a-way. It's more a rotting, abandoned shack, but it's got a dirt cellar that can be sealed—and concealed. And judging from the layer of dust covering everything, no one's stumbled across the place in quite a while."

Sam flinched beside him.

It took him a moment to realize why.

Griff nodded. Dirt cellar or not, she knew as well as he did, it would have to do.

"Good work." He motioned Vince up from rear of the group. Like Deavers, his own copilot and long-time friend was on the Incredible Hulk side. Griff kept his voice low, but loud enough to carry to the others. "Captain Deavers, meet Captain Vince Racey, my right hand. I want you and Vince carrying that stretcher." Between the two men, they ought to be strong enough to keep it steady. "The rest of you, pick up whatever gear you can carry on my signal, and haul-ass behind them. I'll bring up the rear."

Griff turned to find Sam's steady gaze on him. He could tell by the lock to her jaw her arm was getting worse.

"Captain Hall?"

"Sir?"

"You taking anything for that arm?"

"I'm fine, Colonel. We may need the morphine for Major Sloane later tonig—"

"See Kitterman for a hit as soon as we reach the cabin."

The lock on her jaw tightened. Despite the darkness, this close he couldn't miss the flash of anger in her eyes, either. Too damned bad. What Major Sloane might need, she did need. Airmen in pain made mistakes. He couldn't afford to lose her because she was too stubborn to take the relief. He wouldn't. He'd have administered the shot himself before they moved out if they'd had the time. Gunfire riddled the night air once again, underscoring his priorities. He tore his gaze from the swirl of anger and apprehension in those whiskey eyes and nodded down the line of waiting men.

"Let's do it."

She was suffocating.

Sam stared at the thin beam of light struggling valiantly against the moldering dark. Unfortunately, the flickering flashlight had been fighting for over two hours now. It was time to face facts. Slowly but surely, the darkness was regaining ground. That beam of light was losing it. So was she. Another hour in this dirt prison and she wouldn't need the slim switchblade Deavers had slipped her following their crash. The edge on her nerves alone would be honed sharply enough to slice through half the Chechen population.

At first, she'd welcomed the simmering panic. It had given her something to concentrate on after she'd turned down the shot of morphine Sergeant Kitterman had offered her when they'd arrived. But while the biofeedback she'd become so adept at these past three years had allowed the pain in her arm to become bearable, the memories were not.

The cellar even *smelled* like Nana's.

Dank and earthy, with an underlying hint of decay.

Just acknowledging the stench caused her heart to pound against the wall of her chest. If she concentrated, she could even hear her grandmother trying to soothe her beneath the deafening roar of wind and rain. Right before Nana's entire house outside Des Moines, Iowa, had been ripped off its foundation, her grandfather along with it. Sam swallowed the lump of panic, certain her nerves were screaming loud enough for everyone in the cellar to hear. But when the wooden ladder at her back shifted, then creaked she realized the sound had come from above.

Sam forced herself to step away from the base of the ladder and the mental crutch its presence provided. She couldn't be sure if the descending flight boots belonged to Deavers or one of the other airmen assigned to patrol the perimeter. But the moment the man's torso slipped within the glow of the flashlight, she knew who it belonged to. She'd spent half a year cradled against those muscles. With or without a drab-gray flight suit covering them, she'd know that chest anywhere. *Griff.* He stepped onto the packed dirt at the base of the ladder and crossed the twelve-by-twelve cellar, leaving quiet order and a palpable confidence in his wake as he stopped to talk to several of the men. Even the panic thundering through her veins ebbed as she watched him. The faint glow of the flashlight highlighted the planes and shadows of his face, causing his cheeks to appear stronger, his jaw even more square as he stopped at Major Sloane's stretcher and hunkered down to confer with Sergeant Kitterman.

From Griff's sharp frown, whatever assessment Kitterman had offered wasn't good.

He glanced up and their eyes met.

For a moment she swore she saw regret enter his.

But that was foolish. It must have been her imagination. That, or a distortion caused by the flickering light. Even if it was real, it was probably a reaction to whatever Griff and his sergeant had discussed. Griff might have regretted their last fight all those years ago, but it hadn't lasted long.

At least, not long enough.

Griff severed his stare as the navigator approached the stretcher and knelt. Once again, Sam was struck by the compassion and calm authority emanating from Griff as he spoke to the lieutenant. It wasn't Griff's senior rank, or even the additional experience he'd gained in the intervening years. It was simply his nature. Griff Towers had been born a hands-on, fearless leader. Even as a naïve ROTC cadet at the University of Texas, she'd known it. Though Griff had downplayed the tale the one and only time she'd heard him recount it, the write-up on Griff's Air Force Cross she'd stumbled across one afternoon had painted a different picture. As had the testimony of the entire Special Forces A-team Griff had pulled out of a hot-zone in the dead of night while taking ground fire from every conceivable direction. The stunt had earned Griff's copilot a head full of gray hair, what was left of their bird, a complete internal overhaul and new steel skin to replace the shredded one—and Griff his silver bullet. For the first time in his career, Griff had his choice of assignments.

He'd chosen to attend UT to be near his mother for a year while he earned his masters.

From the moment Sam had run into him—literally—in front of the elevator in Russell Steinham Hall, it had been obvious Griff Towers was a unique man. Of course, the more vocal female cadets had gone so far as to vote him *Officer I'd Most Like To Be Stranded And Have Hot Sex With*.

To think she'd done both. Just not in that order.

The dull pain in her arm crept back, but it was nothing compared to the ache in her heart as the memories crowded in. Maybe it was that damned letter. Maybe it was the shock and the stress of the crash. Maybe it was this tiny dirt coffin she'd been buried alive in for the past two hours. She didn't know, let alone care. All she knew was that, suddenly, it hurt to be breathing the same air as Griff Towers.

But as painful as this reunion was, she was truly glad Griff was here. If anyone could get them home, he could.

"How is he?"

Sam tore her attention from the man who'd held it hostage for the past two hours, whether he knew it or not, and fused it on Dimitri. She could only assume Dimitri was referring to the C-130's pilot. "I'm not sure. Griff's discussing his condition with Sergeant Kitterman now."

"Griff?"

She smothered a wince at the slip. Even without the changes Dimitri had proposed to their relationship, she owed him an explanation. "Yes, Griff. He's an old friend."

"Who is?" This time, her wince made it through.

Sam shifted her stare to include the man she and Dimitri had been discussing into their conversation. "You are, sir." Unsure whether or not they'd officially met, she waved her good hand between them. "Colonel Griff Towers, meet Dr. Dimitri Alibek, fellow scientist with Jarco Labs."

"Doctor Alibek." Griff inclined his head. Even in the dim light, she could tell the stare he settled on Dimitri was cool. It was anything but when he fused it to hers. "Let me guess. Doctor Alibek is an 'old friend', too."

Dimitri stiffened.

She could only assume he thought Griff was referring to his age. Friendship or not, she wasn't about to correct him. Nor could she believe Griff had taken offense at the euphemism. How the heck had he expected to be introduced? As the grad student she'd had a torrid affair with back in college? That would go over well with this crowd.

Besides, she wasn't the one who swore she'd come back—and then never showed.

The moldering walls surrounding them seemed to close in as the silence stretched out. The suffocating panic locked back in as well, causing her to wonder if the faint glow from the flashlight had grown even fainter. She wasn't aware that Griff had reached out until his hand brushed her cheek.

She flinched.

What on earth was wrong with her? Why couldn't she control her own mind? The shift from simmering anger to understanding and compassion in those dark gray eyes made her feel worse, not better.

"Sam, why don't you head upstairs? Get some air. There's still no sign we were followed. Just be prepared to head down at a moment's notice."

She nodded and spun around, using her good arm to climb the rickety wood before Griff could change his mind. She gasped as she knocked her splint against the top rung. Despite a series of deep breaths and a crash infusion of biofeedback directed toward her body and her brain, her entire right arm was throbbing by the time she cleared the ladder. Her eyes were watering, too. For all her efforts, the air wasn't even better up here. She passed the scarred table with its splintered chairs and the vermin-infested mattress in the corner of the shadowy cabin and headed for the door. The odor improved marginally as she stepped outside into the swamp.

But it was freezing.

Wisps of white fog swirled around her, sending goosebumps ripping down her good arm. It served her right for leaving the jacket to her Blues in the cellar. Unwilling to return to the dirt dungeon before she had to, she crossed the rotting planks that passed for the cabin's porch and stepped onto the blanket of pine needles covering the ground. She could make out the faint outline of Deavers' flight suit above the low-lying layer of fog, but only because she knew where to look. He appeared to be waiting to see if she was okay.

Sam waved him off silently and he returned to his patrol.

Locating a stump that had lost its thick trunk years before

to someone's ax, she sighed heavily as she sat. She should have gone back for her jacket. The chill seeping into her bones was making the pain downright unbearable. She'd all but given up on the biofeedback when her jacket settled over her shoulders. She forced herself not to stiffen. She wasn't nearly as successful at keeping the subtle musk that'd slipped around her along with the coat from invading her lungs.

"Thanks."

She shouldn't have been surprised Griff had followed. She was under his makeshift command at the moment. He had to keep track of her now.

"I guess I don't have to ask if you've gotten over your fear of dark cellars."

She shrugged, but that was it. There wasn't really anything to add. From her or him. Any explanation he might have was so long overdue, it no longer mattered.

Dammit, it *didn't*.

So why was she waiting?

Truth be known, she'd been waiting since the moment they arrived and Griff had gotten everyone settled, assigned tasks and established the perimeter watch. Well, she was done waiting. She gathered the edges of her jacket with her good hand and pulled it close as the silence sank down into the fog. She studied the blanket of pine needles at her feet. If she stared at them long enough, he just might surrender and go back inside. Then again, this was Griff. He was nothing, if not stubborn. When he wanted to be.

"Samantha?"

It wasn't an order, but she took it as one, finally turning around on the stump to face him.

"Sir?"

He frowned. She knew why. It had been years since she'd addressed him as her senior in private. Too bad. Right now, she needed the reminder. What was he doing out here anyway? But when her gaze fell to his hands, she knew.

He was holding a morphine syrette.

"I'm fi—"

"No, you're not. You're in pain and it's getting worse." He held up the collapsible, single dose, syringe. "Before you argue, you should know that Sergeant Kitterman was able to grab his medical kit before he bailed out of our chopper. But then, you'd have known that if you'd heard him out two hours ago."

Like I ordered you.

He might have left the last unspoken, but she heard it as clearly as if he'd shouted it. Damn him for making her feel like a nineteen-year old girl again.

But then, she'd acted like one, hadn't she?

Shame scorched her neck. "I'm sorry. I didn't intend to undermine your authority. It won't happen again."

"I know. I didn't need to be so brusque, either."

She pulled her jacket tighter and shrugged. "We've both had a hell of a day." A hell of a past.

"*Yeah.*"

The years fell away as he sighed.

The mask of command followed. In that moment, she wondered if she wasn't seeing him clearly for the first time. Oddly enough, without the lingering hero worship of her cadet years or even the flush of first love and first lover, Griff was even more handsome, more capable, more manly.

And more burdened.

The intervening years also allowed her to see how the weight of everything that had happened tonight was sitting on his shoulders. She could see it in the silver that had crept into the deep brown hair at his temples. She could also see it in the faint lines about his mouth and at the corners of those dark, smoky eyes. Lines, she knew, that had more to do with the uncertainty and the pain of weighing one life against another than with the passage of time.

And when Griff's gaze met hers, she knew exactly what he'd discussed with his sergeant. Who.

"Major Sloane is dying."

He simply nodded.

"Oh, Griff."

It was instinctive. It must have been. Because before she knew it, she'd stood up to loop her good arm around Griff's neck to drawn him close to comfort him. The warmth of his body seared into hers so fast and so hot—so *familiar*—that she jumped back. It took a moment for her to realize that Griff had sprung away from her, too. Their rasping, frosted breath filled the icy air, mingling with the translucent mist that had been stirred up from around their feet.

Her breathing finally eased.

Griff held up the syrette.

She nodded, afraid to break this new, precarious silence as it settled between them. She turned away, allowing him to slide her jacket off her shoulders and lay it across the stump before he eased the sling from her makeshift split to get a better look at her arm.

"*Jesus.*"

"It's not that bad."

His low growl filled her ear, scorching the side of her face even as it sent another ripple of goose flesh down her neck. "The hell it isn't. You're arm isn't just broken, Sam, it's been shattered. And you're bleeding again."

"So is Major Sloane."

His answer came in the cold swipe of an alcohol pad. The quick sting of the syrette's hypodermic needle followed and then the slow burn as the morphine spread out into the swollen muscle of her arm. He carefully re-hooked the cloth sling over her shoulder before leaning down to snag her jacket. She gathered the edges of the lapels with the fingers of her left hand as he tucked the coat around her arms.

"Thank you."

"I want Sergeant Kitterman to get a look at that arm as soon as possible. You'll also accept whatever medication he prescribes from his kit, understood?"

"Yes, sir." She stepped off to comply.

"Sam?"

She stopped but refused to turn around.

Why should she? It was painfully obvious Griff had been doing his damnedest to avoid her since the second they'd pulled him out of that chopper. She heard his sigh.

"I should warn you Meg's probably worried to death—"

Meg?

She spun around. "You've spoken to Meg? When?"

"This afternoon."

Oh, God, what had Meg said? Surely she hadn't told him. No. Meg was her sorority sister, her best friend. She refused to believe Meg would betray her confidence like that, no matter how much she'd argued in Griff's favor. But Meg *had* alluded to their conversation. Her dilemma. She could tell by the way Griff's gaze searched her own. Wait a minute— Meg was already in Moscow. They were roughly two and a half hours from Moscow when the C-130 went down—and Griff's chopper had arrived two and a half hours after the crash.

She took a step toward him.

"What were you doing in Moscow?"

Despite the darkness and the cold that might have otherwise concealed it, she caught the slow tide as it washed up Griff's neck and spread through the day's growth already darkening his jaw and lower cheeks. Without uttering a word, he'd answered her question—along with her next one. And the next. Not only had Griff known she was the last minute replacement for Jarco Labs during the Anti-ballistic Missile Summit this coming week, he'd been assigned to attend as well, probably to ferry the Brass. The latter didn't surprise her. What did was that Griff had had no intention of looking her up. In fact, she'd bet Army bullets to Navy beans that if the man hadn't been forced to fly his blasted chopper out here to save their hide, he would have been content to wait another decade before seeing her again.

Eleven years and Griff Towers hadn't changed a bit.

Not in the areas that mattered.

The devil with that dirt prison. The nightmare of her child-hood was nothing compared to the rejection right here, and right now from this man. She truly no longer cared why Griff had broken his vow to come back for her on graduation day. It was clear that his absence had been for the best. She ignored the apology in those smoky eyes, eyes that had haunted her for far too long, and gripped the edges of her jacket before spinning around on her heel. For the first time since they'd arrived at this godforsaken cabin, she was grateful—because it meant Griff couldn't risk ordering her to stop.

She made it across the rotting planks of the porch before she realized he was right behind her.

It didn't deter her.

She wrenched the door to the cabin open and crossed the shadowy threshold. All she had to do was make it to the lad-der and she'd be safe. One word to Dimitri and Griff wouldn't be able to sneak two seconds alone with her ever again. As if he'd even want to. But as the darkness enveloped her, so did Griff's sinewy arms. Before she could blink, he'd locked a hand over her mouth and whirled her around, silently but firmly pushing her back up against the hewn trunks of the cold cabin wall. A second later, the rigid length of Griff's body seared into hers from her breasts right down to her belly and thighs as he trapped her between his powerful legs.

That's all it took. Memories flooded her.

Griff flooded her.

His scent, his touch, his heat. Just like that, she wanted him again, needed him. But this time when she stared into his eyes, she didn't see passion, or even apology or regret. She saw cau-tion. Warning.

That's when she heard them.

Voices.

They couldn't be coming from Captain Deavers, or even the two other airmen Griff had posted outside, around the cabin's perimeter, because these voices were *not* speaking English.

But they were moving closer.

Chapter 3

If there was any hope left in Griff's mind that the explosion that shattered the tail to his bird had also screwed up his hearing, it disintegrated as the achingly familiar curves in his arms stiffened. Sam had heard it, too.

Them.

They definitely had company.

The fact that Deavers had allowed what appeared to be at least two men pass his concealed post unchallenged didn't bode well. Either the copilot wasn't sure which nationality their slowly closing guests claimed…or Vince had already relieved the navigator and signaled the others that the men were definitely Chechen. Griff could only pray the remainder of the American greeting party he'd stationed within the forest were drawing up behind their uninvited guests as instructed. Unfortunately, *he* was not in a position to greet anyone, friend or foe. Not with Samantha locked in his arms.

Griff loosened his grip. "Get downstairs."

"No."

Just like that, every one of their decade-old fights locked in. The reasons why. Damn her for assuming the worst. And damn him for accepting her word that she wouldn't undermine his authority. He should have known better. He'd spent far too many nights confounded by Samantha Hall's willingness to cede to anyone's wishes but his to believe it now. He clamped down on his fury and leaned closer. "That was not a request, Captain, and we're sure as hell not lovers anymore. You will obey me. This is a military mission and I am ordering you—"

"There's no *time*."

He caught her wince as she shifted her broken arm just enough to make her point. It was valid, too. The next burst of Russian and guttural laugh that followed confirmed it. The men were almost on top of the cabin—and Griff swore he could make out another two or three distinct voices at least.

Christ! Just how many men were out there?

Given the speed with which they were closing, he'd soon be finding out. *They'd* be finding out. With Sam's arm in a sling, she'd never make it down that rickety ladder in time. Nor was there time for him to scramble down after, let alone reseal the opening to the root cellar as planned in the hopes that their visitors would stroll in, take one whiff of the rotting wood and putrid leftovers that'd once served as some Russian hunter's dinner at least six months earlier and then barrel right back out to get away from the rats and the stench. The next rumble of Russian damned near reverberated through the cabin's outer walls, grating across his nerves.

What in God's name were they saying?

Griff stiffened at the subdued but pointed cough behind him. The distinctive scrape of wood against wood followed. Vince? About bloody time. Griff spun around, drawing his 9mm from the holster on his flight vest just in case. But it wasn't Vince Racey staring across the shadows or their crew chief. It was Sam's colleague. *Great*. Griff lowered the 9mm and swallowed his disappointment. No help there. Dimitri Alibek had already volunteered that he stunk at hand-to-hand combat. But…the man *did* speak Russian.

Hope surged again—only to shatter a moment later as the physicist captured his stare. From the warning in Alibek's dark, furrowed brows as he cocked his head toward the voices that had reached the porch steps, their company was definitely Chechen. But instead of crossing the room to translate, Alibek turned back to the nightstand beside the rotting mattress, wrenching the warped drawer open with one hand while he yanked the tail to his shirt out of his pants with the other.

What the devil was the guy doing?

Vodka.

Griff's estimation for the scientist shot up a hundred fold as the dusty, half-empty bottle surfaced. It appeared he and Vince weren't the only ones who'd cased the cabin upon arrival, searching beyond the half-dozen stuffed deer and boar heads mounted to the walls for anything they could use. Vince had spotted the bottle first and promptly informed Kitterman the brand was suited more for emergency sterilization than quality consumption. Russian rotgut or not, if Alibek played it right, the contents of that bottle would double as liquid manna from heaven. The man's filthy shirt, missing tie and graying five-o'clock shadow would help.

Griff jerked his chin toward the cabin door, as he pointed to himself, the 9mm and, finally, the hinged side of the door. Alibek nodded his agreement, stomping across the cabin as Griff turned to point again, this time to order Sam deeper into the cabin. By the time Griff turned back to Alibek, the good doctor had swung the cabin door open and launched into a coarse Russian drinking song that put Vince's inebriated off-key bellowing to shame. But then, their lives depended on this particular ditty and Alibek knew it. For a rocket scientist, the man blended into the gutter well, rudely scratching at his groin and swaying convincingly until he broke off his song to fumble with the cap to the bottle.

Using the open door as a shield, the cabin shadows as concealment, Griff moved up behind Alibek, the leading round in his 9mm already chambered as he shot off one last silent prayer before he risked glancing around the door. It died on a curse. They had *seven* camouflaged guests, not four.

And all were armed.

Fortunately Alibek remained drunkenly unfazed as the red-head in the center of the squad raised his rifle, coldly sighting the Kalashnikov on Alibek's chest. Vodka sloshed up the throat of the bottle as Alibek belched and waved in greeting. Griff had no idea what the Chechen on the far right had said in response, but from the rest of the men's collective body language, they weren't quite buying the act. Damn. Griff forced himself to hold fast to patience as the redhead marched up the wooden steps and onto the porch to shove Alibek out of the way. The physicist stumbled convincingly. It was Griff who stiffened as the Chechen stabbed the forward sight on his rifle straight through the cabin's darkened doorway while shooting off his mouth.

Son-of-a—

The cellar.

Griff didn't need to turn to know light wasn't bleeding up. Kitterman had killed the telling glow the moment Alibek had started singing. The Chechen must have spotted the trap door. Neither he nor Alibek had closed it. The three-by-three-foot floor hatch was yawning wide open in the shadows, exposing their sham for what it was. Exposing them.

The guy turned to Alibek and shouted again.

All pretense of inebriation burned off as Alibek swung his arm up. "*Now*, Colonel!"

By the time the bottled shattered across the back of the red-head's skull, Griff had vaulted around the door and onto the porch. He sighted the 9mm on his far right as he'd briefed earlier, plugging the stunned Chechens one-by-one, center mass, as he made his way across the squad. By the time he'd zeroed in on his forth target, the guy was no longer standing, nor were any of the others. Deavers and the navigator had taken out the remaining left three from the tree line as instructed, as well as the redhead who'd started it all. The Chechen clawed at Alibek's arm as he gurgled up at the doctor. Griff had no idea what the guy said, but he'd never forget the look in those stark blue eyes as he dropped his chin to stare at the switchblade protruding out from his gut and the rapidly spreading blood.

Switchblade?

Suspicion sliced in. He hadn't tossed that knife. Neither could any of the others. Not from their positions behind the man. *Sam.* Griff closed his eyes as he turned, praying he was wrong, that she'd the sense to listen to him for once and had stayed back in the shadows as he'd ordered. She hadn't. She was standing behind him, two feet to his right, pale enough to tell him without words that she was going to lose the dinner she hadn't had any moment. He grabbed her shoulders as she swayed, gently but firmly guiding her around and back into the cabin as Vince and their crew chief bounded up the ladder and out of the cellar.

Kitterman stopped at the sight of Sam's face.

Griff waved him off. "I've got her. Check the bodies. If any are alive, tie 'em up. Maybe Alibek can get something out of them. And tell Deavers and the navigator to get back on station. Have them fire up a Prick-112 and see if anyone's out there." He'd had everyone on radio silence since they'd left the lake. It wasn't worth the risk when all the next chopper needed to get a fix on them were the GPS signal tags he, Vince and their crew chief carried. No point in hanging silent now. Those shots they'd fired were bound to bring more company running. God willing, they'd be out of Moscow this time.

Griff turned back to Sam. She was still deathly pale. Despite the past, the sight tore through him. He reached out before he realized what he was doing and smoothed the strands of hair that had fallen from her braid away from her cheeks. Her skin was clammy. He nudged her down into one of the chairs flanking the mold-laden table and hunkered down beside her.

"You okay?"

She blinked up at him, those dark, whiskey eyes welling up as she struggled to focus, and it wasn't because of the shadows or the stench. "I…I've never…killed anyone."

He nodded.

He wasn't surprised. And not only because she was a scientist. Air Force non-combatants had come under fire before. But if Sam had, he knew without a doubt she'd have done her damnedest to leave her enemy alive. The night she'd stumbled across the write-up to his Air Force Cross, she'd asked about it. Killing. He hadn't known what to say. She might have been smarter than he'd ever be, but she'd also been a nineteen-year-old slip of girl and he, a thirty-year-old combat-hardened vet who should have known enough to have left her the heck alone. Hell, the month after they'd met, she'd taken in some homely dirt-gray alley kitten with a body teaming with lice and a belly wound that should have done the thing in days before. She'd tried so hard to conceal her tears when he told her it wouldn't make it, he'd ended up helping her clean the damned thing up and nursing it back to health.

Looking back, that cat had been the beginning of the end for him. The beginning of them—and the end of his dogged determination to see life through as a hardened bachelor.

And look how that had turned out.

God only knew where these silent tears would lead.

Eleven years and the ultimate of betrayals, and they still got to him. He wouldn't have believed it possible…were he not already reaching out to smooth them from her cheeks, struggling to ignore the seductive warmth of the skin beneath. The heady memories. Of how he'd slowly dried those other tears with his hands and then his lips. And the sweetest of kisses that had followed. Their first kiss.

"Colonel?"

He jerked his hands from her face, jolted from the past, from her, as he turned. He had not just been that close to giving in to temptation in the middle of a rancid cabin while a beleaguered group of airmen stood outside. He had *not*.

He was lying.

Alibek knew it, too. He could see it in the man's eyes. Mere colleagues, she'd claimed in that cellar. Friends. According to who? Her? Because the man standing over them thought it was more. At the very least, Alibek wanted it to be. So what? So she had another guy on the string. This one with almost twice as many years on her as he had. It was none of his business. *She* was none of his business. Hadn't been for years.

Griff stood. "Good work, Doctor. If I hadn't forgotten the hatch, it probably would have worked." He extended his hand. Alibek shifted the remains of the broken bottle to his left and returned the shake firmly.

"Please, Dimitri. And I left the hatch open, I'm afraid. Not you."

"Either way, I owe you big time."

Alibek hooked a half smile, born more of relief than victory. "Tell you what. You make it round of Stolichnaya and we'll consider the debt settled." The doctor tossed what remained of the broken bottle and Charodei label on the table. "No decent vodka ever came out of Belarus."

Vince clapped Alibek across the shoulders as he stepped up. "Man after my own heart. Count me in. I'll even buy, save the Temperance King a crisis of conscience. Hell, I'll spring for the whole bottle—but your colleague here gets the medal for taking the guy out." Vince tipped his forehead to Sam, still seated and still pale. "Not bad for a scientist, Sam. Hell, I can't believe you actually hit him. But you did. It was definitely the knife that did him in."

Sam's remaining color bled off.

Griff cuffed his arm across the man's shoulders, cutting him out of the pack before his next comment started her stomach churning again. He guided Vince away from Sam and the table, determined to ignore the way Alibek had automatically assumed the spot he'd vacated—and the way she responded to the guy's embrace as he knelt down to pull her close and comfort her. Dammit, she was *none* of his business.

"Where the hell were you, anyway?"

Vince stiffened at his tone. Instead of answering, Vince turned to the table, his dark gaze honing in on the scene they'd left behind. He didn't say anything as he turned back. He didn't have to. They'd flown together since Desert Storm, long enough for Vince to put two and two together. Vince would expect a side order of twenty questions along with that vodka. His slow, pointed drawl confirmed it. "Well, now, *Colonel*, I was down there in that dirt hole pounding on another pilot's heart."

Major Sloane.

Regret bit in. "Is he dead?"

"Nope. Man's a stubborn cuss. He's still hanging on. Or was when Kitterman and I hauled-ass up here. The C-130's loadmaster stayed with him, just in case. Kitterman's running out of supplies though, options. We don't get help soon, the next pounding ain't gonna do any good."

Griff signed. "I know. And I didn't mean to bite your head off. I just…could've used your ears."

They both knew Alibek spoke better Russian than Oklahoma-born Vince ever would, but he let it slide. Unfortunately, his buddy's gaze also slid back to the table.

Vince waited a beat. Then two.

Finally, he just said it. "Did you tell her?"

"*No.*" It came out harsh enough to draw the attention of the one person he would rather not have drawn. Griff lowered his voice. "She doesn't need to know, either. It's none of her damned—"

"Colonel Towers!"

He and Vince spun around in unison, the lingering friction, his fury and the cause, all forgotten as the C-130's navigator came barreling though the door. They met the huffing man at the table.

"It's Deavers, sir. You were right—they sent another bird despite policy. The rescue chopper's thirty miles out. Pilot said to tell you General Gallagher says he's not letting you off the hook this easy. Copilot's local map shows a clearing large enough to land a bird in half a mile due east from here."

Praise the Lord and pass the ammunition!

Griff managed to remain standing as his buddy whooped loudly and whacked him across the shoulders. "Vince, get Kitterman and Deavers in here. I want Sloane strapped inside that stretcher and upstairs in two minutes. We move out in three." He turned to Alibek. "Doctor, I need you to hide those bodies and quick. If you see anything useful, grab it and we'll turn it in to the locals when we reach Moscow."

The guy clipped a nod with the best of recruits and double-timed out of the cabin after Vince.

That left Sam.

Griff headed back to the table. Her color seemed better, but given the shadows, he couldn't be sure.

He squeezed her good arm. "You okay, now?"

Her nod was even more clipped than Alibek's, the subtle stiffening beneath his hand, slight shift of her body away from his telling him more than he wanted to know. The connection they'd shared out near that stump before he'd given her the morphine was gone. As dead as their past.

It was for the best.

The last thing he needed was to become hung up on this woman again. God willing, he'd have everyone safely in Moscow by midnight. He had no idea if Sam would be staying for the Ballistic Missile summit or if her arm would force her to return to the States. By the time the doctors made a decision, he and Vince would be halfway to Ramstein, Germany, and the 86th airlift wing HQ to fill out the paperwork on their own crash. If he was smart, he wouldn't even look back.

But when had he ever used his brain around Samantha Hall?

She was trapped in a sea of cold, brackish filth, unable to move a single part of her body save her arms and her head as it churned in around her. Within seconds, the water had

*reached her chest, sloshing up to drench the remainder of her
uniform as it continued to push in on her ribs. Crushing her
lungs. And then, suddenly, it surged higher, growing icy and
thick until it finally sloshed up over her chin and into her
mouth—and then she was gasping, choking.*

Sinking.

Farther and farther down into the abyss.

No!

*She gathered her strength and thrashed against it, reach-
ing out instinctively as she tried to grab onto something solid
to pull her out, but nothing was there. She went down again,
and this time the brackish water closed over her nose and her
mouth. Over her head. Somehow, she knew this was it. It was
now or never. She gathered her strength one last time and
thrashed for all she was worth—and collided with something
solid. Cold. She latched on to the form instinctively and pulled
it towards her. It was man. A man she recognized.*

And he was dead.

She screamed—

"Hey, easy now. You're safe."

Who? What—

Someone caught her as she jackknifed up from her back,
her heart still pounding against her ribs, frantically sucking
in air as the images that had been so incredibly real a moment
earlier all but evaporated from her mind. The water, the suf-
focation, *Griff*…she could have sworn he was really dead—

Sam froze.

She stared at the distinctive shade of light blue fabric two
inches from her face, studied the equally telling strip of darker,
deeper blue that formed the tie bisecting the crisp, clean uniform shirt beneath. She'd know that solid, muscular chest
anywhere, no matter how many layers of cloth covered it, or
how many decades had passed.

"Griff?"

"I'm here."

But a moment later, he wasn't. He'd quickly but carefully

withdrawn his sinewy arms and warm, reassuring strength from her body, leaving her embarrassingly bereft as he stepped back into the shadows. "You were dreaming. I'd just hoped to—" He shook his head. "Anyway, you're awake now." His sigh filled the room as he claimed the chair beside her bed.

Bed?

She searched the surrounding shadows, apprehension locking in as she caught sight of the blood pressure cuff draped over the top of an institutional stainless steel bed rail. She spotted the free standing pulse monitor next, bio-electronic lead still attached to her right index finger, machine merrily bleeping away. She was in the hospital? The thin, unisex gown skimming her thighs confirmed it, as did the cast covering her entire left arm. The plaster started just below her shoulder, supporting the near ninety-degree bend in her elbow before extending midway down into her hand. Bemused, she traced the clear tubing from the needle embedded in back of her right up to the IV drip hanging beside her bed. She dragged her stare back to the chair beside her bed.

Back to Griff.

She could make his features out clearly now, though the room was still dim. Not only had her eyes adjusted to the shadows, but whatever medication they'd given her had begun to clear from her head. The thin rays of dawn were just beginning to slip in between the slates of the horizontal blinds behind Griff's head. But which dawn? Griff seemed to be waiting for it to sink in. Unfortunately, she seemed to be missing a few of the crucial details. She dragged the tip of her tongue across her parched lips. "How…when…?"

Griff ran his hands though hair she could tell had been freshly washed as he leaned forward. "You're at Ramstein." He glanced at his watch. "It's almost six-thirty. We landed late last night, remember? We thought you might need surgery on that arm and neither Meg nor her father trusted the Russian orthopedic surgeons."

That's right. She remembered now. Sam studied the pris-

tine cast again. The break had been nastier than she thought.
It turned out she'd broken both bones in her upper arm. While
she hadn't needed the surgery, she had ended up receiving
anesthesia so the bones could be set properly. The specialist
had also recommended she not attend the conference, but instead head back to Kirtland to recuperate. As a result, Valentin
Novosti had gotten his wish after all—namely her slot repre-
senting Jarco Labs at the summit. She'd asked Dimitri to stay
behind and cover the gap until Valentin arrived today, and then
to keep an eye on Valentin after. The rest of the downed crew
had accompanied her and the C-130's pilot here to Germany
in another C-130.

She licked her lips again. "Major Sloane?" The man had lost
so much blood by the time the second rescue chopper had
landed in Moscow at midnight, she was afraid to ask. "Is he...?"

To her relief, Griff shook his head. "Sloane came out of surgery an hour ago. The hospital still has him listed as critical,
but I'm told that's standard given his injuries. His doctors are
pretty sure he'll pull through. They might even be able to save
his leg."

She closed her eyes and offered up a silent thanks, for the
major and his family. She'd spoken to Sloane for all of five
minutes during their stopover in Turkey the afternoon before.
He'd mentioned a wife but no kids. The crayon drawing with
his name on it taped inside the cockpit had filled in the rest.
Because of Griff and Sergeant Kitterman's dogged determination, a little boy was smiling today. Sam frowned as the rest
sank in, lifting her good hand to check her gown. She half-
expected to find a drenched uniform instead.

The nightmare had been that vivid.

Griff had been that dead.

She couldn't help it, she shuddered. Either Griff could still
read her mind after all these years, or she'd done more than
just scream while she was unconscious because he nodded.
"Your nurse gave you a couple Percocets a few hours ago, just
as the anesthesia wore off. That sent you right back under.

Guess it's a good thing your pain threshold's as high as it is. You never could handle anything stronger than a vitamin."

He cracked his lopsided grin. The same grin he'd shot her the day they'd bumped into each other in that elevator in the ROTC building at UT, right after she'd knocked his early-model laptop out of his hands, cracking the Toshiba's spine and decapitating its internal hard drive. She'd snatched the computer off the floor and froze, a freshly-sworn-in Air Force ROTC cadet, out of uniform but still terrified the mighty major was going to read her the riot act, especially when she realized that this major was the same combat vet the two sergeants in the office had been whispering about. But Griff hadn't yelled. Instead, he'd calmly retrieved his computer from her nerveless fingers, accepted her rushed promise that she could bring it back to life for him, if a bit skeptically. And then he'd smiled that amazingly sexy half-smile of his.

Just as it had then, the silence stretched out. This one no less charged than the other had been.

His smile died off.

He cleared his throat. "Need another?"

She blinked.

"Percocet."

"No." Between the lingering effects of the pills and her biofeedback, she was fine. What was he doing here, anyway? She'd already learned he was stationed at Ramstein. Didn't he have quarters to return to? An inbox overflowing with paperwork he'd been able to plow through while temporarily assigned to the Moscow summit detail? A girlfriend?

A wife?

Sloane. Griff had obviously been checking up on the major. She must have been the next obligatory stop. Well, he'd made it. And she'd like to get dressed. Without an audience. Especially him. "Colonel, I've got—"

Percocet?

Anna. Broken arm or not, how could she have forgotten? She was supposed to have checked in with her sorority sister

the night before. Unfortunately, her own laptop and the separate, encrypted communications link she'd designed and installed the week before for the sole purpose of contacting
Anna safely was now sitting at the bottom of some Russian
lake, buried in silt. She cased the room quickly, searching for
a phone. All she found was a set of bed controls and a nurse's
call button beside her right hand. The devil with rank.

"Griff, I need a secure line."

He didn't move. Instead, he shook his head. Firmly.
"You're in no condition to phone the lab."

He would assume that was her intent, wouldn't he?

It didn't matter. She had no intention of kowtowing to this
man's orders after all these years. They weren't trapped out
in Chechen controlled territory anymore. Nor—as he'd so
rudely and succinctly put it in that cabin within earshot of
Dimitri—were they still lovers. She shoved the IV tubing
aside and punched the correct control button to raise the head
of her hospital bed. "Dammit, Griff, I need that line. I have to
talk to Meg and I have to do it now. It's very important—"

"Does it concern Anna Shale?"

Stunned, she lapsed into silence. She finally nodded, completely confused. Yes, Griff knew Anna. He'd known all five
women that made up the founding members of Sisters-in-
Arms. But that was years ago. Even if he had seen the news
and heard the rumors, there was no way he could have known
about her Sister's undercover and extremely precarious mission in Panama City, much less know about Anna's threaten-
ing addiction.

Could he?

She licked her lips once again, this time not so much to
moisten them, but to stall as she tried to figure out how to
phrase it. "Did you…talk to Meg about Anna?"

Instead of answering, Griff stood. He stepped up to the bed
before she could blink, reaching past her head to retrieve the
pitcher of water and crushed ice from the tray table she'd
noted earlier. He poured out a cup of slush and replaced the

sweating pitcher. Griff added an accordion straw to the cup next, even bent the darn thing for her before guiding the tip to her lips as if she were two years old, not bucking thirty.

Trapped against the head of the mattress with no place to go, she sipped. "Thanks."

He kept the cup in his hands, at the ready. She wasn't surprised. She was however intrigued by his hands for the second time in two days. Just as they'd been the previous night when Griff had administered the morphine, his strong, callused fingers were too close to ignore the obvious.

He wasn't wearing a ring.

She shoved the discovery from her mind. A lot of men didn't wear wedding rings. Especially military ones with specialties which put their fingers at risk. "Well? Are you going to tell me what you know about Anna?"

"I know she's about to get her commission reinstated."

"*What?* You're serious? Meg told you?"

Pure joy crashed into relief as he nodded. She grabbed Griff's hands—only to catch more than his startled curse as the contents of the cup sloshed over the rim. Sam gasped as a thousand tiny shards of crushed ice splattered across her chest, drenching the upper half of her hospital gown. Freezing water trickled down between her breasts. Unable to hold her breath against the chill, she inhaled deeply. Unfortunately, the motion caused the gown to stretch and cling, delineating the flesh beneath with zealous perfection. From the sudden flaring in Griff's gaze, he'd just figured out firsthand that her topside bounty had increased significantly since her teens.

Her heart began hammering against her ribs as Griff tore his stare from her chest and fused it to her burning cheeks—and damned if that tattle-telling monitor didn't pick up its pace. She yanked the clamp off her index finger and tossed the lead on the bed before it could condemn her completely. If the situation wasn't so painful, she might have found satisfaction in the matching flush that had crept up from Griff's collar to stain his entire neck. At nineteen to his world-weary

thirty, it wasn't often that she'd been able to get the best of
Griffith Towers. Evidently more had changed during the past
decade than their ages and her bra size.

He dragged his stare down to the slush still clinging to her
chest. "I'm sorry, Sam. I—"

She shook her head. "It was my fault."

Anything to get him to move so she could knock the ice
away. She started in as Griff turned to toss the empty cup on
the tray table. To her horror, he nudged her hands out of the
way as he turned back, drawing the drenched fabric from her
chest as he brushed at the remaining ice. Curse the man's displaced sense of gallantry and incessant need to do. He'd
tugged the hospital gown so high up in his haste, he'd bared
her all the way to her navel, exposing more than the pair of
dark blue bikinis she'd never have worn in the first place had
she not been deathly low on laundry before her emergency
packing. She grabbed the gown with her good hand and
yanked the hem down over her smattering of scars before that
infamous pilot's gaze of his wandered far enough away from
the skimpy lace to zero in on the last of her remaining secrets.

"Sorry."

She nodded as he reached out again, this time brushing his
fingers directly over her chest to remove the last of the ice.
She suffered through his ministrations silently. It wouldn't do
any good to argue. Not with this man. The rate she was going,
the fire in her now full-body blush would dry her nightgown
in under a minute anyway. The ice gone, Griff finally stepped
back. Just far enough to retrieve the covers she must have
tossed off during her nightmare. He drew the sheet and blanket up her legs, tucking the edges beneath the cast and around
her waist.

"Thanks."

He nodded.

"So…what about Anna? I assume you spoke to Meg?"

"Yes. My squadron forwarded a call from her early this
morning. She in turn asked me to pass on a message. She

wanted you to know the Panamanian Defense Forces have arrested Anna's cousin and averted the bombing. Anna's safe and her undercover assignment is over. She's being debriefed now. It may take a few weeks but her Navy commission and security clearance will be restored. Oh, and I'm supposed to tell you the guy Anna was working with checked out. Turns out he wasn't some ex-military thug for hire—but an Army major working undercover for Delta Force. Meg said you'd understand."

Sam nodded. She did. She'd also figured out why Griff had stopped by and it wasn't to make sure she'd survived her surgery intact. The fact that Griff had been asked to deliver a message ambiguous enough that it could have easily been left at the nurse's station proved it. Poor Meg. Her friend would do anything to get her to change her mind about Dimitri's offer. She should have swallowed her pride years ago and told her sorority sisters what really happened after Griff received his masters and left for Alaska—or, rather, what hadn't.

It would have saved her the awkward silence settling in between her and Griff now.

What had she expected? That Griff had spent the night beside her bed in some sort of lovelorn vigil, waiting for her to wake so he could drag her into his arms tell her how sorry he was? How wrong he'd been? Right. The man had sworn his undying love once before. Vowed to come back for her on her own graduation day. Some soul mate. Griff hadn't even had the decency to place a ten-second phone call when he'd broken up with her. Instead, he'd dropped off the face of the planet.

For *eleven* years.

She swore she felt another eleven drag out.

Just when she thought she couldn't stand another second, the door to her room swung open. A moment later, a cheery, "Good morning!" floated across the antiseptic tiles.

Griff reclaimed the chair he'd vacated earlier as a petite brunette bustled through the door, blood pressure cuff and

chart in hand. The nurse laid the chart across Sam's lap and
withdrew a hospital-grade thermometer from one of the pockets on the lab coat covering her Air Force Blues.

The nurse nodded across the bed to Griff. "Sir." Twin dimples flashed as she turned to extend her hand toward Sam's
good one. "Captain—uh, Doctor Hall—I doubt you remember our first meeting. You were still coming out of the anesthesia. I'm Lieutenant Beaumont."

Sam smiled back. "Sorry, I don't. And, please, how about
we just go with Sam."

"Tina." The woman's grin turned impudent as she withdrew her hand to adjust the flow on Sam's IV bag. "Well, Sam,
now that you're fully awake, perhaps you can talk the colonel
into a nap to go with his five-second shower. Lord knows the
rest of us haven't been able to."

What? Griff had been here all night?

No way.

Her shock must have shown, because the woman actually
winked. Before Sam could respond, much less turn to catch
sight of Griff, the nurse had sheathed the thermometer's probe
with a sterile cover and poked the end into her mouth. Sam
bit down on plastic sleeve as Griff stood. Other than the slight
tick flagging at the right of his jaw as he turned to pace his
way to the foot of the bed, she couldn't read his expression.
It didn't matter. That tick told her more than enough.

Griff *had* spent the night in her room.

And he was not happy that she'd been told.

Chapter 4

Griff turned his back on that stunned whiskey stare, executing a clipped retreat to the foot of the bed. So he'd hung out by Samantha's side for most of the night.

Big deal.

It wasn't as if he'd had someplace better to go.

Under normal circumstances, he'd have made a beeline for his quarters. But since he was still technically assigned to the Moscow summit, there'd been nothing to greet him across base but empty rooms. So he'd headed for his squadron instead. There, he'd phoned Grace Larring for the second time in four hours, letting her know he was back on base and would be by for breakfast by nine—before the entire base had a chance to wake and begin gossiping about his crash. That done, he'd taken one look at his overflowing inbox and opted for the five second shower that nosey nurse had accused him of before donning the spare uniform he kept on hand and heading back here. By the time Meg's call had been forwarded, he was already sitting in that chair behind him, waiting like some love-struck fool for Sam to regain consciousness.

It was more than she'd ever done.

Contrary to what that nurse and her starry-eyed coworkers thought, he wasn't hanging around to tear open old scars. He was just doing his job. He knew Samantha well enough to know that the carnage she'd witnessed at the cabin would get to her. That nightmare proved it. Griff steeled himself against the memory of her thrashing as he turned back to the bed. Back to that whiskey gaze still focused on him, still dark with shock. And now, also burning with curiosity.

He ignored it.

The nurse stepped between them, severing Samantha's stare and the other, more painful memories it stoked as she leaned in to press her stethoscope to Sam's chest. She listened to Sam's heart and lungs, then nodded, looping the scope around her neck as she straightened. The nurse retrieved Sam's wrist next, deftly checking and recording her pulse as well as the other data on the chart she'd brought in with her. That done, she tore into a packet of sterile gauze she'd removed from one of the pockets on her lab coat, retrieved a roll of clear tape and proceeded to remove Sam's IV line.

He took it as a good sign.

The nurse swept her gaze toward the wall behind him as she finished. "You might want to turn on the TV, Colonel. Both your crashes are all over the news again. Or will be."

Sam's brow shot up along with his, but he beat her to the punch. "Why?"

The nurse slipped the scraps from the gauze packet and roll of tape into her pocket. "I caught CNN in the lounge. The Russians are scheduled to give a news conference in about—" she glanced at her watch "—two minutes."

Once again, Sam's stare zeroed in on his and once again, it was burning with curiosity.

So was he.

The Russian Minister of Information and the American ambassador had already issued a joint statement regarding the crashes the night before, albeit a sanitized one. He and Sam had caught the bulk of the minister's remarks together via a satellite hookup during the flight from Moscow to Ramstein while Vince, Kitterman and the C-130 contingent wrapped up their incident reports at the rear of the plane. No mention had been made of the Chechens they'd killed at the cabin. Another official statement so soon could only mean one thing. The Kremlin was ready to reveal the extent of the carnage.

Griff retrieved the remote control from the tray table as the nurse grabbed her blood pressure cuff and wrapped it around Sam's good bicep. He turned the TV on and clicked through the channels. The station's camera was already focused on an oak podium rigged with at least a dozen microphones by the time he reached CNN. Unfortunately, no one was manning it. Griff frowned as a disembodied voice began filling the dead air with a recap of the statement they'd caught on the plane. A swift rip filled the room. He turned back to Sam as the nurse finished tearing open the Velcro on the blood pressure cuff. She tossed the cuff on the bed—and froze.

"What on earth happened?"

Sam flushed as the sheet drooped the rest of the way, revealing her drenched gown. Fire torched his own neck as her instinctive shift caused the soggy fabric to cling to breasts he did not remember being that generous. The heat index beneath his tie kicked up another notch as the nurse arched an accusing brow in his direction.

"I'll get a dry gown."

Sam's good hand snaked out before the woman could step away. "What I'd really like, Tina, is a fresh uniform. Heck, a pair of sweats will do. I'm sure there's a flight headed to the States later today. I need to be on it."

"You're leaving? *Now?*"

Her gaze snapped to his. Ice frosted the whiskey within. "Yes, now. The lab was short-handed even before the Moscow conference. It'll be even more so now that another scientist has been sent on to fill in for me. I need to get back. We have several crucial tests scheduled."

"Well, they can wait." He realized his mistake the moment the words—the implied order—came out. Unfortunately, her stubborn streak had already locked in. She'd go home in agony now if she had to, just to spite him. He sighed. "Sam—"

Too late.

She'd turned back to the nurse. "Tina, how long do you normally hold a patient after a break like mine has been surgically set?"

The woman shifted her bemused stare from him to Sam and blinked. "Well, ah, Doctor Caughlin usually lets his similar orthopedic patients go once the anesthesia has worn off and he's satisfied there weren't any complications. You'll just need to check in with the Kirtland hospital within twenty-four hours of your arrival."

"Great. Then instead of a fresh gown, perhaps you could call my doctor and tell him I'm ready to sign my release. Then I'd appreciate it if you could see about a fresh uniform. Heck, I'll be happy with a scrub suit. You've already taken my vitals and removed my IV. We both know you wouldn't have done that if I wasn't healthy."

"Yes, ma'am."

Griff spun around before the nurse finished nodding, marching to the foot of the bed in an effort to bring his frustration to heel. The trip was far too brief and definitely in vain. He waited as the nurse gathered her equipment and hurried across antiseptic tiles to open the door. The moment the door closed, he turned around. "Look, surely no experiment is so critical you can't take a day off. For crying out loud, you just survived a plane crash."

"Yes, I did." She tugged the bed sheet up over her damp gown and locked her arm on top. "I'm also fine."

The curse shooting up his throat ripped free before he could stop it. He clamped down on the next before it compounded the tension between them—and her insane stubbornness. It was amazing how quickly they'd slipped into the old routine. *Their* routine. They'd been through it so many times, he knew it by heart. Griff forced his jaw to unclench as he returned to the head of the bed. He even took pains to soften his stance as he stopped. But before he could open his mouth, the monotonous drone of the CNN day anchor gave way to the cacophony of a dozen voices speaking at once.

In Russian.

Their latest argument would have to wait.

He turned to the television as the minister stepped up to the podium. Fifty-odd camera flashes punctuated the man's initial greeting in his native Russian. A short, smoothly delivered greeting in English followed in deference to the presence of General Gallagher and the U.S. ambassador at the right of the minister's entourage. The initial feminine voice-over resumed, translating the man's remarks into English as he quickly summarized both the C-130 and Pave Hawk crashes, for the first time publicly admitting that Griff's chopper had been shot down by one of two surface-to-air missiles fired by Chechen extremists. A moment later, Sam gasped and he stiffened—and it wasn't due to the minister's subsequent announcement regarding the deaths of the seven-man terrorist squad that located them at the cabin.

It was the revelation that followed.

Griff stood there, transfixed right along with Sam, as the minister detailed a second—and until then, unknown to them—bloodbath at the cabin. He knew then, it was a damned good thing he'd ordered the cabin evacuation when he had, because all hell had literally broken loose in their wake. According to the minister, another nine men—seven Russians and two more Chechens—had lost their lives outside that decrepit pile of logs. The forest surrounding the cabin was now firmly under Chechen control. With that bombshell, the minister ended his remarks and declined to take questions. General Gallagher and the ambassador reiterated the minister's refusal.

Sam was the first to move, retrieving the remote from the mattress as CNN shifted its feed to the anchor desk and began rehashing the minister's remarks. Silence filled the room as she clicked the TV off. He could feel the ache in her heart deepening as it stretched out. Several long moments later, his hand crept up on its own, closing over her shoulder just shy of her cast before he could stop it. He gave into the gnawing urge and squeezed gently. It took several more long moments, but she finally dragged her gaze to his. The unshed tears welling up within those whiskey depths seared through his gut as a bottle of booze never could. He gave into temptation again and pushed the tangled strands from her cheeks to smooth his fingers across the soft skin still bruised from the crash.

"Samantha…there's nothing any of us could have done."

Her chin wobbled slightly as she nodded. "I know. It's just…they were searching for us when they died…and we—" she sucked in her breath "—we were already safe." Several tears slipped free. She tried blinking the rest back, but they followed the others, slowly trickling down her face.

He brushed them aside for her.

She was right. The timing stunk. But according to the minister's remarks, if they'd stayed at that cabin another thirty minutes, they'd have ended up dead as well. They simply hadn't had enough ammunition to defend themselves against what had obviously been a well-planned, zealously executed Chechen uprising. Griff dropped his hand back on her shoulder and gave it another squeeze. "I'll go ask the nurse for a fresh gown."

She tensed.

He took the hint and released her. But he was not giving up. Not with her health at stake. He cut her off before her mouth even opened, "Sam, be reasonable. Your lab's not going anywhere. Why not catch up on your sleep? You can leave first thing tomorrow. I'll make the arrangements myself."

Her gaze narrowed. "You still don't give up, do you?"

No, that had been her department.

He kept the assessment to himself as he stepped away, opting to place a good two feet of the room's now cooling air between them as a downright frigid memory bit in. The familiar ache followed. He slammed both back before they succeeded in ratcheting up his temper. That was not why he was here.

A moment later, she wasn't.

There, that is.

Before he could reclaim the distance he'd relinquished, Sam had shoved the bedcovers to the foot of the mattress and swung her legs to the floor. She padded barefoot across the marbleized gray and white tiles, stopping in front of a modular dresser beside the stainless steel sink. Despite her bulky cast, she managed to rifle through the drawers with ease but she came up empty-handed. She shifted her attention to the narrow closet on the right—and the hospital robe she'd evidently been searching for. He rounded the bed as she slipped her right arm into its corresponding sleeve.

Her palm snapped up as he reached out to help her drape the remaining sleeve over her cast. Her voice snapped with it, "I don't need help." The renewed frost in her stare told him she didn't need *him* at all.

He wasn't surprised. She'd been pissed with him since the moment they'd crawled out of that lake. Hell, the air had all but crackled with it when he'd followed her to that stump outside the cabin. In deference to their situation, he'd ignored it. Well, he didn't have to anymore.

Neither did he have to put up with it.

He held up his own hands. "Fine. Do whatever you want. It's obvious you're going to, anyway." He swung around and headed for the chair he'd spent far too many hours wedged in during the night. He had places to be. Someone who actually wanted to see him. Someone who'd *missed* him. He held fast to the thought as he grabbed the coat to his blues from the back of the chair, donned it, then bent to retrieve his hat. His uniform complete, he rounded the bed for the last time.

But then he stopped at the door.

Why, he couldn't be sure. Maybe he was still holding out hope she'd see reason. Or maybe, deep down, he just wanted one last look at the only woman he'd ever given his heart to. The same woman who'd gone on to grind it beneath her nineteen-year-old, fickle foot. Hell, he didn't know why he was still standing in this cold, barren room. All he knew was that like her inexplicable anger at the cabin, he didn't deserve the shadows of accusation and betrayal that'd slipped into her eyes. She compounded them with a clipped shrug.

"That's it? No polite lies. No, *nice to see you, we should do this again sometime?* Not even a simple goodbye? You're just going to open that door and walk away?" Her voice wavered on the final word, leaving palpable pain and a host of regrets behind as she finished.

Hers and his.

Until white-hot fury purged his own, stunning him with its intensity after all this time. The hell with it. He clipped off his own shrug. "What did you think would happen? We'd exchange phone numbers so I could call you and your lover up some night and get another earful?" He'd expected her flinch. The swift gasp that followed, too. Hell, he'd relieved this moment so many times during the intervening years, he'd even anticipated the loss of color as the blood drained from her cheeks. But what he hadn't expected was the absolute indignation that followed.

"What the devil are you talking about?"

This time, he stiffened.

She wanted to play innocent? Fine with him. He'd nail her to the wall as heartlessly as she nailed him. "The phone call, sweetheart. I know it's been a while, but I do remember making it. Just as I remember getting that goddamned ticket back without so much as an explanation." Not that he'd needed one. Not by then. Ten blistering seconds during the dead of night the week after he'd mailed it had said it all. He opened his mouth to recount those seconds and promptly closed it. Eleven years might have passed, but he still had his pride.

He also appeared to have Samantha's undivided confusion.

She shoved her good hand through her hair, pushing it past her shoulders. "Griff, I'm going to ask you one more time, what the hell you talking about? And please use small words this time. I have a feeling I'm missing a lot here. What ticket? What phone call? For that matter, what *lover?*"

"Unless you married him—yours."

If he hadn't known better—firsthand—he'd have sworn her frustration was as genuine as her shock had appeared to be. "I don't understand. I'm not married. I never have been. Until recently, I've never even seriously considered it." Her stare narrowed, accused. "Except with you."

Until recently? Alibek?

Evidently the old fist of pain hadn't lost its punch, because it socked into Griff's heart with almost as much force as it had all those years before. At least this time he was able to recover quickly. He dragged his attention back to the past. To the lover he could prove. The betrayal that had very nearly consumed him. "That's not what my replacement said."

"What replac—"

"*Chet Osborne.*"

Again, she stiffened. Like the first time, she even managed to do it convincingly. It didn't matter. He didn't care how accomplished an actress she'd become during the intervening years, he'd had enough of her phony innocence. He tossed his hat to the foot of the bed and stalked right up to her, determined to expose her performance for what it was.

"Yeah, you remember Chet? Your no-neck football jock of a neighbor at UT?" He sure hadn't forgotten the man. Especially after the bastard had the cojones to tell him to his face that he'd be moving in on Sam after he left for Alaska.

Less than two months later, Chet had.

"Griff, I *never* slept with Chet."

He ignored the lie and continued, "You know, after you hung up on me, I did as you asked. I spent some time thinking. I realized you were right about a lot of things. I also decided to ask you to fly up to Alaska over Christmas break so we could work things out. The next weekend, I tried calling again, this time in the middle of the night. Stupid me, I hoped you'd be too tired to hang up. You were tired all right—from screwing Chet. Pardon me if I didn't wait for the punk to fumble the phone across the bed." He crossed his arms, anchoring them over the band already clamped about his chest. "Couple days later, my mailbox added insult to injury, punting the ticket I'd sent back in my face without so much as a *thanks, but no thanks* attached. I might not be a rocket scientist like you, honey, but I got the message."

But from the rocked expression on Sam's face, he'd almost swear she hadn't. Gotten the ticket, that is.

She finally recovered, still shaking her head as she grabbed his arm. Her fingers bit into him in way her earlier shock and denial hadn't. "You have to believe me. I never received a ticket from you. As for Chet, I swear to God, I *never* slept with him. The only time Chet was even in my apartment after our last fight was when he—" Her gaze shot wide, as if she'd suddenly found herself staring down the wrong end of a 9mm pistol—held by someone she'd once thought of as a friend. "*Oh, my God.*" Maybe she had.

He did know the shock and indignation in her gaze finally managed to pierce his fury. For the first time in over a decade, Griff was forced to wonder if he'd interrupted what he thought he had all those years ago. Had the only woman he'd ever loved given herself to another man that night…or had Chet been setting the stage to cover up for his own sins?

"Sam?"

She just stood there, her eyes still focused somewhere in the past. His gut fisted in response. Her hand fell away as he grabbed her by the shoulders and tugged her close. "Dammit, this isn't the time to clam up. When Chet *what?*"

He was terrified he already knew.

She might not have had Chet pegged for a rutting stag, but he had. Tutoring his ass. That hulking beast had been after a lot more than a passing grade in calculus. Griff had known it the moment he'd met the steroid-riddled punk. She'd simply been too young and too naive to see it. A decade might have passed, but if the scenario he'd feared most upon leaving Texas had occurred, he'd hunt Chet down. The hell with any statue of limitations. His thoughts must have shown, because she finally returned to the present—and him.

She reached out as she shook her head. This time, she squeezed his arm. "It's not what you think. Let's just say I realized you were right about Chet soon after that fight. He was a jerk at heart. I don't dispute Chet was in my apartment when you called—but I wasn't. I swear it. Griff, I wasn't even in Austin." Instead of continuing, she turned and headed to the bed. The mattress creaked slightly as she turned once more to slump against the edge. "That fight was as hard for me as I think it was for you. For what it's worth, I've always regretted that I hung up on you. But really, what did you expect? This isn't the first time you accused me of sneaking around with Chet and we both know it."

She was right.

She'd also done more than hang up on him during that last fight. She'd given him an ultimatum. If he couldn't figure out how to trust her, he had two options left: get over himself or get over *her*. She'd told him to think long and hard about it, really think, then call her back in two weeks. He'd been pissed as hell at first. Especially after she'd hung up on him again the following morning when he'd tried to jump the gun. By midweek, however, he'd come to understand the wisdom of the delay. Getting through those first three months in Anchorage without Samantha had been hard enough. But those next few days of knowing he couldn't even call just to hear her voice and worse, that there was a chance he might never be able to hear it again, had been living hell.

Fortunately, that hell had forced him to think. More importantly, to realize she was right about a lot of things. Namely, he did have a tendency to be overbearing. Even before he'd graduated, Sam had begun to complain that he acted more like an older brother than a lover, telling her what she should do before she even asked for his opinion. As much as it had pained him to admit, she'd been right about that, too. It was just, she'd been so damned young at the time and even more trusting—regarding Chet and so much more.

Samantha might have possessed one of the more brilliant minds to have ever entered UT's aerospace engineering program, but she'd also been pretty damned naïve about what went on outside the classroom and the lab at the time. Still, she'd been correct about that too. It had been her life to live, her mistakes to make, her lessons to learn. Much as he'd wanted to, he wouldn't have been able to spare her the normal aches and pains of growing up. Nor had he had the right to assume she'd quit college two years from her degree and marry him early simply because the Air Force had changed his orders at the last minute—opting not to transfer him eighty miles away to San Antonio, but practically an entire continent away to Anchorage.

Four days into his hell, and unable to fathom another ten, he'd sat down and written her a letter telling her he'd done as she'd asked. He'd finally come to his senses. He was ready to talk. He hoped she'd be willing to do it in person. He'd signed his letter, enclosed the opened-ended ticket and overnighted both, praying she'd end his misery and call him back early. Four more days of silence and he'd had it. He broke down and tried calling her again…and got Chet.

Shame displaced the anger that usually accompanied the memory. It crawled up his throat, hot and suffocating, even after all this time. He knew Sam could see the evidence on his neck, too, even from ten feet away. She might have been the younger lover in their relationship, but she'd been old enough to know that a long distance relationship couldn't survive without trust. Trust he'd never truly given her.

The night he'd spoken to Chet…and after.

Regret burned through him. Griff cleared his throat in a futile effort to ease it. "You think Chet intercepted my letter, too, don't you? He probably signed for it. Just never gave it to you. He mailed it back to me instead. After that call, he had to know I wouldn't even question it."

"I think so." She hooked a thigh on the mattress and scooted up into the rumpled sheets, carefully smoothing the nightgown and robe down over her thighs as far as they would go. Unlike earlier when he'd tried to assist her with the ice, he knew she wasn't attempting to shield her body from his gaze; she was trying to absorb the pain and regret. She kept that gorgeous stare fused to her fingers as she sighed. "The weekend after that fight, Meg had to drive to Corpus Christi. Her dad was TDY to the naval base for the week and I…I was still too upset to study. You weren't supposed to call and give me your decision for another week. But it was Thanksgiving weekend. Four days of staring at that damned phone, wondering that since I'd hung up on you twice, you might have decided to get over me." She held up her hands. "But I couldn't just leave. I had responsibilities."

Gunter. All this time, and he could still remember its name. That damned alley cat Sam had taken in.

As she had so often in the past, she read his mind. She nodded, confirming it. "Chet told me if I gave him the key, he'd stop in at night, feed Gunter and—"

"—get the mail." Jesus, Mary and Joseph, *no*.

He willed her to deny it. But she didn't.

And he already knew it was true.

The weekend his life had been torn apart only to be stitched back together in ways he never would have imagined, Sam hadn't even been home. And he'd been too busy salving his pride and his heart to even consider that there might be another reason why Chet would be in her bedroom. Not that Chet had given him the chance. He'd bet his pending squadron command Chet had been rifling through Sam's underwear when he'd called. Despite the kid's stunned, academy-award performance at the time, Chet had to have known it was him before he'd even picked up the phone. Who else would be calling Sam's private line at three in the morning?

And he'd accused Sam of naiveté?

He'd been suckered by a punk ten years his junior.

Griff spun around and slammed his palm into the modular closet as the force of the betrayal slammed into him. Even after all these years, he yearned to bash his fist in again, to roar with the injustice of it. But he didn't. He couldn't. As bitter as the revelation was, what did it really change?

Absolutely nothing.

He stared into the mirror above the sink and studied her downcast reflection, mesmerizing despite the bruises from her crash—and now taunting him with the innocence he could no longer deny. She reached over her cast with her right hand and pulled at the tie to her hospital robe, twining the thin strip of cloth around and around her first two fingers until the tips had turned white. She didn't seem to notice the loss of blood even though she was staring straight at them.

"You know, there's something I still don't understand. Chet's deception explains why you never called back with your answer, not to mention why you didn't show up at my graduation like you swore you would, but—" The thin layer of her gown rose as she stopped to draw her breath in deep, her gaze finally rising to meet his as well. "Griff, I broke down and called your room at the Bachelor Quarters Christmas morning. You weren't there. The clerk at the front desk said you'd checked out a couple days before. He also said, you said—"

His heart constricted as she closed her eyes and searched for the strength to continue. If he'd only known then what he knew now. But he hadn't. So he did what he'd unwittingly done all those years before. He finished it for her. "I told him not to give out my forwarding address or number."

"*Yeah.*"

If he'd harbored any hope, any fantasy, that somehow they could make it through this, the raw edge to that simple word slashed it. How had he thought this would end, anyway? Had he honestly believed he could confess his sins and she would forgive all? And then what? She'd stick around for a day or two before heading back across the ocean, perhaps even stop by his house for an intimate dinner? For *three*. Hell, he hadn't even been able to kill his feelings for this woman years before when he'd believed she'd betrayed him with another man. If nothing else, sitting beside her bed through the night had proven that. He could never hurt her. Not like that.

Not now. Not ever.

So what did he do? His cell phone rang before he could decide. He ignored the first ring as he turned to face Sam, determined to let whoever it was leave voicemail—until the door to the room swung open on the second ring. Fate was definitely against them. Still. He caved in to the third trill, retrieving the phone clipped to his belt as the nurse entered, a stack of blue sweats and what could only be Sam's battered leather uniform oxfords in tow. He flipped the phone open as the nurse reached the bed in his stead.

"Towers."

His copilot's voice filled his ear, rapidly filling him in on the latest, not entirely unforeseen, change to their schedule as the nurse handed the sweats and shoes to Sam. The woman murmured something he couldn't catch due to Vince's sudden bellow as well as the chopper now powering up in his ear. Their chopper. Her impromptu humanitarian mission complete, the nurse retreated across the room. By the time the door closed behind her, Vince had finished, too.

Griff severed the connection with a frown. So much for the breakfast he desperately needed to have across base. He shoved his disappointment aside and tucked the phone home.

"Sounds like you're headed back to Moscow."

He nodded. "Seems Meg's father had a couple courses of the local cuisine sent in while we were holed up in that cabin. Four Jarhead pilots came down with food poisoning this morning." He cracked a grin, hoping to lighten the mood. "Marines. They're not as tough as they'd like us to think."

She returned his smile, but the attempt was half-hearted and faded quickly. The silence returned, heavy and resigned. He knew why. She'd already asked the question. He knew her well enough to know she wouldn't repeat it. Just as she knew that if he intended on answering, he'd have done it by now. Eleven more years seemed to pass before she spoke.

"You have to leave now, don't you?"

He should agree and be done with it. Cauterize this raw, seeping wound right here and now—for the both of them. But again, he couldn't. God only knew how many more years would pass before fate sent their worlds crashing down around them, leaving them staring at each other across the same room, breathing the same tortured air. He already knew the answer.

Never.

"You sure you can't take a day to rest?"

She shook her head. "My boss died unexpectedly two days ago. The lab's going through an upheaval as it is."

There was nothing left then, was there?

And Vince was waiting.

Leave.

He tried to. He just couldn't seem to get his feet to cooperate. Her gaze darkened as the seconds continued to tick out, dampened. Maybe that's what did it, what finally allowed his feet to move. But for some reason they were moving in the wrong direction. Unable to stop, or perhaps simply unwilling, he stepped closer. Before he knew it, he'd reached the bed. Her. He drank in the soft features he'd never forgotten, absorbing the changes time had wrought. Later, when he was back in Moscow and the shroud of night had closed in, cloaking him with privacy, he would drag this moment out again.

Savor it. Savor her.

Dammit, just one kiss. On the cheek. That's it.

Just one more time.

He dipped his head before sanity had a chance to set in, but the moment his lips brushed her soft, smooth flesh, she turned. A split second later, their lips brushed. He felt the swift rush of warmth as her startled gasp pulled the air from his lungs into her own, but he didn't move. Neither did she. God as his witness, he hadn't meant to do *this*. But once again, he couldn't seem to move forward—and he sure as hell couldn't find the strength to step back. He just stood there, holding, hovering, a fraction of an inch from the sweetest taste he'd ever known. Wanting, craving. The moment her soft, tremulous sigh bathed his lips, his restraint shattered.

His hands snapped up, tunneling into her hair as his mouth crashed down.

"Oh, my!"

They tore apart.

Griff spun around as the edge of door slipped away from the nurse's fingers, his own goddamned guilty hands looking even guiltier as they raked through his hair before he could stop them. He forced them down and locked them to his sides. "Good God, lieutenant—don't you ever knock?"

Scarlet flashed into the woman's cheeks. "I'm sorry, colonel. I didn't mean to interrupt. It's just— It's your phone, sir. It was busy, so he called here."

"He?" He'd just spoken to Vince.

Who else knew enough to know he was here?

"Staff Sergeant Garza. It's about your daughter."

For the second time in as many minutes, Griff felt more than heard Samantha's gasp. He forced himself to ignore it as the panic slammed in. "What happened? Is she—"

"She's fine, sir. Physically. Sergeant Garza said to tell you she called the squadron in tears a few minutes ago. Apparently she and her friend woke early and turned the radio on. She knows about the crash, colonel. Garza told her you were okay, but he doesn't think she believes him."

Ah, Christ. It was barely oh-eight-hundred in the morning. He'd called Grace the first chance he'd had following the rescue. Unfortunately, Christy and the friend she'd begged to stay with while he was TDY to Moscow had already fallen asleep.

A pilot herself, Grace had already heard the news and anticipated his concern. She swore she wouldn't breathe a word about the crash until Griff had a chance to call back. When he'd phoned before his shower at the squadron two hours ago to let Grace know he'd be by for breakfast instead, she'd informed him she'd unplugged the TV just in case. So much for Saturday morning cartoon withdrawal.

He had to go.

"Sir?"

He'd forgotten the nurse was there. "Yes?"

"The sergeant's still on the line. He wasn't sure you had her friend's number—"

He held up his hand. "Tell Garza I said thanks. I'll take it from here."

The door closed behind her, its soft swish magnified a thousand-fold by stark silence as he turned to face Sam. He'd never seen her so pale. He knew why. Just as he knew he'd have given anything to have spared her this moment and not for the reasons she obviously thought. They'd spent many an hour lying in bed after she'd agreed to marry him, doing nothing but discussing children. How many, when they'd have them, girls, boys. Names. With four older brothers all she'd truly wanted was a daughter. The daughter he was supposed to have given her. The daughter he'd given to another woman instead.

He reached out instinctively.

She flinched. "Don't."

"Samantha, please, I—"

"Just *go.*"

His cell phone shrilled. He nearly snarled aloud with frustration, but he grabbed it just the same. Just in case.

It wasn't Christy.

"What's the hold up, old man? The blades are already turning. You ready to rock-n-roll, or not?"

Not.

Unwilling to hurt Sam more than he had, he cupped the

phone and turned away, lowering his voice as he briefed his copilot on the unexpected delay as well as his concerns for his daughter. Christy had had a rough enough time worrying while he was in Afghanistan and then Iraq. If Sergeant Garza had mentioned he was at the hospital visiting someone when Christy called the squadron, she'd never believe he was okay by simply hearing his voice. She needed to see him for herself. To his eternal relief, Vince offered to contact the scheduler and buy them the time he'd need to stop by and calm Christy down face to face. One crisis staunched, Griff hung up on Vince—just in time to catch the soft swish of another door and the resoundingly cold clunk that followed.

Samantha.

No!

He spun around, but it was too late. She was already gone. So were the sweats and the shoes the nurse had dropped off. She'd locked herself in the bathroom. A moment later, he heard the bathtub water gushing. Loudly. The message was clear. He could pound on that door until North and South Korea reunited, she wasn't coming out. He even knew why. As much as he'd hurt her, she was offering him one last gift, doing what he hadn't been able to do. Leave. Nor did he have any choice but to accept it. Christy needed him. Moscow wanted him.

The irony of it ripped through him.

He loved his daughter and believed in his career. But, dammit, why did embracing Christy and the Air Force have to mean turning his back on the only woman he'd ever loved?

Again.

Chapter 5

Kirtland, Air Force Base
Albuquerque, New Mexico

Griff had a daughter.

Twelve weeks later and half a world away, the realization still had the power to sear through Sam with more force than the combined thrust of the twin solid rocket boosters that had propelled the shuttle Endeavor into space the day before. Unfortunately, the inescapable heartache that came with it also forced Sam to accept that no matter how many times she refocused her attention on the stack of requisition forms she'd carted from her office across base, she was too preoccupied to plow through them. Even if the man hadn't managed to invade her brain for the millionth time since her return home, she was still trapped in yet another suffocating hospital, albeit this time, in a waiting room. Might as well give in and wallow in the only pain all the biofeedback skills in the world wouldn't be able to dent.

Griff.

He'd actually fallen in love. Gotten married. Fathered at least one child. With someone else.

She still couldn't quite believe it. Or maybe she just didn't want to. It wasn't as if she'd expected that he'd lived the life of a monk during the past decade. Nor would she have honestly wished it. But in her own selfish heart, she had wanted to believe the promise Griff had made all those years ago. Eleven years ago, when she'd pressed his engagement ring back into his hand and begged him to hold on to it for just two more years, he'd not only sworn to her that he would, he'd also vowed if she didn't wear his ring, no woman *ever* would.

Evidently he'd been wrong.

Worse, she couldn't even blame him. Not when she knew he believed she'd thrown him over for another man. But marriage? That truly hurt. She also knew it was true. A by-blow himself, Griff would never have knowingly had a child out of wedlock.

But was he still married? That she didn't know.

Frankly, she'd been too chicken to ask.

The fact that Griff was by her side when she'd woken in that hospital at Ramstein pointed to no. But the guilt flooding his face after that nurse interrupted their fiery split-second kiss pointed to yes. Once she'd recovered from the shock of watching Griff turn away to discuss his daughter during that second conversation with Vince, she'd done the only thing she could. She'd left. An eternity later, she'd screwed up enough nerve to unlock that bathroom door and reenter her room. To her relief Griff was gone. By the time her doctor arrived, she'd managed to shove Griff back into the past where he belonged. Then she'd changed into that pair of oversized sweats and slightly pinched shoes and boarded a plane to Kirtland—and the present she'd carved out for herself…the future Dimitri still wanted to share. A future she was pretty sure she wanted to share with Dimitri, too. If she could keep Griff from haunting it.

And her.

Then stop thinking about him.

Difficult to do with the first test flight for the optical target recognition experiment scheduled for later this week, now wasn't it? Sam sighed and gave up on the requisitions. She tapped the pile of forms into a tidy stack and reached for the briefcase she'd left on the unoccupied chair beside her. It wasn't there. Startled, she jerked her gaze up—only to have it collide with the worse case of walking conceit she'd ever had the misfortune to work with. Trapped between two hospital appointments in the same day, and now him. Could this day get any worse?

Don't tempt fate.

She mustered a polite nod. "Valentin."

"Samantha." The man's matching, overly-polite smile gleamed down at her as he shifted her briefcase in his hands. Instead of handing the case over, her former officemate studied the distinctive scarlet Jarco rocket emblem stitched into matte-black leather. "Please excuse the fright. With your head bent and so many of the same blue military uniforms, I didn't recognize you. I saw the lab's logo and thought perhaps it might be the missing briefcase."

Wrong. He'd been hoping to get a look at what she was working on and they both knew it.

"Well, it's not Phil's case. It's mine."

"I see." The flint sparking in his light blue gaze claimed otherwise, as did his slightly exaggerated sigh. "Though I suppose since you have already helped yourself to the man's office and its contents—as well as commandeered his work on improved target recognition—technically his briefcase would now be yours as well…for the time being."

Jerk. She was the only Ph.D. at the lab who hadn't put in a bid to assume Phil's position as section head and Valentin knew it. With no less than a dozen research projects on her plate—*before* the addition of Phil's target recognition work—she didn't have the desire or time to fill their boss's shoes, much less his office. Even temporarily. But since she wasn't a civilian like Valentin, she'd duly followed orders, sucking up her chagrin at the added mountain of bureaucratic paperwork until a replacement could be hired or promoted from within.

As for that briefcase, she wished it was Phil's. She hadn't even learned about the missing briefcase until after her return from Ramstein. In the fruitless rush to get their boss to the emergency room during his heart attack, no one had noticed that the briefcase Phil kept in the bottom right drawer of his desk during the day had disappeared. They'd only discovered the discrepancy upon her return. She'd needed the disc to a report Phil had brought home the night before his death. Security had locked the entire facility down and conducted a detailed sweep of the premises, as well as a painstaking search of Phil's on-base housing. Both the report and Phil's briefcase were still missing. The full extent of its contents, a mystery. Or so, Valentin had implied.

She didn't care if Los Alamos and its shredded security reputation *was* practically down the street. Phil Haskell would never have taken classified material out of the lab. Ever. The briefcase would turn up—and when it did, she'd take pleasure in rubbing Valentin's arrogant nose in it.

As for the man's phony excuse for snagging her case, "Besides, I could have sworn the ambulance brought Phil's body here to the hospital, not the contents of his office."

Valentin's smile didn't falter. "One lives in hope."

No, but his ego sure did.

Personally as well as professionally.

Even now while Valentin was supposedly conversing with her, he was furtively scanning the main patient's lounge over the top of her head, all the way to the Medical Records Desk. No doubt searching for some young, naive airman to impress. With Valentin's canned tan, religiously sculpted physique and dark Russian accent, his barely-pubescent target probably would be. Heck, with the man's unusually light blue eyes and slick, black hair just barely touched with silver, most single and quite a few married women would be, too. Until Valentin opened his mouth and his self-inflated ego swelled out.

His gaze finally dipped, his attention with it.

Lucky her. "May I have it?"

He blinked. "I beg y—"

"Please, Valentin, never beg. American women find it so…unseemly."

It took his usual beat to translate the double-entendre to his native tongue. The instant he caught it, anger stained his cheeks.

Somehow, she managed to kill her grin. "Sorry, it's been a rough morning. The briefcase. I believe we've established it's mine. I'd like it back before my appointment."

Liar.

What she'd really like is to walk—no *run*—out of here faster than a laser-guided bomb bearing down on its chosen prey. But at least Valentin had handed the case over. He'd also noted the discrepancy. Granted, he'd had help. At the staff meeting that morning, her secretary had announced there was a chance Sam's arm would be pronounced healed today. Though she detested having her personal life discussed in public almost as much as she hated hospitals, Sam hadn't been able to stay piqued at Lucinda. If she had to type her own work plus someone else's for three months, she'd be giddy too.

Valentin pushed his nose in farther. "I thought Lucinda said your appointment was at ten-thirty."

Sam nodded.

"But…it's twelve-thirty now."

"Sure is."

My how those brilliant wheel could turn. Quite visibly, too. "You…have another appointment as well?"

Valentin waited for confirmation.

He waited in vain.

She'd yet to tell Dimitri that Dr. Stan The-Insistent-Man Burrows had finally made her an offer she couldn't refuse. She sure as hell wouldn't be telling Valentin Novosti. Especially when he'd run to the lab director with the information. She might not want Phil's job, but she damned sure wouldn't let some preening Russian stud use her own body against her so he could steal it. To her relief, a svelte, dark-haired airman fitting Valentin's remaining *too young to know better* criteria strolled within view. She took advantage of his instantaneous distraction and stood.

"Well, gotta run. See you at the lab."

She didn't wait for him to argue. Not that he would have. The man's supersonic libido had already locked on a target. God willing, Valentin wouldn't get shot down until she'd had a chance to clear the runway herself. She crammed the stack of still-unapproved requisitions in her briefcase and leaned down to grab her flight cap and the newly opened can of Diet Coke that was supposed to have doubled as her lunch. Ten steps and a right turn at the far hallway, and she'd be home-free. In her haste to evade Valentin as quickly as possible, she ended up juggling her hat, the briefcase and the can of Diet Coke as she passed the Medical Records Desk, losing her grip on the latter two as she slammed into the hard masculine form that rounded the corner first.

The edge of the briefcase hit the freshly waxed floor, splitting both latches as well as the case wide open. Papers went flying, shooting up and then raining back down around her along with a violent spray of Diet Coke. She gasped as the soda splattered everywhere, leaving dark brown splotches on the walls, the institutional-gray floor, herself, the once-white requisitions forms and, of course, the crisp blue uniform of the colonel she'd nearly flattened.

Only it wasn't just any colonel. It was—

"*Griff?*"

Sam closed her eyes, certain the hospital wait had caused her to see things. People. Him. She waited through four more thunderous heartbeats, then reopened them.

It was Griff, all right. He seemed as stunned to see her as she was to see him. For exactly two more seconds.

Before she could ask what he was doing at Kirtland, much less how long he'd be there, he'd snagged her arm, deftly nudging her over the ring of Coke-stained litter at their feet. She turned back toward the patient lounge as he released her, spotting half a dozen airmen bearing down on them, all clearly eager to help the colonel out. Griff waved them off and bent down himself. She bent down beside him, scooping as many of her papers together as she could while he culled his own folders from the mess. He set his files aside and helped her gather up the remaining papers she'd stuffed into her briefcase earlier that morning. He tried to close the case, but the latches had wrenched askew during the fall.

It wouldn't lock.

He finally settled for tucking his files beneath his left arm as they stood and presenting the briefcase to her as if it were a book. She accepted it silently. Her initial shock bled off, she had no idea what to say. Where to begin. Griff didn't seem to know either—until a lieutenant on crutches hobbled within their view, the man's right foot encased in a dark blue cast that matched his uniform trousers.

"I didn't hurt your arm, did I?"

"No."

He nodded. "Good."

She shifted the briefcase beneath her arm, hinged side down to hold in the mess. "Griff, what are you even doing here? I thought—" She paused as the case slipped, causing the bottom edges of several forms to dangle free. She regained her grip and reached down with her right hand to shove the forms back inside the case—and froze. Griff instinctively shifted his own, lighter burden, discreetly tucking it higher and more snuggly beneath his arm.

It was too late.

The significance of the form that had gotten mixed up with her requisitions had already locked in. The rest fell neatly into place as well. Griff, hand-carrying a stack of outpatient medical records past the main hospital desk, dressed not in his usual flight suit, but his Blues, complete with coat, ribbons. and the golden scrambled eggs that were now embroidered along the bill of his hat. "You're checking in."

He didn't deny it.

And she was still trying to process it.

Griff had been *transferred* to Kirtland. In other words, she had a million of these quaint little unexpected run-ins to look forward to over the next couple of years. The ache she'd been ignoring in her abdomen all morning began to throb, surpassing the painful knocking of her heart. "Well, it's been nice seeing you again, Colonel. I've got to go. I'm supposed to be somewhere soon." Too much. Just leave.

"Samantha, wait—"

She stopped, barely holding her tongue in check as she swung back. What the devil did he expect? A round of polite chit-chat? Or was he honestly hoping she'd hang out long enough so he could introduce her to his wife and kids? No, thank you. She tightened her grip on her battered case and heart as he raked his right through his hair.

"You probably won't believe me, but I'd planned on stopping by your house this evening."

"Well, now you don't have to." In fact, with a bit of conscious effort on her part, they never needed to see each other again. Jarco Labs were as far removed from the hangars as they could get. She lived off base. She could start shopping off base, too, clear across town if she had to. In fact, she would. Tonight.

"Sam, please. We need to talk."

"I'm sorry, but I really do have somewhere to be." In fact, she'd never been so thrilled to have a doctor's appointment in her life. "Goodbye, Colonel."

Unfortunately, those damned pilot reflexes of his were still quicker than hers had ever been. Before she could move much less blink, he'd snagged her elbow and guided her away from a passing captain's curious gaze, right up to the side of the

sheltering corridor. The papers still dangling from the center
of her briefcase brushed the wall as he stopped.

"Griff, please, I really do have to—"

"Daddy!"

"—go." She choked on the last of her protest as Griff
flinched. God, *no*. Not here. Not now. Even before he released her arm, she knew what would eventually happen.

She couldn't do it.

Not today of all days.

Blood began roaring through her head as Griff shot her a
look born of apology and supreme frustration…and something she couldn't fathom—or maybe she just didn't want to.
All she knew was that by the time Griff had released her arm
and turned to the childish summons, her heart had gone completely numb. She stood there, as frozen as the chunk of metal
and circuits she'd soldered together during robotics lab the
year they'd met, watching as Griff smiled and waved to a
young girl, no more than seven or eight. The child's blond
ponytail swished from shoulder to shoulder as she picked up
her pace, until she was all but running across the lounge.

Sam was dimly aware of an older woman, too, her stocky,
nylon-clad legs working overtime to keep up. The woman gave
up and slowed her pace as the girl barreled straight into Griff.

"Daddy, daddy! We saw a signup sheet in the cafeteria.
There's a summer space camp nearby—I can go for a whole
week."

"That's great, honey. We'll talk about it in a minute. First,
there's someone I'd like you to meet." And then, Griff was
turning around once more, this time with his right hand firmly
planted upon the girl's shoulder as she smiled up at her. Every
single matching feature the two shared sliced in deep. Other
than the blond hair, it was all there. The same arch to her
brows, the same thick, curling eyelashes. The same solemn
gray gaze. She could even see the stamp of Griff's quirky,
half-smile in the girl's pink lips.

But there was more.

"Sam, I'd like to meet my daughter. Christy, this is Dr. Samantha Hall. She's the scientist I told you about…and an old friend." The throbbing awkwardness deepened at the euphemism. Still, she couldn't condemn him for it. It was the same one she'd used in that cabin back in Russia when she'd introduced Griff to Dimitri. But she could and would condemn him for the other. And when Christy smiled and offered her own soft though guarded hello, she did. The girl was definitely older than she'd originally thought.

Much older.

The sheet spilling out from her briefcase whispered to her, seducing her with the promise of confirmation…or exoneration. She caved in, reaching down to tug the medical form free. One swift glance at the correct information block, told her all she needed to know. More than she ever wanted. When the guilt and hope in Griff's taut stare gave way to pleading, she knew—he knew she'd figured it out. Just as she knew without asking what he wanted. What he craved. Her understanding. Forgiveness. Her blessing.

How in God's name could she give it?

Here? Now? Like this?

When every raw, jangled nerve in her body hurt so damned much? She'd never know where she found the strength to breathe, much less speak, but she did. She used it before it fled. "It's nice to meet you, Christy. Unfortunately, I just finished telling your dad I have to go." She told herself her voice had been slow enough, smooth, and light.

Friendly.

She hadn't fooled them, either.

Panic snapped into the darker gray, wariness into the lighter. "Sam—" Griff broke off, retrieved the files from beneath his arm and pressed them into his daughter's hands. "Honey, can you give this to Mrs. Schulz? Ask her to wait in line for me at the desk? And…stay with her. Okay?"

Wariness tightened into suspicion, but the girl nodded. "Sure, Dad."

Sam purged the breath she hadn't even realized she'd been holding captive as the girl turned and headed for the lounge. She was about to step after her when Griff snagged her arm.

She flinched.

"Sweetheart, I—"

"*Don't.*" Her fury finally accomplished what her pain hadn't been able to since the moment that little girl had called out to him. She met his stare squarely. "I don't know what you expected, but I'm sure your *wife* wouldn't approve."

"I'm not married."

The revelation bounced right off her—almost. "I don't *care.*" Dammit, she *didn't.* She couldn't afford to.

And he knew why.

"I'd like a chance to explain—"

"No."

"Please. You name the time. As late as you like. Wherever you like."

"I said, *no.*" With that, she wrenched her arm elbow free. She slapped the sheet of paper onto his chest, leaving him no choice but to take it. "You'll need this. It's part of your daughter's health record. It doesn't note much. Just the fact that she broke her own left forearm when she was three. Oh, and of course it includes her birth date."

She didn't wait for him to answer. She simply left.

Why not? He hadn't bothered to wait for her. She'd spent the past three months agonizing over her decision to hang up on him all those years ago, consumed by what could have been. She needn't have bothered. Not only would they never be, for all their struggles and all his apologies and solemn vows, she and Griff had never stood a chance. And it had nothing to do with Chet Osborne or his lies. She'd lost Griff long before the night she'd hung up on him. The proof was right there on that sheet of paper. While she'd been pining away for her long-distance fiancé and suffering through their on-and-off phone spats, Griff had been busy conceiving his daughter.

With someone *else.*

* * *

Eight hours, five meetings, three ducked phone calls, two scientific spats refereed and one near fender-bender later, Samantha finally turned into her driveway. She killed the engine to her VW Bug and slumped forward onto the steering wheel, grateful she'd left the top down that morning despite the promise of rain. The oversight paid off as the lingering warmth from the setting sun began baking the back of her neck and shoulders, slowly evaporating the fog that had coalesced inside her brain and around her heart since her run-in with Griff that afternoon. She was almost sorry to feel it leave. The numbing mist had served as a cocoon of sorts. Without it, she wasn't sure she'd have made it out of the hospital, much less through the rest of the day.

Bad enough to learn Griff had been sleeping around on her from the moment his plane had touched down in Anchorage, she'd had to discover his infidelity within full view of Valentin Novosti. Evidently sidling up to some brunette hadn't been as riveting as watching her heart shatter. Valentin might not have gotten close enough to hear what she and Griff had said, but from the smirk on his face as she'd passed him on her way out to the parking lot, Valentin had seen enough to piece her shock and horror together. She still couldn't believe the jerk had used her distraction back at the lab that afternoon to try and push his flaky rocket guidance experiment ahead of not one, but two other experiments. If Dimitri hadn't stopped by her office to bring the scientists' complaints to her attention, Valentin might have succeeded too. One more reason to make sure she never ran into Griff again.

Anywhere.

She could *not* afford to let Griff affect her work.

Unfortunately, she'd seen the look in Griff's eyes when she'd made her escape. It looked a lot like the determination she'd seen in the middle of the night years before—after Griff had woken up in her arms, drenched in a yet another cold sweat. She'd finally succeeded in getting him to talk about the team of SF soldiers he'd rescued during the first Iraq war, learning more from Griff's woefully understated remarks than he'd intended to reveal. If a dead buddy slumped over in the copilot's seat and relentless barrage of ground fire hadn't dissuaded Griff from his chosen mission, how could she hope to? Heck, she'd half expected him to stop by the lab the moment he'd dropped his daughter off at their quarters.

To her surprise, he hadn't even phoned.

Or had that been part of his strategy? Had he simply changed his tactics in an effort to knock her off guard? If so, it wouldn't work. She wouldn't let it. She'd worked too hard to accept the reality of the decisions she'd been forced to make regarding her body. She did not need Griff Towers back in her life, making her feel all over again.

Or worse, making her hope.

Sam tugged the key from the ignition and bailed out of the Bug, hurrying up the flagstone path that led to her stucco ranch as quickly as her heels let her. She'd deliberately stayed at the lab later than usual—even for her—just in case Griff decided to lie in wait and follow her home. He hadn't. With her home address and phone number unlisted as per Jarco policy, she was safe until tomorrow at least. Unfortunately, due to the accident she'd narrowly avoided outside the main base gate, she was also late. She had ten minutes to make it inside, strip off her uniform and grab a shower.

With the help of her shower cap, she made it with three minutes to spare. Still a bit thrown from this morning's revelation, she slid her closet open and passed on the simple dress Dimitri would have preferred, tugging on her favorite pair of faded jeans and a buttery lace-trimmed T-shirt, instead. The outfit would serve double duty. The dull pull in her abdomen had kicked up a notch since her run in with Griff—probably more psychosomatic than anything given the discovery. Or so she hoped. Either way, she'd be comfortable enough given the elastic at the waist and the choice would let Dimitri know she wasn't up to their usual spot. She probably should have cancelled. Dimitri would have understood. But that would mean giving in to the heartache and distraction that had become all too familiar these past three months.

Dimitri was right. She might have wavered for three months now, it was time to make a decision. Hell, Griff had made his, albeit earlier than she'd have ever thought.

Christy.

She purged the sight of that little girl from her head and her heart as she headed back into the bathroom. Yeah, it was past time to move on.

So get started.

A quick pass of the mascara wand and she was ready to attack her mane. She retrieved the large bobby pins that held the tail to her usual French braid tucked neatly beneath the rest of the bulk and tossed them into the bathroom sink. The elastic band followed. Halfway into unraveling the rope, her doorbell rang. *Shoot.* She'd already asked Dimitri to push dinner back by an hour. Sam grabbed the brush and tucked it in her back pocket. She'd have to finish in the car. The doorbell chimed a second time as she headed out of the bathroom to fish her leather flats out from under her unmade bed.

"Just a second!"

Shoot. Her pills. She grabbed the shoes and dashed back into the bathroom to snatch the pink container up from the back of the sink. It took some juggling but she managed to pop one of the tiny pills from the blister pack and swallow it dry. She followed the birth control pill up with a pair of prescription strength ibuprofen. Gripping her shoes in her left hand, she raced out of the bedroom, down the narrow hall and around the corner, coming to an abrupt halt to wrench the front door open with her right. "Sorry, but Valentin would *not* get out of my office. I just got home a few min—"

The shoes fell along with her lower jaw. She winced as the slight heel to one of the flats cut into her toes before bouncing off. She was dimly aware of the shoe skidding across the ochre tiles of the foyer and onto the hardwood floor of the open living room beyond. She managed to snap her jaw shut as Griff's right hand dropped away from the door jam.

"Hello, Samantha."

For the life of her, she couldn't figure out how to release her jaw—until Griff leaned down and casually scooped up her other shoe. The one that had bounced out through the doorway and onto the small porch, landing inches from his gray cowboy boots. She stared at the boots, transfixed. Eleven years and he still preferred the same brand. In fact, she'd almost swear that was the same pair of Dan Posts she'd bought for his birthday the month he left Austin. The suspicion deepened as she spotted the deep scratch running down the outer length of the left tip. He'd gouged out a scratch just like that the last time they'd headed over to Sixth Street to go dancing. But that was ridiculous…wasn't it? He would have had to have held onto them all these years. The possibility disturbed her more than she was willing to admit.

He held out her shoe.

She snatched it from his hand. By the time she dragged her gaze up, she was forced to squint. Another few minutes and the setting sun would've been obscured by the tops of the trees opposite the gravel road that led to her house. As it was, she was nearly blinded by the huge orange disk clinging to the horizon two inches from Griff's steady stare.

"What are you doing here?" Good Heavens, she had not just invited conversation, had she? It had to be the sun. A sudden, massive case of heat stroke. She tossed the shoe into the living room beside its mate and threw up both hands as Griff opened his mouth. "Don't answer that. I don't want to know. In fact, I thought I made my feelings on the matter—this matter—exceedingly clear this afternoon."

He nodded. "You did."

She shoved her half-woven braid over her shoulder. "Then what makes you think you can change my mind?"

"I don't. I just came to give you something."

She stood silent, refusing to take the bait. As if she wanted anything from this man after all this time.

He glanced past her shoulder. "May I come in?"

"No."

His sigh filled the tiny outer courtyard she'd crafted.

She ignored it. "This is *my* house."

Another nod followed. "I know. Took a bit of research to find it. You're not in the phonebook."

She crossed her arms over her T-shirt and locked them into place. "Yeah, well, you never know when some uninvited nut is going to decide to show up at your door."

This time, he ignored her. He just stood there, staring into her house, shamelessly casing it. He took his sweet time, too, silently studying the sliver of dining area behind her before shifting to his right, sliding his gaze across her living room, pausing every so often, as if he was searching for something he recognized. Some stamp of his presence in her life that had survived the test of time. The moment he spotted the antique seven-foot couch, she knew it. Dammit, she knew she should have changed that fabric. But then…she'd have had to let go of the memories too, wouldn't she?

Get it over with. "Okay, I give in. What do you want?"

His stare returned to hers. Uncomfortable with how well she could still decipher those dark gray shadows and the iron resolve within, she stepped backwards.

The shift helped with the glare from the sun.

"I told you. I have something for you." He shrugged. "I'd hoped to be invited in, maybe even sit down so I could explain it, but—" He tucked his hand beneath his dark blue pullover and withdrew a sheet of tightly folded paper from the front pocket of his jeans. He held it out.

"What's that?"

He frowned. "I'd rather you read it for yourself."

She weighed her curiosity against her better judgment. Every time she'd learned something new about this man since he'd barged back into her life, it had caused her nothing but more heartache. She should slam the door in his face and be done with it. Except, that wouldn't be the end of it—

this. If Griff had gone to this much trouble to track her down, there was no way he'd leave until she did as he'd asked. And unfortunately, Dimitri appeared to be running later than she.

She snatched the offering from Griff's hand and opened it. From the distinctive lines running across the sheet, it appeared to be another military hospital entry form. Her curiosity ratcheted up another notch as she unfolded the sheet of paper completely—until she spotted the name and the date on this one. LeAnn Towers, 30 June '93. His wife. The mother of his child. Her replacement in every way that mattered.

In every way that hurt.

Her eyes blurred and her chest tightened. She pushed the form at him without finishing. "I'm sorry, I don't—"

He pushed it back. "*Please*. Just read the first notation. That's all I'm asking."

Well, he was asking too much, damn it!

Unfortunately, he didn't give her a choice. Griff had taken advantage of her distraction and crossed over the threshold of her house before she could stop him. He stepped deep into the foyer, invading her home, her personal space and most of all her heart as he pushed the form closer, a mere twelve inches from her face. Furious at his audacity, she blinked. The tears stinging her eyes cleared, causing the words to snap into focus whether she wanted them to or not. She sucked in her breath at the first notation, the only notation, he'd asked her to read—but by then, she was unable to stop.

Just as he'd known she would be.

Griff's deep voice filled the foyer, reverberating through her as he paraphrased what she read in places, adding details that weren't there in others, "We'd had a fight, the last of many. But this one was worse than all the others. Much worse. She took off, hit a patch of black ice. She was barely seven months pregnant. By the time I found her and got her to the hospital, she was already hemorrhaging. Christy was born that night, by emergency C-section. She was two months premature. It was touch and go for the both of them, during and after the birth. Christy made it. LeAnn didn't."

He paused to draw his breath in deep. When he continued, his tone was darker and hoarse, riddled with self-loathing. As if he'd memorized this all years before and had forced himself to drag it out on occasion to torture himself. "As for Christy's conception, I slept with LeAnn once. I never loved her and she sure as heck didn't love me. Hell, we never even got to the point where we liked each other. I'm not proud of that. Nor am I making excuses. It's just the way it was. What happened was both our faults. But I should have tried harder. I've had to live with that—as well as that fight—for a long time. But at least I've been able to live. And I've had Christy. I regret a lot of things in my life, especially after what I learned in that hospital in Ramstein, but I don't regret my daughter. I could never regret her. She's the only reason I made it."

His hand fell away as he finished and Sam dropped hers, clutching the form as she slumped against the foyer wall.

It wasn't enough.

One slight evening breeze and she'd be sliding down.

She forced her legs into motion, pushing one bare foot in front of the other as she made her way into the living room and to her couch by memory alone. She sank into the cushions they'd refurbished and then baptized together, dimly aware of the front door closing, of Griff's boots thumping slowly across the foyer tiles and then onto the hardwood floor. The area rug she'd purchased from a Taos gift shop muffled them as he tracked her to the couch. He had the grace not to join her though, lowering his frame into the armchair she'd bought at another San Antonio estate sale a year after they'd found the couch.

She still couldn't face him.

She stared at her feet instead. At the fine lines running through her frosted coral polish. A decade of practice and she'd never been able to paint them as perfectly as Griff. The

first time he'd offered, she'd laughed. Until he'd confessed
that he'd done it for his mom all the time growing up. It made
sense. Madeline's tiny Datsun hatchback had been hit by a
pickup while she was headed home from work when Griff was
nine. She'd been in a wheelchair ever since. Sam had often
wondered how Madeline was doing over the years. She'd
even been tempted to call once or twice. She never had. Nor
did she ask about his mother now. She didn't say anything.

She did, however, realize she was still holding the hospital form. It appeared to be the original, so she carefully re-
folded it and held it out. Griff retrieved it silently. His initial
confession offered, he appeared to be waiting for her to ask
for the rest. God help her, she did. She had to know. "Wh-what
happened?"

"I got drunk."

What?

She jerked her head up, finally meeting Griff's tortured
stare. He never drank. Ever. His mom hadn't just been hit by
any pickup; the driver had been drunk. He'd detested alcohol
ever since. She sucked in her shock, still not quite able to grasp
it. What in God's name could have been so bad that he'd
taken a drink, let alone gotten soused? She was afraid to ask.

Had Madeline—

She slammed the thought out of her head. No. Please, God,
no. She couldn't take that. Not now. Not after today. Not after
this past year. Sam swallowed firmly and held fast to her
hope. "Griff…I don't understand."

The shadows in his eyes deepened and this time, she
couldn't read them. All she could see was the absolute desolation settling in. "Neither did I…at first. It happened the
night I called you back—and got Chet."

Her stomach lurched. Her heart burned.

Hell, her heart *screamed*.

Suddenly, she knew what he was going to say. She shot to
her feet, unwilling to sit and listen. She escaped to the far side
of the room, stopping at the fireplace she rarely used because

it reminded her too damned much of that first time with Griff. She stared at the photos on the mantle, deliberately settling on the commissioning picture in the center, drawing strength from her Sisters-in-Arms even though they weren't there: Eve and Carrie, and especially Anna and Meg. She needed them now like she never had before. More than when they'd all gathered around her to pull her heart and her pride back together whether she'd wanted to or not after Griff dropped out of her life without so much as a phone call.

Only now, she finally knew why.

Chapter 6

He'd argued this moment damned near every second of every waking hour these past three months. Now that it was here—now that *he* was here—staring at Samantha's rigid spine as she stared into that photo of her sorority sisters, visibly trying to hold herself together, he was still debating whether or not he'd made the right decision. Griff clamped down on the hospital form as he fought the urge to stand, to go to her and draw her in his arms, all the while knowing his comfort wasn't wanted. That it might never be welcome again. Maybe Vince was right. Maybe this idea had been doomed from the start.

But, dammit, he had to try.

And he would. As much as this was killing the both of them, there was no turning back. He'd known that when he'd stared into the utter disillusionment in those gorgeous eyes at the hospital. Fortunately, the worst was over. Griff forced himself to push past the regret as he waited for Samantha to turn around. He hadn't come all this way to retreat, much less wallow in his mistakes. He'd come to own up to them, yes, even accept her eternal hatred if that's all she had left to give when he finished. But if not—and, God willing, it wasn't— then he was also here to find out if there was any way this incredible woman could find it within herself to help him move past those mistakes…with her.

When she'd first opened her door, he'd feared it was too late. She'd obviously been expecting someone else. Someone she felt comfortable enough to invite in while getting ready to go out. The brush tucked in her back pocket told him that.

Alibek? Or someone else?

Someone she might feel more for than the solid, but limited friendship he'd felt in that cabin in Russia?

As much as he wanted to ask, he had no right. All he could do was wait and pray the information Vince had culled from the base rumor mill upon his buddy's own transfer to Kirtland six weeks earlier was accurate. Griff strengthened his resolve to do just that—until he caught the sound of a car approaching. His apprehension returned as Samantha tensed. With the blinds drawn over the living room window, he couldn't determine its make or model as it passed. By the time Sam had relaxed her stance, he'd changed his mind about waiting for her to face him. Whoever she was expecting, it was probably best to push through, before the next car turned into her driveway and she turned even further away from him. Not to mention, it might be easier for her if she didn't have to look at him.

God forgive him, it was easier on him.

He dragged his stare from those achingly familiar curves and fused it to the hospital form she'd returned, rolling the folded sheet between his palms until it formed a tube. He clenched his fingers around it to keep from chickening out. "A couple days after your ultimatum, I wrote you a letter. I was ready to admit you were right. Our relationship did have problems, most of them stemming from my insecurity over you. Mostly my fear that you'd find someone your own age…and, yeah, some pretty deep-seated fears that, age-span or not, you'd eventually walk out on me anyway like my dad had."

She'd tensed again—but she was listening.

So he continued, "I mailed the letter along with the airline ticket you never got, certain you'd call me. But when Thanksgiving came and went and you still hadn't, I got scared—wondered if I'd finally blown it. A couple buddies had asked me to serve as designated driver that Saturday. As you know, not my preferred way to spend a night. But frankly, I was going insane staring at the walls of my BQ room waiting for you to phone. I agreed. A couple hours into the night and fed up with shooting pool when all I really wanted to do was talk to you, I got to thinking about the time zone difference, about how you'd probably be too sleepy to hang up on me…so I called you." He paused to roll the form tighter and drag in a fortifying breath before forcing himself to finish.

She turned before he got the chance. "But you got Chet instead."

"*Yeah.*" Despite the fact he knew Chet had lied, the memory still burned. He sucked in another breath as he stared up into that gorgeous, glistening gaze. The same one that matched the color of the poison he'd chosen all those years ago. "I was still pretty shaken when I joined the guys at the bar." More rattled than he'd been while pulling that SF team out of Iraq the year before they'd met. "I downed the wrong drink. Coke and something. Don't remember what. I do remember choosing Scotch, straight up, for the next round."

The resulting burn had barely registered. All he'd cared about was that the contents of his glass had matched those incredible eyes. Unfortunately, the more he'd stared into that glass, the more he could see her eyes…and the more he drank.

Griff sighed. "Eventually, I stopped remembering. You, me, Chet, everything. To this day, I have no idea how I ended up in LeAnn's apartment and she wasn't exactly forthcoming the next morning. Not that I gave her a chance." He'd been too busy holding his splitting head together while trying to locate his clothes.

"You left?"

He nodded. As fast as he could. "Until she showed up at the base two weeks later, I wasn't even sure we'd had sex."

The color bled from her cheeks at that, leaving taut, pale skin behind. His heart began burning as the tears welled up again. His arms began to ache as they finally spilled over. He forced himself to remain seated as a second wave trickled down. There was no way she'd let him touch her. Nor would it help to admit he was a bastard. Just as there'd been no way to soften the blow. All he could do was wait. He knew it was coming. He'd done the math himself ten years ago and reached the same conclusion. The only conclusion.

A moment later, it did. "Two weeks?" Her frown cut deeper. "Griff, she was trying to get pregnant."

He let the statement stand. The fact that it was true didn't change anything—now or then. LeAnn might have set out to trap him, but he was as guilty as she regarding the consequences. LeAnn hadn't poured that bottle of Scotch down his throat. He had. And there was Christy. The one innocent in the entire mess he'd made of his life. Because of her, he couldn't even regret what he'd done.

Not completely.

He finally caved into the urge and stood, pacing his way to the living room window. There, he reached for the control rod and twisted the blinds open. The sun had finally set, leaving a cooling, soothing dusk behind. Several fireflies lit up the lawn as he sighed. "I admit, I was furious when LeAnn showed up. I couldn't even be sure the child was mine. Even if it was, I'll be honest, I wasn't prepared to marry her. Nor did it have anything to do with losing you. Support the child? Absolutely. But a life together? I didn't even know her." What he had learned about her, he sure as hell hadn't liked.

He'd told her so, too.

LeAnn had been just as brutal in return. Not only had she freely admitted she'd set out to trap him, any airman would have done. As far as she was concerned, he was her ticket out of Alaska and down to the lower, warmer Forty-eight.

Sam's bare feet padded across the floor. A moment later, he caught her reflection in the window several feet to his left and behind him. "She threatened to call your commander, didn't she? She said she'd ruin your career."

He shook his head.

"I don't understand. You just said—"

"She threatened to have an abortion." He turned around as Sam gasped and stared down at her. She was less than two feet away. Close enough to touch. Just like that, the craving returned. The piercing need to pull her in his arms and comfort her. He didn't give in to it.

Nor did she reach out to him.

He pressed on, determined to finish it. "LeAnn gave me until the first of the year to decide. If I didn't marry her by New Year's, she was going through with an abortion. She already had it scheduled. I know because she brought the proof. Apparently she'd gleaned my views on the subject while I was plastered." He shook his head. "That's something else I don't remember. But it wasn't what sealed the bargain."

He watched as regret washed through that soft, gold gaze. "The ticket and the letter. You got them back."

He nodded.

Ironically, LeAnn hadn't even known about the letter. But in the end, it was that letter that sealed his fate. "Within the week, we headed down to the courthouse." Their mutual hell started that same night. LeAnn might not have known about the letter, but she'd known all about Samantha. Apparently he talked when drunk. And LeAnn had used her newfound knowledge to painful perfection. Six months of never-ending fights and ice-cold shoulders had followed. On both their parts. Until their last argument had led to LeAnn's death...but given him Christy. He swallowed the regret that had never quite left him and shoved the hospital form into the rear pocket of his jeans. "You have to understand. My daughter doesn't know any of this. She thinks her mother and I had a whirl-wind courtship and got married. I couldn't tell her the truth."

The regret deepened, darkening the gold in that beautiful gaze to bronze. "Why are you telling me?"

"Because you deserve to know."

Her lips quivered as tears crowded into the regret. But this time, they didn't fall. Instead, they hung between them, unshed, right along with her soft sigh of resignation.

"Griff…it's too late."

The hell it was. It couldn't be. He wouldn't let it be. He didn't care if that kiss they'd shared in Ramstein had lasted less than a second. It had been enough. He'd felt her response. He *knew* she still cared. Because of that kiss—because of her—he'd spent the next three months moving mountains. Hell, he'd risked more than his career. After this morning's unexpected run-in at the hospital and the fiasco that resulted, he'd managed to alienate Christy even more than he had when he'd finally gotten the official okay from Washington and told her they weren't moving to Hawaii as he'd originally promised. They were headed to New Mexico instead.

To *this* woman.

He gave in to the blistering urge and reached out, wrapping his hands about Samantha's arms as he pulled her close. "Honey, I know this is a shock. And, yes, I probably should have told you I was coming. Tonight, and especially to Kirtland. But I needed to say this one-on-one, without some ocean or continent between us. Frankly, I wasn't willing to take the chance you'd hang up on me again. I tried to tell you this that day in Ramstein but you refused to come out of the bathroom. I went back to the hospital after a buddy offered to fly back to Moscow with Vince. I was hoping you'd cooled off. Instead, you'd left. So had your flight."

Damn, but he hadn't meant to sound so accusing. He started to apologize, but she cut him off.

"What did you expect? That I'd hang around and wait? Griff, I've got a newsflash. I'm not some nineteen-year-old kid anymore. I'm all grown up and in case you haven't figured it out, I stopped waiting for you *years* ago."

He clenched his fingers against the blow—until he realized he was still holding on to her. He released his hands immediately and forced his anger down as well. Holding on to it wouldn't accomplish anything. He nodded instead.

"I deserved that."

To his surprise, she pushed past her own anger as well. "No, you didn't. Nor did you deserve what Chet and LeAnn did. Neither did I. But it happened. And as a result, you have a sweet little girl who obviously thinks the world of you." Relief swept through him—until a darker shadow entered her eyes, a shadow he'd never seen before…and it scared him. The fear cut deeper as she shook her head, slowly. Sadly. "Go back to your daughter, Griff. Be the daddy we always talked about. It's clear you're good at it. As for me? Us?" This shake was even slower. Firmer. "I can't go back. The past is over. Too much has changed. I've changed. I've moved on. I've had to."

No!

"Samantha, please, I'm not asking you to go back. I wouldn't want to, even if we could. I want a present with you. A future. All I'm asking is that you withhold final judgment for a while. Get to know Christy. Heck, get to know me again. I've changed, too. Give me a chance to prove it—"

The doorbell rang.

The sound seemed to startle her as much it had him. Evidently she hadn't seen anyone come up the walk either. He stepped closer, determined to ignore whoever was on the other side of that door until they'd finished this. Or she at least agreed to pick it—them—up again later.

He was encouraged when she stepped closer as well. His optimism faded as she spoke. Calmly, softly. The way he spoke to Christy when he needed to explain something she was too young to understand…or something she didn't want to. "Griff, you have listen to me. I meant what I said, I've moved on. It took me a long time to realize that I needed to. I'm not talking about the past eleven years right now, either. I'm talking about these past three months."

Three months. Ramstein.

He swallowed firmly. "Because of Christy?"

Was she saying she simply couldn't get past the fact that he'd a child with another woman and never would?

That same frightening shadow slipped back in. "No. Though I admit, it hurts. She hurts. But it's not her fault. It's us. Griff, we weren't meant to be. Not really. It took me a long time to understand that. To accept it. And it has nothing to do with LeAnn or your daughter, or even what did or didn't happened with Chet. It has to do with the host of things—life— that have happened since you left Austin."

What on earth was she talking about?

The door bell chimed again.

They both ignored it again.

"I'm sorry, Griff. More than you'll ever know. But my decision is final. Please accept it. I don't have anything to offer you. Not even friendship. You need to leave now and, please, don't come back. Don't stop by my office. You'll only make me hurt you more than I already have." He was dimly aware of someone thumping on the door in the moments that followed. Though in all honesty, it could have been the thudding of his heart. He did know it was Samantha's breath that washed his jaw as she tiptoed up to gently press her lips to his cheek, her voice that slipped into his ear to deliver the final blow. But it wasn't until she stepped back and turned to head for the door that her murmured, "My date is here," sunk in.

Date. That simple word and all implications that came with it, stabbed in.

He wasn't sure why he followed her. Maybe he was hoping the motion would help staunch the massive ache slashing through his chest. His heart. Or maybe he just wanted to get a look at whoever was behind that door. All he knew, as she reached for the knob and slowly pulled the door open, was that he didn't want to recognize the man. He'd never know how he managed to clip a nod. He could only pray it appeared polite.

"Doctor Alibek."

From the genuine warmth that infused the scientist's smile, Griff knew Sam hadn't discussed what happened in that hospital room in Ramstein—and that terrified him more than the way she'd leaned into the man's embrace. The good doctor brushed a perfunctory kiss across her right temple and turned to extend his hand. "It's good to see you again, Colonel. And, please, after what we survived together, you must call me Dimitri. Samantha told me she ran into you at the hospital this morning. I understand you've been transferred here."

"Yes. And it's Griff."

Another friendly smile as they shook. This time, he wasn't surprised. But the curve Alibek turned on Samantha did. Griff swore the smile was almost…fatherly. Date his ass. He might not have a clue as to what was going on between these two, but it sure as heck did not involve romance. So why had Sam implied that it did?

To throw him off?

No. He didn't care if eleven hundred years had passed, she knew him better than that.

"Are you ready to leave, Samantha?"

She nodded. "Just need to finish my hair." She finally turned to include him in her stare. "Griff was just leaving."

His polite nod surprised her.

Good. It was the first of many. He might not understand what was going on here, but he would. And when he did, he'd be back. He'd lost this woman once before. He had no intention of losing her again. Samantha was wrong, she did have something to offer him. Something he'd been searching for since the day he left Austin. He'd found it again in that hospital room in Ramstein, in that brief, searing kiss they'd shared. So had she. Whether or not she was willing to admit it. All he had to do was figure out a way to prove it to her.

Before it was too late.

The Pave Hawk was already outside the hangar, fueled and ready to go, just as Captain Swanson had promised. Relieved, Samantha killed the Bug's engine and tugged the keys from the ignition. Despite the fact that no one appeared to be within fifty feet of the chopper already rigged to fly her experiment, Sam remained in the driver's seat and studied the aviation apron, studying each of the pilots, crewmembers and maintenance techs as they returned from lunch and headed back to work. It had been three days since Griff had stopped by her house. Three days spent vigilantly checking the caller ID on her home, work and cellular phones before she picked up. Three days of countless moments spent just like this, nervously scanning the hallways, exits and parking lots each time she walked out of Jarco labs. But the longest and most painful stretch of torture had occurred each night as she'd lain in bed, sleepless, trying *not* to think about Griff lying in another bed somewhere across town…and wondering when and where he was going to show next—and why he already hadn't.

Had he really given up so easily?

Or was he simply executing the time-honored military tactic of patience while he plotted his next move? Knowing Griff, she'd put money on the latter. All the more reason to be cautious. She was on his turf now.

Or rather, his tarmac.

She'd made a few phone calls since the night Griff had knocked on her door. According to a friend at HQ, there'd been an unexpected change in base staffing. The colonel who'd been slotted to take over as commander of Kirtland's 58th Special Operations Wing had suddenly and mysteriously been offered another assignment. Griff had taken the man's place. Due to the change-of-command ceremony that'd taken place two days earlier, Griff was now ultimately responsible for all aspects of aircraft operations for Kirtland's Huey, Pave Low and Pave Hawk helicopter fleets…including the Pave Hawk parked out on the cement aviation apron dead ahead. Fortunately, her optical target recognition experiment had been tasked weeks before. There was a chance Griff wouldn't even realize she was in his backyard until her experiment was over and she was safely back at Jarco, results in hand. Even as she clung to the hope, she knew it was false. Griff knew she was here, all right.

He might be new to Kirtland, but he was thorough.

To her surprise, Griff also appeared to be truly absent.

Sam scanned the apron again, then the hangar beyond. Griff was nowhere to be seen. She shoved the disappointment down. She should be thrilled Griff had honored her request and stayed away from her. At the very least, relieved. A quick, clean and complete break was for the best. In the long run it would be easier on her and on Griff. It might have taken his presence in her house last Monday night, but she'd finally made her decision. A decision long overdue. She should be getting on with her life, focusing on Dimitri and the future—their future. But that was the problem, wasn't it?

She couldn't.

If anything, Griff's conspicuous absence had her thinking about him all the more.

Dammit, *don't*.

Dimitri didn't know how right he'd been. What did she have left to offer Griff, anyway? The only area they'd been completely compatible in had been the bedroom. She didn't even have that to offer him anymore...or anyone else. Griff might have changed but unfortunately, so had she.

At least her body had. And not for the better.

Sam sighed as a particular portion of that same body increased the tempo of its insidious throb. The throb increased as she leaned forward to dig her spare bottle of prescription-strength ibuprofen from the Bug's glove box. She palmed two of the pills, washing them down with a sip from her rapidly warming Diet Coke and sighed again. It might have taken that botched trip to Moscow and her subsequent meeting with Griff in her hospital room in Ramstein, but she'd finally come to terms with her body's failings. Running into Griff three months later in yet another hospital, might have rattled her so much that she'd skipped out on her second appointment, but she'd also finally accepted the wisdom of her doctor's advice—and what that advice ultimately meant for her. She and Griff were over. They had been for a very long time. To try and rekindle anything with the man now would only hurt the both of them. Eventually, her heart would figure that out.

Fortunately, Griff's had.

She scanned the apron and hangar beyond one last time— still no sign of Griff. He truly had given up.

She sucked up the disappointment she couldn't quite kill and retrieved her briefcase and capped bottle of Diet Coke. She bailed out of the Bug and then the parking lot, determined to push Griff out of her mind as well—if only for the next hour. She studied the flight suits strolling about the apron as she closed in on her own waiting Pave Hawk, this time searching for Captain Rick Swanson, the pilot scheduled to fly her initial optical recognition experiment.

There. Sam spotted the lanky pilot, helmet crooked under his right arm, departing the hangar beyond.

She quickened her pace, juggling her briefcase along with the soda scheduled to double as her latest missing lunch. Despite the sweat trickling down her back, she was actually grateful the increased ache in her abdomen had led her to choose slacks and low-quarters that morning. Her usual uniformed skirt might have been cooler, but in heels she'd have fallen flat on her face for sure as her right shoe snagged a metal tie down embedded in the cement. Grace was so *not* her middle name. She proved it yet again as she pitched forward, rudely slamming into Swanson's chest as he rounded the Pave Hawk's tail. Her Diet Coke went flying, the plastic bottle exploding at their feet as the captain lunged to the left to save her briefcase before it, too, hit the tarmac.

"Got it!"

Good thing, because she suddenly did *not*. This was not her pilot. Sam blinked up—way up—into a partially obscured face she hadn't seen since their plane touched down in Ramstein three months earlier.

"Vince Racey."

It was him, all right. Even with the mirrored aviator sunglasses, she recognized him. The Race-man, in the flesh. All six-feet-five-inches of rugged, dark-haired, NASCAR-doll with a drawl. Like Vince's infuriating mentor, not an ounce of pretty boy had ever tainted the man's blood. Probably why the two got along so well, even before an enlisted Vince had crewed for Griff in Desert Storm. Griff's Texas A&M alumni protégé flashed a grin as dazzling as ever as he brushed the splatter of Diet Coke from his flight suit before wiping her briefcase down with his sleeve. He held the case out. "Good to see you again, Samantha. Especially with two good arms. I take it everything's healed up okay?"

As if he hadn't heard—in detail.

She snatched the briefcase from his paw. "I'm fine. Good to see you again, too…I think." She stared at him as he flushed—both of them knowing what she meant. Vince refused to confirm or deny the unspoken accusation, evading her suspicion as he leaned down to scoop up yet another of her fallen Diet Cokes, though this bottle had been split clean through and was now completely empty. So much for lunch.

Worse, so much for her hope that Griff had gotten the message that she wanted to be left alone.

Vince squashed the remains of the bottle, folding the plastic over and tucking it into the pocket at the front of his flight suit with an absentmindedness born of countless foreign object walk-downs. Awkwardness set in along with silence as he drew the zipper shut. She shifted the briefcase to her left hand as he removed the mirrored shades and tucked them inside his helmet before setting both inside the chopper.

"So, tell me, who arrived first? Damon or Pythias?"

The latter blinked.

She refused to fall for the feigned ignorance in those dark brown eyes. Vince knew full well whom and what she was referring to, and it wasn't the Greek legend concerning two friends, one of whom had pledged his life as guarantee that his condemned friend would return to face execution—at least, not directly. Mostly because neither this man nor the friend Vince was fronting for would be pardoned. Not by her.

She hiked a pointed brow as the awkwardness strung out.

He finally cleared his throat. "I did."

Figured. "When?"

His flush deepened. "Six weeks ago."

That would explain the mysterious Operations Group's commander swap. Upon his arrival, Vince had obviously discovered the 58th would be hosting a change-of-command in the near future. He must have passed the information regarding the potential assignment switch to Griff. That didn't surprise her. What did, was the inescapable reality that Griff had actually traveled halfway around the globe just to try and date her again. She couldn't help it. She was flattered.

What woman wouldn't be?

But she was also ticked. The discovery also explained why she'd seen neither hide nor hair of Griff these past three days…including here. Now. He didn't need to be standing out on this apron. His buddy would make sure every second of her afternoon was relayed back to Griff. Heck, Vince had probably hoped to play matchmaker while he was at it. Most grown men might balk at the job, but not Vince. Not for the man who'd once saved his life in combat. Though she doubted the matchmaking portion of the plan was Griff's. Griff preferred to do his own work—dirty or otherwise.

No, Vince had planned this little reunion on his own.

Well, said reunion was also *over*. She had work to do. Thank God. Sam turned to stow her briefcase inside the Pave Hawk's wide-open steel belly. "Where's Captain Swanson?"

"Kansas."

She swung around. "That's impossible. I just talked to him yesterday afternoon. He helped me rig the core modules inside this bird. He promised he was good to go for today."

Vince dragged out a shrug along with his drawl. "He was. Unfortunately, his father's tractor overturned last night. Swanson's on emergency leave 'til they find someone to take over the farm while his old man's laid up in traction."

Great. She felt for the guy, she truly did. But it'd taken her three weeks and countless arguments with an increasingly cantankerous General Luft to get this experiment worked into the Jarco queue. Luft had never quite bought into Phil's proposed improvements on the Army's existing target recognition systems. Luft simply didn't think the benefits the optical and infrared radar upgrades Phil had designed were strong enough to warrant the amount of money needed to see his initially proposed experiments through—until she'd come up with a way to combine her own work on target acquisition with Phil's. Though Luft was still more skeptical than excited, the general had at least given her enough funds to move from the planning board to an initial flight.

Unfortunately that was all she had.

One flight.

Two measly hours to see if she could generate enough results to convince Luft that Phil's legacy would save lives someday, in the cockpit and elsewhere on the battlefield. If she couldn't produce today, Luft expected her to cancel the remaining two initial experiments as well as the entire second, laser countermeasures stage and move on. Her frustration must have shown.

"Not to worry." Vince pulled a crescent wrench she hadn't noticed until then from his pocket. "Just need to finish a couple checks, tighten a few nuts to keep the computer modules and other equipment you installed bolted down, and we can crank this baby up."

We. That meant Captain Litton wasn't far behind.

Relief seared in despite the fact that her day's work would eventually become fodder for Vince's pending, private debrief with a certain, blessedly absent colonel. It wouldn't be long before Griff felt he had enough encouragement to come pounding on her door again. Griff wasn't stupid. He'd eventually add that chopper crash in Russia to the debrief on today's experiment and reach the one conclusion she'd prefer he didn't: that her continuing nightmare over his crash had led her to make the leap to take Phil's original work to the next level. She shoved the realization from her head, determined to keep Griff out as well. Vince was right, they'd best get a move on, before fate tossed a wrench into more than the chopper's engine. Fortunately for her, from the way Vince had crawled into the Pave Hawk's belly and began firing up her gear and double-checking the various cable connections she'd hardwired into the cockpit two days before, it appeared Swanson had briefed Vince thoroughly before he left.

She shoved her briefcase out of the way and leaned in alongside him, already back to wishing she was wearing her skirt and low heels as the heat index around her instantly kicked up another ten degrees. Even with both the chopper's side doors slid all the way open, the Pave Hawk's belly was stifling. Sweat glistened on her forearm as she reached for the wrench. "I'll do that. You'd better go find Litton so we can get started."

To her surprise, Vince didn't budge. Nor did he relinquish the wrench. But he did swing his stare to hers. It was filled with reluctance. Guilt. "I'm, ah, not filling in for Swanson. I've got Litton's seat."

Good Lord, was anything to go as planned today? She shoved a wisp of hair from her forehead as she straightened. Granted, this was her first experiment with the chopper-side of the 58th, but what kind of wing had Griff inherited?

Griff.

No.

The dread locked in, before she could prevent it, snapping her nerves in tight. The dull tug in her side kicked up to a bona fide rip. She pulled her breath in slowly and concentrated on relaxing until the pills she'd taken in the car had a chance to kick in and take over. Her heart rate ebbed until finally, the pain receptors in her brain eased up off their message as well. Only then did she speak. "Vince, Captain Litton was supposed to copilot this bird today."

"Yup."

A fresh wave of sweat trickled down her back and this one had nothing to do with heat. It had been milked on pure nerves. She dragged in another breath. Blew it out. Neither helped to calm the fresh surge of panic that crashed into her stomach, much less the increased throbbing that had all but taken over her lower abdomen. She braced herself against the next answer, even before she located enough nerve to ask the question. "Vince…if you're the copilot today…who's flying this thing?"

"I am."

She jumped, banging her right temple against the steel lip of the open chopper as she swung around to face that second drawl. The one that didn't carry the distinctive underpinnings of an Oklahoma twang, but the smoother, deeper, more mellow tones of middle Texas. The precise drawl that had invaded her dreams more times than she cared to remember during the past eleven years. During the past three months.

Good Lord, did Griff look good in a flight suit.

Damned good.

She'd only seen him wearing one twice before. The first time, two months after they'd met. She'd gone on a field trip to Bergstrom airbase just outside Austin. Low and behold, who should she and her fellow AFROTC cadets spot logging a couple hours of flight time on a Saturday morning but Major Hunk himself. She'd taken one look at this man in that uniform, noting the way the fabric lovingly clung—still clung— to his broad shoulders and tight buns, and made up her mind right then and there. She was done playing the virginal friend and neighbor Griff had relegated her to. The memory seared in deeper as Griff dragged his sunglasses from his eyes slowly, so that he could capture her gaze just as he had that day. A half smile eased into his lips, just as it had that day.

Damn him, he knew he'd turned her on.

Just as he had that day.

It was in that easy, confident stance she remembered all too well. In those gray smoky eyes. In his leisurely nod. "Afternoon, Captain Hall."

She managed a return nod. "Colonel."

The lines at the corners of his eyes deepened as he tipped his head toward the chopper beside them. "I understand you've got a target recognition experiment you'd like me to take up."

Oh, she'd love for him to take something somewhere. But it wasn't her experiment and it wasn't necessarily up—in the sky that is. Whatever he thought he was doing, she wasn't falling for it. Swanson might be in Kansas, but that didn't mean she was headed for Oz. "Where's Captain Litton?"

"The hospital, I imagine."

The hospital? Great. "What happened to *him?*"

Griff shrugged as he folded his sunglasses and hooked the outer wire into the front pocket on his flight suit. "Nothing as far as I know. His wife on the other hand, was admitted at eighteen-thirty last night—OB ward. She's—"

"Let me guess. In labor."

He nodded.

Peachy. If the woman had been lying on the concrete at her feet, she'd have groaned along with her. Louder, too. To make matters worse, Vince picked up on her exasperation as she slumped back against the copilot's door. He took off toward the chopper's tail, shamelessly abandoning her. "Left something in the hangar. Back in a sec."

She briefly entertained escaping with him but didn't. This was her slot, darn it, and she wanted it. *Without* Griff Towers breathing down her neck. She glared up at him. "What do you think you're doing?"

"Flying."

The heck he was. Not for her. She'd planned on using the same set of pilots for all three stages of the initial target acquisition experiment. There'd be better continuity that way. If Vince and Griff signed on now, and today's results were able convince Luft to finance the remaining experiments, she'd have to see the men again and again. And that didn't take into count the debriefs. Let alone the second, lengthier laser-countermeasure phase. "Damn it, Griff, this is so like you."

His brow shot up.

The confusion that came with it succeeded in knocking her fury up another notch along with it. She wasn't surprised he hadn't understood. He never had. Because he'd never wanted to. For once, she was in the mood to elaborate to his face instead of over the phone. "Three days ago, you stood in my house—uninvited I might add—and swore you'd changed. Hogwash. You're still as pig-headed and overbearing as ever. Well, guess what? I don't have to put up with it anymore, much less you." She shoved off the side of the Pave Hawk and turned to grab her briefcase from the bird's belly. She'd grovel to General Luft if she had to. God as her witness, she'd even agree to take Phil's blasted job—so long as Luft allowed her to reschedule today with a set of pilots of her choosing.

"Samantha, don't—"

"—*touch* me." She winced as her words came out louder than she'd intended. Three enlisted airmen two choppers over turned to stare. Griff released her arm immediately. His frown bit in deep, along with his palpable regret.

"I'm sorry."

She rubbed her forearm, and not because his touch had hurt. But because it hadn't. She could still feel the electric sparks zinging through her insides, knocking down the dull ache in her abdomen. That stunned her more than the desire. She covered both. "It's okay. I shouldn't have yelled."

He shoved his hands through his hair, ruffling it.

Damned if the familiar sight didn't send a fresh wave of sparks snapping though her.

"Look, I know you're upset, but—"

Her cell phone trilled.

He broke off and waited while she tugged the phone from the belt clip at the small of her back. She glanced at the read out, frowning as she spotted the one number she'd been dreading more than Griff's this past week. The phone trilled a second, then a third time as she continued to stare.

"Do you need to take that?"

His comment snapped her out of her trance. She hooked the phone on her belt as it trilled a fourth and final time before shunting her doctor and his latest, undoubtedly affronted message to her voicemail. Given the way she'd been ducking Stan's calls for months, he'd never believe she'd honestly meant to phone him back and explain after she'd run out of the hospital after running into Griff. She was certain when the trilling started up again. She didn't bother checking the number. She already knew Stan had reached the end of his rope. Unfortunately, it didn't matter. There was no way she was taking that call in front of Griff. Not even if it meant Stan would follow through on his threats to call Luft and issue an official medical profile against her.

"Well?"

Blast that tone. She no longer had to answer to him. "Not all of us are control freaks, Griff. Some of us can actually let a phone ring." She regretted the words the moment they tumbled out but it was too late. The shadows had already entered his eyes. Like her, he wasn't thinking about all the calls he'd been driven to pick up at her place because she wouldn't— he was thinking about the one she'd refused to take the morning after their last fight.

And the one he'd made a week later.

Suddenly, she was tired of the games. The pain. "Please, isn't there anyone else who can fly this bird?"

He shook his head. She took one look in those dark gray eyes and knew he was telling the truth.

She felt like a heel.

Fire singed her neck and cheeks. For all her insistence that she'd changed, here she was jumping to conclusions like her old nineteen-year-old insecure self. She hadn't even given him the benefit of the doubt. That wasn't like her. Not the woman she'd worked hard to become. Worse, the crime she'd automatically assumed Griff guilty of wasn't like him either. Griff would never abuse his rank to further his personal life.

"I'm sorry. I had no right to accuse you of manipulating the flight schedule for personal gain."

She swore he'd flushed as well. "It's okay. The truth is, I wasn't above capitalizing on the vacancy. But the vacancy is real. Vince and I are the only ones not already tied up. You want that experiment of yours off the ground today, we're the ones who'll be taking it up."

"*Damn.*" She winced as the curse slipped free. "I didn't mean that the way it sounded. It's just…this experiment is important to me. For a lot of reasons."

"I know."

She blinked.

He shrugged. "Swanson and Litton filled us in. They said your mentor did the initial work—an aerospace engineer by the name of Haskell—but that he died recently. He was the boss you mentioned in Russia, wasn't he? The one you were supposed to replace at the summit in Moscow?"

"Yes." She fell silent as the memory bit in. The regret. Phil had been a great scientist, but an even better friend. She wasn't sure why she felt the need to elaborate, but she did. "Phil had a heart attack in his office. I was there when it happened. I started CPR while his secretary called the paramedics, but—ah—he didn't make it."

"I'm sorry for your loss."

He was. He'd even reached out, only to pull his hand back before he touched her. She was grateful for that, too. As rattled as she still was, she might have given in to the urge to step closer and accept the comfort she suddenly craved from this man. She covered the need and dragged her breath in instead. "Thank you. Anyway, your pilots were right, this experiment is a continuation of Phil's work. But I believe in it as much as he did." More so since her return from Russia.

Though she could not afford to let Griff know that.

Much less why.

"Sam…let me help."

The offer hung between them, warm and seductive, along with his even more seductive, though unspoken plea.

It was ironic. So much so, it wasn't funny.

Yes, she'd originally continued this experiment for Phil's sake, but she'd also hoped its success would get this very man out of her head. Not only hadn't she succeeded, she now had him in her face. As much as she needed to turn her back on his offer, for her own sanity if nothing else, she couldn't. General Luft might be pushing her to claim Phil's job permanently, but she knew her heart wasn't in it, much less the mind-numbing bureaucracy, scientific infighting and the hangar-sized stack of added paperwork. It was here, in the belly of that bird, despite the man standing beside it.

Who was she kidding? *Because* of the man standing beside it. She'd known that the moment she'd woken up in the middle of the night with the connection locking into her brain. If she could successfully apply the optical recognition parameters she was working in her Star Wars satellite research to helicopters along with her experimental laser system, she just might be able to prevent the next Pave Hawk from getting shot down over some lake in Russia—or elsewhere in the world.

And maybe, just maybe, that chilling flashback would disappear from her dreams as well.

She sighed.

Griff frowned. "You're going to cancel today, aren't you?"

She slipped her arm across her abdomen and pushed in on the ache at her side as she shook her head. The slight counter pressure helped. "No. I will need a couple minutes with you and Vince though, so I can run you through—"

"No need. Swanson and Litton took us through everything yesterday. It looks like a fairly straight run. You can go on and head up to the control tower while we finish the preflight checks. Ten minutes, tops."

He was right.

This first flight was designed to serve as a control to base the others on more than anything. The targets were all stationary. All Griff had to do was ride the Pave Hawk's controls while her onboard computer flew a set of carefully scripted automated runs on five separate stationary targets. The recorder she'd installed would hopefully soak up enough improved radar data to thrill even General Luft while the computer went on to execute a set of preprogrammed basic evasive maneuvers. In other words, Griff could fly this one with his eyes closed. She waited while he turned to retrieve her briefcase from the belly of the chopper.

He held it out.

His fingers brushed hers as she took the case. Though the contact had been brief, it succeeded in reminding her of a host of other things Griff could do extremely well with his eyes closed, every one of them involving those hands…and her flesh. She turned her back on the resulting heat and open invitation in his gaze, before they combined to seduce her into something more foolish than what she'd just agreed to. She headed past the remaining choppers as Griff called Vince out of the hangar. Her phone shrilled as she reached the edge of the concrete. This time she grabbed it and punched the connection open immediately, willing to promise Stan surgery that very minute if it would staunch the throb.

Not the one in her abdomen, the one in her heart.

It wasn't Stan. It was the lab.

She paused at the far end of the hangar to settle yet another infantile spat between two scientists who should've known better. By the time she'd started up and reached the control tower, she'd taken two more calls, both from Jarco as well. She hung up on Valentin's latest whine-fest and climbed the steps, glancing at her watch as she reached the door. Shoot. Griff had given her ten minutes. She'd eaten up almost twenty.

She'd asked for a hot mike on this one, specifically so she could listen in on everything that went down in the cockpit from the get go. Griff and Vince had probably finished the pre-flight checks and taken off by now.

She shoved the door open.

They had. The rhythmic thunder of chopper blades filling the tower told her that. But it was the sight of every single airmen, officer and enlisted alike—some leaning forward, ears cocked, some with binoculars in hand, staring out the windows in vain, *all* ramrod stiff—that told her the rest.

Something was wrong.

Very wrong.

She dropped her briefcase and vaulted forward, digging her clipped nails into the meaty shoulder of the closest air traffic controller. "What is it? What happened?" Somewhere, a mike was still keyed on their end, because the controller didn't answer her, Griff did.

"—not working!" *Static*. "—won't relinquish...control. Christ! Can't...hold it—"

Another burst of static cut off the rest.

By the time Griff's voice returned, his next words—and orders—were directed toward Vince. She could tell by Griff's tone that now was not the time for twenty questions with some armchair scientist, even her. She wasn't offended.

She was terrified.

Sam listened in vain along with everyone else in the control tower as Griff issued order after counter order as he and Vince worked together, trying anything and everything they could think of to break the rogue hold the computer she'd installed had somehow claimed over the Pave Hawk's automatic evasive maneuvering system. Damn it, she could not just stand here and listen to this. She raced across the tower to join the remaining air traffic controllers at the panoramic bank of windows overlooking the test range. She wrenched a pair of binoculars from someone's hands and jerked the eyepiece to her face. Her stomach bottomed out as the Pave Hawk snapped into focus. The bird was definitely going down.

And it was headed straight for the Abrams tank her blasted program had been designed to avoid.

She watched the chopper's entire airframe shudder in response to Griff's latest desperate command—and curse. He shouted another order and this time, he and Vince cursed together. Griff's deep voice picked up again, damned near topping the chopper's roar as he pelted Vince with a continuous stream of rapid-fire suggestions.

A fresh wave of adrenaline crashed through Sam as she watched the chopper continue to scream towards the massive tank despite each and every one. Sweat popped out along every inch of her flesh, drenching her uniform. Her heart rate damn near tripled, ratcheting so high, the blood roaring through her head rivaled the chopper's blades—until instantly, mercifully the Pave Hawk banked at the last second. The sudden, jarring motion sent the bird thundering sideways over the top of the tank instead of smack into it. Paint ground into paint as the Pave Hawk's belly scraped along the top of the tank's turret. A split second later, the hot mike cut out, leaving stark, screaming silence in the tower.

No!

A vicious curse punctuated the silence as the trailing tail of the Pave Hawk clipped the tip of the tank's turret. At that speed, the force of the resulting, glancing blow sent the bird spinning up and a hundred and eighty degrees about, just as Griff's other chopper had after it had taken that missile hit over that lake in Russia three months before. But instead of slamming back to earth, this chopper hung there, suspended for a brief, terrifying heartbeat before descending slowly, almost gracefully, in what could only be the most amazing, miraculously controlled piece of flying Sam had ever seen.

The moment the chopper touched down, something inside her just snapped.

The binoculars slipped from her fingers before she could

stop them. She was dimly aware of their weight crashing down onto her ribs as her heart continued to slam into them from within. Unable to control the wave of tremors that had taken up residence in each and every one of her muscles, she slumped forward, pressing her forehead into the window for support as the hot mike's connection kicked back in. And then, Griff's smooth deep voice filled the tower as he assured everyone that he and Vince were fine. His voice cut out again as he powered down the engine before bailing out of the bird along with Vince to make sure it, too, was fine.

She was dimly aware of the air traffic controller turning and asking if she was okay. Somehow, she managed to regain control of her body long enough to ease off the glass and nod.

Though the sergeant nodded back, he was clearly unconvinced.

Maybe her wobble had been too shaky. Maybe she simply looked as pale and clammy as she felt. She didn't know. Nor did she care. She had more to worry about than convincing some airman she'd never met before that she wasn't going to faint on his boots. Despite the tangle of red tape that had just been dumped in everyone's collective lap, she figured she had three, maybe four hours before she'd have to face Griff. A man who, from the moment they'd met, had been able to read her more thoroughly than her own mother could. How the hell was she going to ever convince Griff she no longer cared for him now? That she did not want him back in her life?

How was ever going to convince herself?

Chapter 7

Samantha was still inside Wing HQ when he signed his statement. At first, Griff thought—hoped—she might've been waiting for him. But as he caught the tail end of her discussion with one of the Army captains from the mobile safety board, he realized not. She'd simply finished wrapping up her official version of the day's events as well. Griff waited as the guy stuck out his hand. He could tell from the set of the man's jaw as Sam returned his shake the captain was cursing his luck. There he was, talking to a woman smart and gorgeous enough to bring every blessed one of the Pentagon's super-computers to instantaneous, testosterone-charged life…and the guy couldn't date her. Not while he was part of the mobile accident investigation board that was also investigating her part in the day's events, too.

Join the club, buddy.

Some guys got all the truly rotten luck.

And damned if his just didn't keep getting worse. He'd been straight with her out on that apron. He might not have used the eagles on his shoulders to muscle in on her experimental flight, but he'd been damned quick to pick up the slack when the opportunity presented itself. He'd known at the time the pilot change wouldn't go over well. Hell, even Vince had warned him. Now look at him. Them.

He'd made a mess of all three of their careers.

He had no idea what the devil caused that chopper to react the way it had. But the moment his own smart-ass investigator had brought up the smoldering bird he and Vince had left on the bottom of that Russian lake—and that, low and behold, Captain Hall had been there, too—he'd known they were in for a long, painful ride. He just hoped he didn't take either of them down with him. Fortunately, said smart-ass investigator had already departed for the test range. And he?

He was headed in the opposite direction.

Away from that mesmerizing smile. Griff watched as Sam dipped briefly to retrieve her briefcase from the waxed tiles at her feet before leaving the soldier's side. She headed down the corridor, stopping again to talk to another captain, this one Air Force, three feet from the main doors. Sam appeared to know the woman well. He took advantage of their quick catch-up to catch up with her, reaching Sam's blind side as the two exchanged a wave goodbye. She turned and shifted her briefcase to her left hand and reached for the door with her right.

"I'll get that."

She flinched.

He focused on the ache in his collar bone and not the tightening in his chest as he shoved the glass door all the way open and waited for her to walk through.

Damn it, get it over with.

The demon lodged in his brain was right. It was time to back off—for good. He might still care about this woman more than flying, but too many years had passed for her to ever feel the same way about him again. Too many sins. His. All his continuing to butt into her life would accomplish would be more of the same heartache and career-ache he'd given the both of them this afternoon. He opened his mouth, intent on issuing the polite kiss-off and promise to stay the hell away from her that she'd so desperately wanted—until she turned. He took one look in those dark whiskey eyes and knew.

She still cared.

It was in the way her gaze clung to his before traveling down his face and over every blessed inch of his flight suit as if she were reassuring herself that all his parts were still attached and still functioning. It was in the way her fingers bit into the handle of that briefcase as she pulled it close to shield herself, as if she was terrified she was going to give into the urge to reach out and drag him in as hard and as close as he was dying to hold her. He tugged his blue flight cap from his pocket instead and took his time donning it as he waited for her to finish drinking her fill—because he'd seen something else in those eyes too.

She might still care.

But she didn't want to.

She tightened her grip on the case. "Hi."

"Hi."

"You, ah, finish your statement?"

He nodded. Though they could legally discuss the crash now that they'd each given their separate, official version of events, he didn't want to. Oddly enough, despite the fact that it was her experiment—that as a scientist she had to have a hundred questions for the pilot who'd flown and then blown it—she didn't appear to want to discuss it either.

It gave him hope.

Time. That's what they needed.

He'd hurt her terribly. Destroyed her trust. No matter what the circumstance that had driven his actions. It would take time for her to heal. Time he planned on giving her. She'd been wrong about him out on that apron this afternoon. He had changed. He was going to prove it, too. He started right then, determined to suffer the awkward silence that had setled between them for as long as it took for her to decide on the next move. For the both of them. Unfortunately, a pair of enlisted airmen forced his hand and hers as they chose that moment to head up the steps behind her, popping simultaneous salutes his way as they approached.

He bit down on his grunt as he returned the salutes.

But his wince made it through.

The briefcase fell back to her side as the pair passed. "You're hurt."

"No, I'm—" He cut off the instinctive denial every pilot lived and died by from their flight-school physical on. Sam was right, she wasn't some nineteen-year-old kid anymore. She was grown woman. A woman he desperately wanted back in his life, this time as a solid equal. He gave her the truth. "My shoulder took a hit when we clipped that turret. It's not bad. Probably won't even rate a thump from the doc. But, yeah, it stings."

"Is that where you're headed? To the hospital?"

He nodded. Vince had finished his statement early. He was probably already halfway through his post-crash medical workup.

"Are you…okay to drive?"

The moment the words tumbled past those lush, pink lips, he knew she regretted them. Almost. He forced himself to wait. To let the memory help her figure the answer out. The moment her gaze softened, he knew it had. They eased back through the years together. To another hotter, much later, summer night. To a deserted parking lot on the outskirts of Austin. His new Jeep Wrangler. She in the driver's seat of the stick shift for the first time in her life, he in the passenger. Her utter frustration and rapidly skyrocketing irritation with his fifteenth painstaking review on how to drive a clutch…until he'd slid his palm over the back of her hand, gently but firmly knitting their fingers together as he guided her hand down and then up the gear shift in a slow, deliberate caress of supple leather designed to remind her about the night before and

everything that was right about them. Just before they'd show
each other, in that same darkened parking lot, how *very* righ
it could be again.

He bit down on another errant groan.

That time, he could've sworn she had too. He did catch he
soft sigh of resignation as they crawled out of the past and int
the present. Again, together.

"Your rental has a stick."

He pushed up a one-sided shrug. His good side. "You know
me, Major Control in the flesh."

She glanced at the bird on his hat. "Colonel now."

He cracked a grin. "Would you believe some flaws dimin-
ish with added age and rank?"

She actually laughed. His heart swelled at the sound.

"No."

He stepped out, way out, on the limb anyway. "Give me
chance, and I'll prove it."

Her smile faded. That same stark, lifeless shadow he'
seen three nights before in her living room slipped back int
her eyes. "I'm sorry, Griff, I can't. I meant what I said at my
house. But…I will give you a lift. As long as you understand
that's all I'm offering."

He'd take what he could for now.

And continue to pray for the rest later.

They headed for her electric-blue VW Bug in silence. Neither of them commented on the manual shift as he wedged
his frame into the passenger seat. But for the slow, throaty
tones of a bluesy alto he didn't recognize, the trip across base
passed in the same silence as their trip across the headquarters' parking lot. Still, he drew comfort from the fact that he
musical tastes had evidently remained the same. Despite he
date with the amiable, if somewhat stiff Dr. Alibek three
nights earlier, it gave him even more hope that her taste in me
might have survived the years intact as well. He was sur
prised as she pulled into a parking slot at the hospital and
bailed out of the Bug along with him.

He refused to comment on it.

If she was willing to kill a couple of hours outside his exam room with just that ever-present briefcase in tow to give him a return lift, who was he to stop her?

Given that Evening Colors had come and gone by the time they reached the main doors of the hospital, along with sunset and the majority of Kirtland's workforce, he was spared any further salutes and the jarring stab that came with them. He stopped at the entrance to the flight clinic to sign in.

"Do you want to come in or wait out here?"

For a moment, he swore she'd forgotten where she was—and that she had no real need to be there. She shrugged. "Here's fine. But, ah, I missed lunch earlier as well as dinner. I'm going to go grab a soda, see what's in the vending machine. Do you want something? A snack, coffee?"

"No, thanks."

He'd had three cups during his statement. One more hit of caffeine and he'd be flying, whether or not he'd been temporarily grounded due to the crash investigation. It wasn't until Sam had departed that he realized she'd forgotten her briefcase. Moments later, a nurse motioned him into an exam room. Though he sincerely doubted there was anything sensitive inside the locked case besides her wallet, he brought it with him. The nurse left him with a checked, backless gown that was a dead-on match for the one Sam had worn that day in Ramstein and instructions to don it. He managed to unzip the front of his flight suit with his good arm as the door closed, but peeling the fabric off proved more painful. He turned as the door reopened, the unforgiving fabric still hung up at mid-biceps.

"Would you mind giving me a—"

It wasn't the nurse.

"—hand."

Samantha's brows shot up as she stepped completely into the room, the briefcase and wallet she must have come back for clearly forgotten as she closed the door. "Good God, Griff. You made it sound like a bump."

He stared down at the four-by-twelve-inch band of black-ish purple that started just above his collar bone and tracked down into his chest, tracing the line of his now absent safety harness perfectly. It hadn't looked this bad in the bathroom during the debrief. Of course, that'd been a good three hours ago. He shook his head, hoping to soothe the panic in her eyes. "Trust me. It looks worse than it is."

She stepped closer.

He held his breath as she reached out and skimmed the tips of her fingers down his flesh.

"I don't know. It looks pretty bad."

Yeah, but it felt pretty damned good.

Her fingers slipped lower as she bent to examine the length of the bruise, including the thick knot that'd swelled up mid-ribs since he'd first looked. His breath caught as one of her fingers scraped the ring of his right areole, a part of his body he'd never thought erotic, much less sensitive until she'd gotten a hold of it…and him. He closed his eyes as he struggled to absorb the sensations he'd craved for years, even when he believed she'd betrayed him. The memories slipped in as well. The dark, sultry ones that had only escaped deeper into his fantasies each and every time he'd banished them. The ones that had continued to sneak out from their cage in the middle of the night as he slept, seducing him all over again when he was powerless to resist.

Her head still bent, she gently traced his centermost right rib all the way to the knot and stopped. "You don't think it's broken do you?"

His ribs? Or his heart?

He knew she wasn't ready for the truer answer, so he gave none. He inhaled instead. Slowly. Deliberately pulling the soft peach fragrance wafting up deep into his lungs. He held it there, jealously guarding it against the stronger antiseptic stench of the room, as well as the tang of jet fuel still clinging to him. He was forced to release his breath and her essence, however, as she finally stepped back.

"You're going to need more than a thump from the doctor, Griff. You're going to need an X-ray."

He doubted it. But again, he didn't argue. Nor did he argue when she reached out without thinking—or at the very least, remembering—to help him peel the upper half of his flight suit down. Unfortunately, *he* remembered that night quite clearly. He'd logged more flight hours than he'd intended one weekend. Already late for dinner, he'd left his flight suit on and bypassed his apartment to head directly for her place. The dessert that followed was one he'd never forget. Mainly because not only had it occurred out of the usual culinary order, it had started out on him. He banished the list of ingredients from his brain, lest they both find the crucial one snapping to attention years later.

Too late.

Her fingers fumbled as they and his zipper reached his hips. God forgive him, he captured her hands, trapping them lightly but firmly in his as he hooked his thighs against the exam table and leaned back into the edge to ease himself down to her level. He parted his legs and drew her in close, so close, he could feel the heat radiating off her body and into his. She refused to meet his gaze, keeping hers leveled on his exposed chest. But neither had she pulled away. Emboldened by her silence, he shifted her hands to one of his and reached up to tuck a loose strand of silk into her braid. He smoothed his index finger across her temple next, slowly soothing the thin bruise that still marred her temple from where she'd bumped her head against the edge of the chopper that afternoon.

When she didn't stiffen, he trailed his fingers over the light flush staining her cheeks, then traced the tempting curve of her jaw. Lord, she was beautiful. Even with her lashes downcast, her most intoxicating feature still avoiding him.

He caved into the need and leaned closer.

"Griff…*don't.*"

He stopped, less than an inch from the warm, honeyed promise of her lips. But he didn't move away.

"Why?"

"Please, just don't."

He skimmed his fingertips up and traced the tiny lines that had begun to form at the corners of her eyes, so damned sorry he hadn't been around to have seen the first one sneak in. "Give me a reason, a good one, and I won't." He waited, knowing in his soul if anyone, flight surgeon, nurse or the base commanding general himself, so much as touched the knob on the door across this room, he'd kill them.

On the spot.

But when several more moments passed and she still hadn't answered, he did back off. Not much, just far enough so he could slip his fingers down and feather them across her lips. He savored the swift, telltale hitch of desire in her throat, the warm wash of her exhale against his flesh. The sweet, achingly familiar scent of her breath.

"Sam?"

"Griff, please, just don't. It's…complicated."

"Sweetheart, we've always been complicated."

He knew she wouldn't deny it. She couldn't. Not when everyone who'd known them all those years ago had assumed he was the one who'd seduced her…and couldn't have been more wrong. By the time he'd given in and given *her* the nineteenth birthday present she'd stood as close as this while brazenly demanding, it was too late. Samantha had not only lost her virginity that night, she'd also become absolutely, completely, his. When she finally raised that soft gold gaze, he knew she was thinking about that first time, too. Her eyes darkened with the stirring of passion he remembered so well, deepening to that exact shade of whiskey that had altered his entire life and hers. Unable to prevent himself now any more than he had then, he drank the transformation in, drank her in, deeper and deeper until he was completely drunk. The way he'd wanted to be that cold, desperate night in Anchorage.

Only this time, she was also reaching out to him…

——until that blasted cell phone of hers pierced the air.

The mood.

Them.

He closed his hands instinctively, but she was already gone, slipping out of his grasp and away from his empty arms as he backed up all the way to the set of stainless steel cabinets behind her. He swallowed a curse as she wrenched her phone from the small of her back and brought it to her ear.

"Captain Hall."

A brief silence followed…and a scarlet flush. Hers. "I'm sorry, Dimitri. I didn't realize it was you."

To Griff's disappointment and frustration, he missed the rest as she lowered her voice and turned away. Eavesdropping would have been moot anyway, since the flight surgeon chose that moment to shove the door open. His fellow colonel took in his half-dressed state, Samantha's shrinking presence and cocked an amused brow between the two of them. Griff clamped down on his jaw as her flush spread.

"I'll, ah, take this outside."

Before he could argue, much less open the door for her, she'd snatched her briefcase from the floor beside him and fled. He was left listening to her making excuses to another man as the door snapped shut behind her.

The flight surgeon had the brains to kill his smirk. "I hope I didn't interrupt."

The smile he forced hurt more than his shrug. "It's complicated."

The surgeon was clearly puzzled as he turned to hook his hand beneath the base of a low stool and roll it closer.

So was he. But he wouldn't be for long.

Alibek. Somehow, the good doctor had become his complication. While he knew in his gut the assessment was valid, it didn't make sense. Not entirely. Yes, she'd referred to the man as her date that night at her house. Even if the label was true, that was all Alibek was. They weren't sleeping together. There was no way that would have escaped his internal radar. Not with her. That just made him all the more curious—and

determined. He might not understand what exactly Dimitri A
ibek shared with the woman he'd traveled eleven years, thre
months and six thousand miles to claim, but he would.

And soon.

"This is it."

Sam nodded and pulled the car into the driveway.

Vince Racey's driveway.

Other than the black Ford four-by-four parked in front o
the garage door and an antique-white stucco wash instead o
blushed pink, the ranch was disconcertingly similar to her
Worse, the house itself was disconcertingly near hers, le:
than ten blocks away. Meaning that for the next few weeks–
until Griff's household goods caught up with him and he an
Christy moved into Griff's on-base quarters—*Griff* lived le:
than ten blocks away. With both houses facing east, they eve
shared the same breathtaking view of the Sandia Mountain

How on earth was she supposed to sleep now?

All thoughts of sleep fled as Sam killed the Bug's engin
but only because Norah Jones' debut CD had kept on pla
ing. This afternoon, the woman's velvety voice had calme
her nerves after she'd left a seething Valentin in the lab'
parking lot, closing her car door on his latest demands for a
increased chunk of their new projects budget. Right now, th
suggestive longing in Norah's voice as *Feeling the Same Wa*
All Over Again kicked in took on a whole new meaning. E:
pecially as she switched off the Bug's headlights, allowing th
full cloak of night to ease in around them. Maybe Griff wasn
listening to the refrain, let alone thinking about the memorie
and that kiss they'd very nearly shared in his examinatio
room two hours earlier.

"Interesting lyrics." The velvet in his voice might b
rougher, but it was a whole lot more suggestive.

She stabbed the CD player's off button.

It was a mistake.

The thrumming quiet that swirled in along with the dar

carried even more suggestion…as did Griff's hand as he deliberately skimmed the top of the Bug's stick shift while reaching for the CD's cover. She waited while he turned the plastic case toward the whisper of light bleeding in though the passenger window from Vince's porch. His brow kicked up higher with each title she knew by heart: *Come Away With Me, Turn Me On, I've Got to See You Again.*

"Mind if I borrow this?"

No doubt about it. This ride had been a bad idea from the start. If she hadn't been so rattled after that crash, she never would have offered. But she had been. No, she'd been more than rattled. She'd been downright terrified. More scared than she'd been in her entire life. And after the C130 crash and subsequent confrontation with that squad of Chechen terrorists in Russia, that was saying something. Even the nightmares about Griff's downing that'd been tormenting her these past three months had nothing on reality. Watching today, knowing all the while that Griff was piloting that bird? That he could have died right then—that she could have killed him? Her stomach rolled at the memory. She punched the player's eject button and retrieved the CD.

She held it between them. "Keep it. I've got another copy."

His fingers brushed hers as he snagged the disc. "Thanks."

Might as well picture him listening to the same music to go with the identical view behind that house. She ought to recommend he start with the last track. *The Nearness of You* seemed particularly appropriate as he unzipped the front of his flight suit and slipped the CD in over his heart.

"Ready?"

No. But there was no other polite way to do this, now was there?

Griff had taken a call on his own cell phone as they'd left the hospital. It seemed one of the air traffic controllers was intent on sucking up to the new commander. Everyone knew Griff was staying with Vince. They had to, in case of an emergency. The controller had taken advantage of the temporary living arrangements and burned an extra copy of the tower's recording of the Pave Hawk's flight. The sergeant had dropped it off with Vince on his way home. While the favor might be unorthodox, it wasn't illegal. And she was definitely interested in the third-generation copy Vince had offered to burn for her. She'd be up all night going over the afternoon's events and double-checking her experiment in preparation for the accident investigation board's trip to her lab the following morning, anyway. The cockpit recording would help. A recording that was inside that house.

Along with Christy Towers.

She didn't need the intermittent flicker of light behind those drapes to tell her the girl was still up, killing time with TV until her father came home. She did not want to go in there. It was just too painful to look into that little girl's gaze—and not for the reasons he assumed. "Griff, I know you said your daughter was okay with the near miss when you called, but are you sure you wouldn't rather go in alone?"

He shook his head, refusing to give her the out she'd suggested at the hospital. She knew why. She could read his hopes just as clearly. But they wouldn't come to pass. As humiliating as it was going to be, she was going to have to tell Griff the brutal facts about just how much she had changed since he'd last seen her, and soon. Otherwise, he'd go on thinking that if he could just get her and his daughter together often enough, she'd get over the circumstances of Christy's conception and let him back in her life. Truth was, she probably would have. If that was all there was to it.

But it wasn't, was it?

Damn it, this was so unfair!

Tears born of frustration and self-pity stung at the corners of her eyes. She tugged the keys from the ignition and bailed out of the Bug before they could fall. She'd tell him. Just not now. Not after the ringer her heart had been through today. Unfortunately, Griff caught up with her at the triple steps leading up to the postage stamp of a courtyard landing and snagged her elbow. "Samantha, don't—" He broke off as he spun her around. To her utter embarrassment his hand came up. He snagged her chin and tipped her face into the light streaming down from the porch. His fingers shook as he smoothed the tears from her cheeks. "Oh, sweetheart, please don't cry. I'm sorry, I shouldn't have pushed you. Not today. You don't have to come inside. Just stay here. I'll get the recording—"

"No. Don't go. It's not—" She closed her eyes, reopened them. "—Christy." But it was…and it wasn't.

She reached up and closed her hand over his, gripping it tight as she searched for the strength to just say it. Now. While she could escape. He could have Vince drop the recording off later, or she could just wait until tomorrow. But this couldn't wait. Whether or not she wanted to, she had to say it. End this. While she could. She sucked in her breath and forced the tears down. "Griff—"

She snapped her mouth shut as the front door flew open, immediately stepping into the shadows as Christy barreled out, straight into her father's waiting arms.

"*Daddy!*"

Her heart ripped as the girl gave into what was probably her third or fourth bout of tears since Griff's call that afternoon. The rip widened as Griff swung his daughter up in his arms, no doubt grateful now for the combination muscle relaxant and painkiller the flight surgeon had forced on him before they'd left the hospital. "Hey, hey. Easy now. I told you I was okay." Griff gathered the girl closer as she buried her face in his neck, stroking her ponytail over and over as she vented the worst of her fears.

Her heart ripped clear through. Pending confession and cockpit recording be damned. She couldn't do this.

Sam edged toward the steps, intent on slipping away.

"Wait."

She froze as Griff shifted his daughter to his left hip so his good arm could take the brunt of the girl's weight. Fortunately, Christy was a tiny slip of a thing.

Probably like her mother.

She pushed the thought aside.

"Christy, you remember Dr. Hall. We met her at the hospital on Monday."

To Sam's surprise, the girl all but glared down at her. Griff caught the stare, too. Like her, he chose to ignore it. "Samantha's here to pick up something."

"*No.*"

Griff lowered his daughter to her feet, immediately. "Christy—"

The girl ignored the same note of warning that had put Sam on edge in years past. "I don't want her here." Christy swung around and faced her directly. "I hate you. *You're* the reason we didn't go to Hawaii."

Stunned by the girl's vehemence, Sam stiffened.

Griff didn't. He stepped forward. "Excuse me?" He reached out with his sore arm. "Young lady, I don't know what—"

The girl whirled about before he could finish, deftly evading his grasp as she ran back into the house. She turned down what Samantha assumed from her own home's floor plan was a hallway leading to Vince's guest and master bedrooms. The loud door slam reverberating into the foyer confirmed it. Sam would have escaped then, heading in the opposite direction back to her car but for the fact that she had no choice. Griff had latched on to her arm with his good hand and pulled her into the house with him.

"Griff, I don't think now's a good—"

He tugged her through the parquet foyer and down the carpeted hall alongside him. "Now's the perfect time. For an *apology*."

No way. She did not want to get in the middle of this.

Hawaii? She'd hate herself, too.

"Please, I think you and your daughter need to settle this without me."

"The hell we will. She involved you with that comment." He tried the door knob at the end of the hall. It was locked.

He rapped his knuckles against the door. "Christy!" He glanced down as silence greeted his summons. "Samantha, I'm sorry. I've never seen her so rude. I have no idea what's gotten into her."

Gee, dad changes duty stations—from exciting Hawaii to land-locked, boring New Mexico of all places—and introduces an "old friend" at the hospital. A *woman* friend. Then brings said woman home the night of yet another crash? What's not to understand? The girl might be ten, but she was still female.

And Griff was *her* dad.

This time, he banged on the door with the flat of his palm. "Young lady, do not make me get—"

The door unlocked. Opened. Slowly.

And just a crack.

Reddened, watery gray eyes stared up at them.

"Apologize. *Now*."

The girl nodded—and sucked in her breath. Deep. "Okay. But you have to leave first, Dad."

"Like hel—" Griff cut himself off. He sucked in a breath five times as deep as his daughter's. "Christy, I don't know what you think you're pulling—"

Sam laid her hand on his arm. "Please."

He stared down at her.

She nodded. "It's okay." It would probably be better this way.

Griff gave her the same look of utter exasperation her own father used to give whenever he got in the middle of her and her mother while she was growing up—and realized his mistake. She'd have laughed if the situation wasn't so serious. And so very painful.

"Fine. I'll get the recording."

Christy waited until he'd turned and reached the end of the hall before she opened the door any farther. To Sam's surprise, the girl motioned her inside the room.

Why not?

She entered a generic guestroom consisting of a tall oak

dresser, nightstand with lamp and a full bed with a matching oak headboard. The dark blue comforter had been softened by half a dozen small, colorful Beanie bears, a worn cloth pastel patchwork pony and—not so surprising after the girl's excitement over the summer camp signup discovery—a plush black and white space shuttle similar to the one Sam had on her desk at the lab. She waited at the foot of the bed as the girl shut the door before she bounded up onto the bed. Christy pulled the patchwork horse into her arms, her denim clad legs beneath her as she leaned back against the pillows and headboard and just stared.

When a good two minutes had passed and Christy didn't offer the promised apology, Sam decided to risk a bit of rudeness herself. She hooked a uniformed knee onto the mattress and settled down at the edge of the bed. The girl shoved her pony tail past her shoulder, but she still didn't speak.

"This is about more than Hawaii, isn't it?"

The girl nodded slowly.

Okay. Glad they got that out of the way. Sam glanced down at the exposed sole to her right oxford. The dusty wedge looked as out of place in this pristine room as she felt. To her surprise, the girl moved, leaning across the rest of her stuffed toys to tug the top drawer of the nightstand open. She pulled out an oversized zippered binder with large yellow daisies stitched over the front. Curious, Sam waited as the girl unzipped the binder and withdrew a slim, lockable diary from a pocket within. Whatever Christy was after must be special, because she'd taken pains to hide it. The girl reached down the neck of her pink T-shirt next and withdrew a chain with a tiny key at the end. She used the tiny key to release the miniature flat padlock and open the book.

The moment Christy withdrew a folded sheet of paper, acid seared up Sam's throat.

It was yellowed and worn with age.

No! Please God, *no*.

The girl held out the sheet of paper. Again, silently. Daring her to take it. To read it.

Samantha had no idea what that letter said, but she already knew, deep inside her heart, who had sent it…had meant it for her alone…eleven long years ago. Tears stung at the corners of her eyes as she took the sheet of paper and slowly unfolded it. They slipped free, scalding her cheeks, as she skimmed the letter's date before moving on to the explanation, the impassioned plea and the promise that followed. Some of the tears were purely selfish, meant for herself, for having never read these words until it was too late, but the rest of her tears were for this innocent child for ever having had to read them at all.

> *14 Nov '92*
> *Dear Samantha,*
>
> *Since you've refused my calls, please accept this letter. Honey, I'm sorry I came down on you again. You're right, I can be an overbearing ass. It's just…you're so damned trusting. It's one of the reasons I love you, yes. But, sweetheart, I've seen things—life—and I'm not just talking about the war. There's so much I want to spare you; mistakes and pain I'd give anything to help you avoid. But you're right, I can't. It is your life and I don't want to live it for you. I want to live it with you. I know there's a balance. Help me find it, Sam. Help me find my way back to us. The Air Force can't do anything about my orders, I tried. I'm stuck in Alaska for the next year. Please accept this ticket and visit so we can talk about it, about us. The dates are open-ended. I'll be waiting. For as long as it takes.*
>
> *Lost without you,*
> *Griff*

Sam wiped the tears from her cheeks before they could drip down and stain the yellowed paper. Then she slowly reread

the words, Griff's words. She'd gotten an apology all right,
just not the one she'd expected. The worst part of all was, it
was years too late. Griff had evidently kept the letter. Three
nights ago, he'd sworn to her that he'd changed, right there
in her house. He'd probably brought the letter to Kirtland to
show to her. To prove to her that he had changed, that he'd
been willing to work things out. Not now, but years before.

Why he hadn't brought the letter with him that night, she
didn't know. Maybe he thought he'd misplaced it. Maybe he
thought it was still on some container ship in the middle of
the Atlantic with the rest of his household goods. She didn't
know. Nor was it important right now. What was important—
critical, in fact—was that someone else had gotten a hold of
this letter first. Read the words, the pain and the love.

The date.

She folded the sheet up and passed it back to that someone. The hurt in Christy's eyes confirmed her worst fears. This
little girl might be ten years old, but she was bright enough
to do the math and figure out that this letter was written far
too close to her birth date for the fairytale romance her father
had spun for her to be true.

There was only one thing to do. One gift she could give
this child that would come close to making up for the
heartache and doubt she'd unwittingly caused her.

The truth.

"Christy, I never got this letter."

The girl nodded solemnly.

"And even if I had, I honestly can't say what it would have
changed. But I can tell you that this letter doesn't change anything now. Not for you. Not for your dad. Not even for me.
Most especially, not for your dad *and* me."

She waited as Christy slipped the letter back into her diary,
locked it, then secreted the diary inside the binder and the
binder into the nightstand drawer. She tucked the key beneath
the collar of her T-shirt as she straightened against the headboard. "We were supposed to move to Hawaii."

Sam nodded. "I know. Now. But as of three days ago, the day I first met you in the hospital, I didn't know you and your dad would be transferred here. Christy, I'm going to tell you something I haven't had a chance to tell your dad, not really. I have a boyfriend. A boyfriend I just agreed to marry. Do you understand what I'm saying?"

Those dark gray eyes looked so much like Griff's it was unnerving. Especially when the disbelief hit. The similarities in their thought processes was more telling than even their looks. Like her father, Christy hadn't even considered that *she* might not want to get involved with Griff again. "You—you're not going to marry my dad?"

She shook her head slowly. Firmly. "No."

"But…*why?*"

Why, indeed? "Because I don't want to." Damn it, she *didn't*.

"And my dad doesn't know you're getting married?"

"Not yet. I just accepted Dimitri's proposal."

The girl actually smiled. Grinned. The relief spreading across her face was humbling. And hurtful.

Sam forced herself to suck up the pain. In her heart…and in her side. She turned more fully onto the bed and adjusted her crooked knee to help alleviate the latter.

It helped.

Christy retrieved the patchwork pony. Her smile faded as she stroked the worn ears and mane almost pensively, as if she needed time to process the transition from potential threat to possible friend. She wasn't surprised when the minutes began to drag out and Griff didn't arrive. He probably thought, or at least hoped, they were in here bonding. Oddly enough, it felt like they were. Especially when Christy finally pulled the pony close and sighed. "My dad says you're the smartest person he's ever met."

She blinked. "Really?" Wow.

Griff had flattered her with similar comments while they were involved in college. But frankly, she'd always assumed he'd made them because, well, they were involved. That he'd

repeated the flattery to someone else—his daughter, no less—
floored her. She was even more surprised Christy had admitted it to her. Until the girl added, "He also thinks you're a
klutz."

Sam couldn't help it, she laughed.

Score one for the kid.

Her laughter deepened. It felt good, too. It warmed her,
bolstering her hope that this girl might be able to get past that
letter she'd found. She was definitely strong enough. The
laughter also helped to relieve the stress of this whole damned
day. Unfortunately, Christy was staring at her as if she were
an exhibit in the zoo. She seemed genuinely surprised someone could laugh at criticism intended as an insult. "I'm sorry,
honey. It's just, I *am* a klutz." She turned her head so the girl
could see her latest bruise, the one on her temple she'd gotten compliments of the Pave Hawk that afternoon. "See, I got
this today on your dad's helicopter."

The moment the explanation came out, she realized it was
a mistake. Any suggestion of something positive and friendly
between her and Griff would bruise this girl's ego for some
time. She searched her brain for more and added it quickly.
"That flight today? The one that almost crashed but didn't?
It had my experiment inside it. Vince and your dad were supposed to take it up for me. See if it worked."

In other words, just business.

"Oh." But the suspicion was still there.

"That's why I'm here. I need to get a recording of what
happened. So I can figure out what went wrong."

"My dad's a good pilot."

In other words, it wasn't his fault. That, she already knew.
She'd always had been the klutz between the two of them, not
Griff. Griff was right about her eye-hand coordination. It truly
stunk. That was the real reason she'd never applied to the pilot
program herself. "You're right. Your dad is a good pilot. Very
good. So's Vince. But…don't tell them I said that. They'll just
get swelled heads."

This time, Christy giggled.

Darn, but she really could like this kid. She was sharp. Not that that surprised her.

The girl's giggle faded into a shy smile. "I'm going to fly someday, too. I'm going to be better than my dad, though. I'm going to fly jets and be an astronaut."

Sam returned the smile. She believed it. Not only had she decided on her own career path at this age, the girl clearly had her father's ballsy confidence. A necessary trait in any pilot, rotary or fixed wing. She watched as Christy traded her patch-work pony for the plush shuttle. She smoothed her fingers along the wings, showing even more care than she had with the horse. Given the girl's excitement with the signup sheet she'd seen at the hospital for the space camp, it made sense. "Did your dad call about camp yet?"

To her surprise, Christy's face fell. She studied the shuttle glumly. "Yeah."

Oh, no. She'd been so rattled at the hospital, it hadn't even occurred to her. "You missed the cut-off." May 15th. Even before Christy nodded, Sam knew she was right. She'd helped Dimitri distribute the leaflets across base.

Dimitri.

He could do it. He would, if she asked him. "You know what? Maybe I can help. If it's okay with your dad, that is."

Christy's head snapped up. The wariness was still clearly there amid all that dark gray surprise. But this time, there was a distinct glint of hope in the girl's gaze, too. "The lady at the museum told my dad all the fifth-grade sessions were full. She said I could go next year. But if I do that, I'll be stuck with the fifth-graders when I'm in sixth, 'cause you have to go to the sessions in order."

A woe to be sure. But it was true. Alamogordo had a strict policy on meeting session prerequisites.

Fortunately, she had an in Griff didn't. "I'll let you in on a secret—but you can't tell anyone else but your dad. Especially anyone at camp." The girl nodded, completely hooked now, and even more hopeful. Christy wanted that slot. Really, really wanted it. Enough to accept help from the woman in that note to get it. Sam just hoped Griff didn't have a fit when he heard. "My fiancé? He's a scientist, like me. Dimitri designs rockets at the lab where I work. He's also friends with the man who runs the shuttle camp."

"You mean he can get me in?"

With that beatific grin as thanks? "I think so."

"*Really?*" Christy all but vaulted the center of the bed. But then, just as quickly as she'd lurched forward, she pulled back, her initial enthusiasm tempered by the returning wariness and suspicion. As if she'd just realized she still should be. "I mean, are you sure you want to?"

In other words why would she *want* to? It had to be because of her dad, right?

Sam knew then, this girl had experienced shaded kindness before. At least one woman had extended a hand to her in the past, but had really been reaching for Griff. She pushed the realization from her mind. The jealousy. This wasn't about her. Let alone what she would never have. It was about this child. She might not have moved around as a kid, but as the accidental, late-in-life *oops* of farming parents who'd already raised four sons, she knew what loneliness felt like. She'd become even more familiar with it after her mother had given in and agreed to home school her so she could meet her educational goals early.

She nodded firmly. "I'm sure."

"Oh, wow! I gotta email Jen. She'll be *so* jealous."

Sam had no idea who Jen was and she told herself it didn't matter. Not to her. she couldn't afford to get to know this child any more than she already had. It was time to leave. The room and this house. It was late and the pair of ibuprofen tablets she'd swallowed in her car before she'd met Griff and Vince out on that apron had worn off hours ago. Unfortunately, both times she'd been inside her Bug and within arms' reach of her prescription, Griff had been inside the car as well. As a result, her abdomen was beginning to smart like the devil. "Christy, I have to go. I haven't had dinner yet."

Just like that, the girl quieted. Turned pensive once more. Wary. But this time, Sam knew it wasn't due to just her. She was sure of it when the girl faked a yawn. "Okay. I'm kind of tired. I'm going to go to bed. You'll ask about the camp?"

"I'll talk to your dad." She turned to leave.

"Doctor Hall?"

She swung back. "Yes?"

"I'm sorry for what I said. I don't really hate you. I mean, I thought I did. In Germany. But now, I…"

Sam nodded as those gorgeous gray eyes she knew so well filled with tears and finished it for her. "It's okay. I understand." She did. More than this girl could know. For three months she'd done her best to avoid thinking about Christy at all. And now that she was here, standing across this room from her, she was experiencing the beginnings of the one emotion she never thought to feel towards Griff's child.

Affection.

She honestly wanted to get to know Christy better. Worse, she suspected she was capable of more than just liking her. And that was even more dangerous than the renewed desire Griff had been able to ignite within her inside that exam room two hours ago. She closed the door behind her as the girl burrowed down into her pillows, knowing the real reason Christy had chosen to remain behind was her dad's temper.

Smart kid.

She'd run into that temper a time or two in college. The first had been the night Griff had unknowingly taken her virginity. She would never forget his fury at being duped.

Yeah, she definitely recommended avoiding an angry Griff if at all possible.

Unfortunately she couldn't avoid him. Not right then.

He was standing in the foyer with Vince as she reached it, audio CD in hand. He held it out as she nodded to Vince.

"Did Christy apologize?"

"Yes. And we talked. Speaking of which." She glanced at Vince. "Could we, ah…"

Vince tipped an informal salute her way. "Gotta run. Griff's housekeeper held dinner. Not often I can get a woman to cook for me." He winked. "Best grab it before she changes her mind. 'Night, Sam."

"Goodnight."

She waited for Griff to open the door and close it behind them, stopping once their privacy was assured.

"I'll see you to your car."

She shook her head. "What I have to say won't take long."

His sigh was born of embarrassment, rather than exasperation. "If it's about what happened, about Christy's attitude, there's something you should know. We *were* supposed to go to Hawaii."

"I know."

"Yeah, well, she probably didn't tell you that her best friend Jennifer is slated to transfer there in six months with her mom. Christy's still a bit ticked over the change. Anyway, with school just out for the summer and no new friends yet, she's lonely, too. Mrs. Schultz is a great housekeeper, but not much of a fellow tomboy." She caught Griff's wry smile in the dark and knew that was an understatement. She also knew he was rambling on deliberately. He didn't want her to leave.

And she didn't know how to tell him.

Dealing with this scar was harder than dealing with the ones knitted all over the inside of her belly.

She didn't want to think about that letter, much less remember those words. The past. What could have been…but would never be. Unfortunately, he needed to know. There was a little girl in there with a hundred questions. Questions that needed answers. Now. "Griff, Christy's not mad about Hawaii. Well, she might be. But there's more. More than loneliness. You two need to talk." She dragged the cooling night air into her lungs and held it there. It didn't help.

Any moment, she was going to shatter.

"About what?" He shook head. Exasperation had crept into his voice, too. "Sam, you're not making sense."

Dammit, just say it. "Christy found the letter."

"The letter? What—" He stiffened. Cursed.

She nodded. "Yeah. That letter." The stinging had returned to her eyes. She refused to wipe them in front of him. The hell with space camp. Christy could fill him in. He could yell at her later if he wanted to. She needed to get out of here. Before the tears started falling again.

Too late.

She jerked away as he reached for her, spinning around as another curse filled the landing, this one of frustration. She was halfway down the steps by the time he shouted her name. She blessed the electronic key on her ring as she unlocked the Bug and scrambled inside while he stood on the porch, rocked by the implications of what she'd just confessed.

What his daughter now knew.

Probably wondering what the heck he was going to tell her. She shoved the key in the ignition and started up the car, pressing her hand into the now throbbing ache in her abdomen, trying to offset it with counter pressure as Griff slowly turned and headed back into the house. Back to his little girl. The little girl she'd never had.

The little girl she never would.

Chapter 8

"So, you ready to talk?"

Samantha shot straight to her feet as Griff's voice rumbled through the Pave Hawk, cursing as the top of her head slammed squarely into the chopper's steel overhead. She dropped the wrench she'd been using and rubbed her fingers over the lump already swelling beneath her scalp. As she turned toward the aircraft hangar's distant, yawning doors, a shadowy, denim-clad Griff stepped out of the night and into the artificial light. Her heart continued to pound against her chest as Griff crossed thirty-odd feet of oil-stained concrete—and it wasn't due to the gray T-shirt clinging to the man's ever-impressive chest and arms.

A good twenty-four hours had passed since she'd fled Vince Racey's house. She'd spent each one of them dreading this moment, too. But if Griff's intent was to grill her over her interference with his daughter's summer plans, let alone the bombshell she'd inadvertently left in the girl's care in her haste to leave, he should have headed for her place after

Christy went to bed. The middle of an Air Force hangar—whether or not that hangar was deserted but for the two of them, a battered chopper and a strip of expired yellow, *Do Not Cross* tape—was not the place for a personal dressing down.

Even if this was technically Griff's hangar.

To her disappointment, he was still frowning when he reached the chopper. It wasn't until he reached inside and snagged her left hand to gently but insistently guide her out that she realized he wasn't mad, he was concerned.

"You okay?"

Before she could answer, he pushed her other hand out of the way, the one she hadn't realized was still massaging her scalp. He threaded his fingers through hair she'd loosened half an hour ago in an attempt to stave off a growing tension headache. A headache she'd ended up with anyway. She winced as Griff prodded her newest bump.

His frown deepened. "Sorry."

"It's o-okay. I just—"

"—cut yourself." He brandished his fingers.

The blood.

She lowered her gaze and spotted the matching evidence on her own fingers. She wiped the smear of blood into the thigh of her dark-blue coveralls, directly beside a set-in splotch of oil. By the time she'd glanced up, Griff had tugged the hem of his T-shirt from his jeans and a Swiss Army knife from his back pocket. He used the latter to slice off a good three-by-six-inch strip of the former. He closed the knife and returned it to his pocket before rolling the swatch of gray cloth up and sealing it over the lump atop her head.

"Hold this."

Her embarrassment deepened as Griff turned around and pushed a mobile tool chest aside before heading across the hangar to the first aid station. She freely admitted the whack stung, but it didn't feel that bad. He returned with an antiseptic towelette, sterile packet already torn open. He nudged her fingers out the way again, this time pressing the alcohol wipe to the cut. Several moments passed before he removed the wipe and tilted her scalp toward the bank of overhead lights and his darker, steadier stare.

She hiked her brow dryly as he released her. "Well, Doc, am I going to die? Or do I just need stitches?"

He shook his head. "No, and no. But take it easy, will you?" That half smile she loved so much dipped in, softening his own deadpanned tone. "Steel skin or not, that poor bird might not survive your next wallop."

She couldn't help it, she laughed.

His smile spread.

And the heat index in the hangar tripled.

She heard his air rush out as Griff turned to hook his forearms against the upper ledge of the Pave Hawk's open door and stare into the chopper's belly. Several moments passed before he spoke. "So, have you had a chance to figure out what happened?"

For the second time that night, she stood mute, and not because of what he'd asked. Because of what he hadn't. She still couldn't quite believe he didn't intend to read her the riot act regarding her engagement to another man.

Had he really changed that much?

Or had Christy simply not had a chance to tell him?

The two had had more to discuss last night than her eventual wedding plans. Either way, now was not the time to obsess over her personal life. She and Griff had more pressing matters. She stepped up beside him and stared into the chopper. Other than the innards of a stripped Pave Hawk, there wasn't much else to see. The core modules Phil had designed had been removed the day before by investigators from the safety board. All that remained were half a dozen pieces of auxiliary equipment and a set of dangling cables that been left behind for someone else to retrieve—and those had yielded precisely squat.

She sighed. "No, I don't have anything yet."

He tensed. So slight had the motion been that someone

else, anyone else, probably wouldn't have picked up on it. But she wasn't just anyone. She'd lain in this man's arms for nearly a year. During that time, she'd learned to read every one of his moods, whether or not Griff had been willing to share the source of his darker ones with her.

"What's wrong?"

He continued to stare inside the chopper. Blindly.

Her stomach bottomed out.

No! It couldn't be.

But it was. Every nerve in her body screamed it. Her hand crept up before she could stop it, sliding up his T-shirt-clad back. The thick muscles of his shoulders bunched as she reached them. And Lord help them, she knew why.

"You've been grounded."

He finally sighed. But still, he wouldn't turn. Wouldn't face her. And, again, she knew why. He couldn't. She shook her head as the shock, the utter disbelief, reverberated through her body, slamming full force into her heart. Denial screamed back up into her brain. Of all the scenarios she'd considered last night and today, this was not one of them.

"I don't understand. *Why?*"

He laughed. Harshly. "You have to ask?"

"You're damned right I do." That anyone could even think Griff was capable of screwing up blew her away. Completely. But that was the board's preliminary determination. The fact that Griff still wouldn't even look at her confirmed it. She dragged her hand down and gripped his arm. She tugged hard, forcing him to turn and face her. The distance in his stare as he focused not on her, but through her, tore deep into her soul. She'd give anything to ease that look, the pain and humiliation within those dark gray pools.

And worse…the doubt.

"Griff, this is insane. You did not cause that accident. I don't know how the board managed to reach that conclusion, but they don't have a shred of evidence to support it."

He focused on her then, for a split second—just before he

jerked his chin toward the chopper's tail. Specifically, the chunk of steel that was conspicuously missing from that tail. "Yeah, well, seems all the evidence they need is right there— or rather, isn't. Unless you've got something better, that's what they're going with."

And she'd already told him she didn't.

Frustration ripped through her for the hundredth time since the safety board had shown up at her lab at 0700 that morning, only this wave was a thousand times more intense. She'd spent the past twelve hours biting her tongue as a trio of technicians coldly and methodically dissected every aspect of the experiment Griff had attempted to fly for her. By the time the techs finished, the men had examined every keystroke in every piece of software she and Phil had ever written as well as every single circuit in every piece of hardware. Nothing had been overlooked. And, no, not a single flaw had been detected. But that did *not* mean Griff had screwed up.

But it did explain why Griff's voice had sent her shooting into the overhead of this bird five minutes earlier. Only the anger she'd picked up on hadn't been directed toward her. He must have just heard.

And the first person he'd sought out had been her.

Her heart lurched as Griff finally moved. He turned and sat down inside the belly of the chopper as he sighed. Like the distant stare that was now focused on the oil-stained hangar floor, the sound stabbed clear through her heart. And it drew more than mere blood. A lot more. She forced herself to shove the compassion aside, along with the surge of something stronger and a whole lot more powerful. Something she hadn't felt in years. Something she'd never been able to feel for another man, no matter how hard she'd tried, after this man had disappeared from her life.

Don't. Dammit, he didn't need it. Not now.

What he needed was a solution.

She stepped closer, risked seating herself down beside him on his right. Risked reaching out to touch him. Like his shoulders, the muscles of his thigh locked beneath her fingers. She withdrew her hand—but his had snapped out. He twined his fingers into hers and held on tightly as he settled her hand back on his thigh. His gaze finally met hers. It seared in hot and deep, pulsing with honesty. With need.

"I'm sorry. It's just…been a long time since a woman has touched me." His voice grew darker, lower. Rougher. "An eternity since the right woman's touched me."

He fell silent.

She knew he wasn't waiting for an answer. They both knew an Air Force hangar wasn't the proper place for his confession. Much less the one she knew she was going to have to make, and soon. She forced herself to wait until he was ready to continue the conversation they needed to finish. When he gave her hand one last squeeze and released it, she knew he was. He kicked his legs out and stared at his boots. The same boots he'd worn to her place four nights earlier. Boots she was now positive he'd hung on to for over a decade along with a certain letter. She curled her fingers around the edge of the chopper floor between them and held on tight, determined to ignore the achingly familiar warmth beside her and how desperately she wanted to reach for it…and him.

"Griff, I don't understand. I thought the board was going to issue its preliminary finding Tuesday morning—because of the Memorial Day Weekend." A weekend which had technically kicked off four hours earlier.

He nodded. "They were."

"Then…you got this through the backdoor?"

Another nod.

She didn't press him for more, let alone a name. Passing along a copy of that cockpit recording might not have fallen within the bounds of career-suicide, but preempting the board's decision did. Griff wouldn't finger his source. Nor would she want him to. "Does Vince know?"

He nodded. But again, he didn't elaborate.

And again, she had a pretty good idea why. She'd wager

their source had come to Vince, not Griff. That way after
Griff was vindicated—and Griff *would* be vindicated—he
wouldn't be in the awkward position of knowing who broke
the rules while he was serving as Wing commander. Her re-
spect for their informant and his faith shot up.

She drew strength from it.

Earlier that afternoon, when a tech revealed that the Pave
Hawk's flight data recorder had somehow been fried by the
same surge of power that knocked out the chopper's communications during the flight, she'd been surprised but not
worried. She'd believed in Griff's skills. She knew he hadn't
screwed up. She still did. She reached over and squeezed his
hand. Hard. "I'm not done yet—and neither are you. If you
know the board's decision, then I'm sure you also heard they
didn't find anything wrong back at the lab. Yes, the computer
modeling we've been working off went down without a hitch.
But that doesn't mean there wasn't an unexpected deviation
in the data or the equipment that ended up in here." She released Griff's hand and stood, turned to gesture into the Pave
Hawk's belly to make her point. "They've pulled the core
modules. There's a rider program attached to the main experiment. It's designed to record normal instrument readings
during the flight, not just our new ones. Once the tech gets a
look at it, you and Vince will have all the proof you need."

To her disappointment, Griff didn't perk up as expected.
He shook his head. "They just finished looking at it—or trying to. According to Vince's source, the whole damned core's
shot. Just like the flight data recorder. The board's tech ripped
it apart. Twice. They think the surge of power that knocked
out my comms when I clipped the turret fried your modules
as well as the cockpit recorder."

She stiffened. "But that's impossible! There was back-up."
She'd designed it with just such a scenario in mind.

Griff shrugged. "You'll have to talk to the tech."

She intended to.

Stranger things had been known to happen during test

flights, yes. But this was just a little too strange. Unfortunately, it was eight o'clock at night. A Friday night before a three-day Memorial Weekend, no less. The very reason why the board wouldn't be reconvening until Tuesday morning. *Damn.* She slapped her palm on the pilot's door. What the devil was she supposed to do until then? Sit on her hands?

Wait— "What about the control tower recording?"

Griff crossed his boots. "Vince already thought of that. So have they. Doesn't prove anything."

"The heck it doesn't. It proves you didn't screw up. I know, I ran through it at least twenty times last night."

He shrugged. "Doesn't matter."

"It doesn't matter?" How could he sit there so calmly?

He held up his hand. "Think about it. All that voice recording shows is what I said I did, not what I actually did." This time his shrug pushed her fury through the roof.

She spun around and stalked a good ten feet across the hangar, stopping only because she'd reached the mobile tool box Griff had pushed out of the way earlier. She whirled around, not even bothering to lower her voice. Even if the hangar hadn't been empty, she plain didn't care. "So that's it? You're lying? A colonel with twenty years, three wars, and countless police actions. What about Vince? I suppose he's lying too? Protecting you. Old combat buddies and all."

"They're not saying. But they are looking into Russia."

"*What?*"

He straightened. Stood. "Samantha, please."

"*No.*" At that moment, she didn't give a blessed care who might walk into the hangar. This was too much. "Do not stand there and tell me they're going to drag that crash into this."

"They have to."

"Bull."

He crossed the ten feet of concrete still separating them. One of the Pave Hawk's main rotor blades hung dormant above his head. "There's no sense getting riled up. It's a normal connection, especially since both crashes dealt specifically with evasive maneuvering, one in real time, one in theory. And when you add on that Vince was involved with both, too, they have to look into it. Hell, at this point they'll be crawling through every mission I've ever flown. By the time they're done, they'll know what I ate before and after my first check ride."

That may be true, but the thought of having his record called into question wasn't what was really bothering Griff. What had gotten under his craw was knowing his best friend was under scrutiny because of him. The evidence was still churning through those smoky depths. But there was more. She was sure of it. And whatever it was, it was bothering him at least as much as the potential career fallout for Vince.

"There's more, isn't there?"

He sighed. Heavily.

Oh, God. No. Her stomach clenched. "You told them we were lovers." She closed her eyes and waited for him to deny it. But he didn't. When she opened them, he nodded.

"I'm sorry."

She pushed the embarrassment down. Now wasn't the time to wallow in that, either. "It's not your fault. They'd have found out eventually." Which was why Griff had come clean first. This way, he kept the focus on himself and his own possible reasons for taking that flight yesterday and off her. Even now, at his lowest, he was trying to protect her. Damn this man's innate sense of honor. Didn't he get it? She wasn't the one who needed protecting, he did.

And she should have made the connection sooner.

A month ago General Luft mentioned that someone high up in the Air Force chain of command was still pissed they'd lost an eighteen million dollar chopper to a ragtag band of Chechen rebels. This second accident, though the cost was pennies in comparison, would give that someone the perfect patsy to blame both on—along with that all-encompassing and insidiously ambiguous reason. Pilot error. "You have to fight this."

He nodded. "Oh, I intend to."

She shook her head. "No, you don't understand. Someone's gunning for you. Someone who may have his next star riding on the outcome."

His brow hiked. And she knew she was caught. She'd bet her Ph.D. Griff already knew about the lingering questions over who was ultimately responsible for the Pave Hawk he and Vince had left at the bottom of that Russian lake. What Griff hadn't known until she'd given herself away just now was that she'd known. It wasn't common knowledge. That she was privy to high-level information about his career could only mean she'd sought him out since that hospital room in Ramstein, albeit indirectly. The warmth that settled into Griff's eyes told her he was more than pleased by the discovery. Encouraged. Fortunately, he moved past the revelation.

For now.

He nodded. "I've heard the rumors. I suspect there may be a bit of truth to them. But I also know the general in question. He'll want proof. Between you and I, Vince and I are working on that proof. You're not supposed to know this—hell, neither am I—but two weeks ago, Russia regained control of the lake where both my bird and your C130 are buried. A joint Russian-American team is investigating the joint wreckage as we speak. And Vince has an in with that team."

"What if you can't get the information you need in time?"

"We will."

"You can't be sure."

He pushed up another of those blasted enigmatic shrugs of his. "Then it comes down to my record. I'm not afraid to stand on it. It'll support me."

Exasperated, she marched forward, stopping directly in front of him so he'd be forced to listen. To take her—this—seriously. "Griff, we both know there are times when a pilot's record doesn't count for squat. Remember Eve Paris? She was one of my fellow Sisters-in-Arms in college."

He nodded. "I heard about the Black Hawk crash."

"Well, did you know she almost lost her wings over it? If the Special Forces captain who survived that crash with her hadn't risked his own career and hide to lead her back into that jungle, the Army would have Eve flying a desk by now." A desk, she didn't have to add, that the Air Force wouldn't bother offering Griff if this preliminary decision became final. Not for a wing commander removed for cause. They'd be forced to make an example of him to support the decision.

His career, his command. Griff would lose it *all*.

Tears stung the corners of her eyes, and they weren't a result of all the added hormones in the birth control pills her doctor had her taking. They were from flat-out frustration and a triple dose of fear. If this witch-hunt reached its natural conclusion, not only would Griff be drummed out of the Air Force, he'd never fly again, not even as some local yokel, eye-in-the-sky air traffic reporter.

The loss would kill him.

He reached out and smoothed his thumbs beneath her eyes, catching the first, errant drops. "Hey, don't do that. It's going to be okay. You'll see."

She pulled away slightly, scrubbing her cheeks as his hands fell away. "How can you be so calm? So, matter of fact? You have no idea the hell Eve and Rick had to go through to get her reputation restored."

"Rick? Is he her SF captain?"

She had no idea why it mattered, but she nodded.

Griff actually smiled. No, he downright grinned. "Not a problem. I've got an Air Force captain on my side. Damned bright scientist, to boot. But don't be telling that scientist I said so, okay? She's liable to get a swelled head."

Sam couldn't help it. She laughed. Those were almost the exact words she'd used with his daughter the night before.

His grin deepened.

And once again, the heat index in the hangar shot up.

He tipped his head toward the chopper. The gear she'd

long since finished with but had been going over yet again out of desperation. "You ready to leave?"

No. If they stepped out of this hangar and he followed her into that parking lot, they'd be on No Man's land. He'd be free to say what was in his eyes and in his heart. And she'd be forced to tell him what was in hers. She couldn't do that now. She could not tell him he had no chance of a future with her, because she had no chance of a real future with anyone. He had more to worry about than her worsening health.

And he would worry.

Where would his efforts to redeem his reputation be then?

But she couldn't stay here either. She needed to get home, get some sleep and get back to the lab. She had another diagnostic to run—and then another and another. Until she figured out what in tar hill had gone wrong.

"Hey, you okay?"

She tugged her gaze from the chopper. "Sorry. Just thinking. I'm going to grab a couple pieces of the auxiliary equipment they left and run them over to the lab. Who knows? With some sleep I might get lucky."

"If anyone can, it'll be you."

He shouldn't be so sure. Because, lately, her luck stunk. How else could she explain finding this man again after all these years—and still being unable to truly have him?

Griff snagged her elbow just beneath the rolled sleeve of her coveralls and turned her toward the Pave Hawk with him. "I'll grab the modules. You get your briefcase."

"What about—"

He shook his head, cutting off her concern before she could voice it. "That prescription strength ibuprofen they gave me is working fine. Good stuff."

Yeah, it was. To a point.

Unfortunately, her last dose was wearing off. Her sole remaining ovary was beginning to throb like the dickens along with half her belly. Moments like this, she swore she could see the adhesions spreading out, crisscrossing her abdominal cavity, connecting two more organs that had no business being connected, ratcheting them in closer, tighter. She bit down on a wince as they reached the chopper and she bent down to grab her briefcase. She waited while Griff stacked one of the modules she'd unhooked earlier atop the other and hefted them. They turned in unison, crossing the hangar and heading out to the darkened and otherwise deserted parking lot in silence.

They passed two trucks, his rental Jeep, two sportier cars and a van before they reached her Bug at the far end. She unlocked the trunk and opened it for him.

"Tight fit."

"Yeah, but they won't rattle on the way to the lab."

He closed the trunk. "You headed there now?"

"Yup." Then home to swallow another set of those pills he'd vouched for, crank up her air conditioner and crawl onto her heating pad. "It'll be a quick stop, though. I didn't get much sleep last night. I'm exhausted." There, that ought to stave off the offer of a late dinner or at least coffee she could see brewing in his eyes despite the shadows of night.

Wrong.

If Griff did know about Dimitri, he was not deterred. He proved it by tracking her up the driver's side of the Bug. He reached down and deftly slipped her car keys from her grasp and unlocked her door. He snagged her briefcase and tossed it into the car. It landed on the passenger seat with a soft thump. She was about to escape in after it. Unfortunately Griff's fiercely-honed reflexes thwarted her once more as he reached out again and snagged something else—her. She allowed him to use her arm to gently turn her around.

It was a mistake.

Somehow he'd managed to shift both their bodies a good twelve inches toward the rear wheels. With the side of the car pressing squarely into her back and Griff's broad, T-shirt clad chest planted six inches in front, she was trapped.

"Aren't you going to ask how it went?"

She knew what he was talking about. Who.

Christy. The letter.

She kept her stare fused to the T-shirt and forced herself to ignore the solid, generous muscles beneath. Yes, she was dying to ask how it went. She had been since the moment he'd walked in that hangar. But if she asked him about Christy, then—

"You know."

He nodded. "I know. Got it coming and going."

She snapped gaze up. "Coming and going?"

Another slow nod. "Christy, bless her, was a bit more gleeful in the telling last night. But your fiancé also managed to slip it into the conversation when he called my office this afternoon to tell me about the camp opening he'd finagled. As a matter of fact, the man seemed to think you'd already told me."

She jerked her head down. Fused her stare to that T-shirt, not even noticing the muscles this time. She couldn't focus on anything but the shame coursing through her. Maybe she had wanted Dimitri to do it. Or Christy.

Anyone but her.

She forced her lips to move, starting with the safer topic. And that was saying something. "How…did it go? The letter, I mean."

"About as well as can be expected. Turns out she's known about the letter for almost a year. Makes sense. It probably also explains why she's still hurt, but not nearly as torn up as I expected. The night you left Ramstein, I went through my lock box looking for it. The ticket was there."

"But the letter wasn't."

"Nope."

"I'm so sorry."

"Yeah. It'll take time. Understanding. Some careful discussions I'd hoped to avoid in this lifetime." He shook his head ruefully. "A lot more of those damned bossy lectures of hers, I'm sure. But she'll get over it. Hell, she's already done most of the work—the adjusting and accepting—without my even knowing she knew. Can't say I'm surprised. Nor does the credit go to me. It's all hers. She's a smart girl, tough. Always has been." He stepped closer, whittling the night air between them down to a mosquito's breadth. He slipped his fingers beneath her chin and tilted her face, forcing her to meet his steady stare. "Like someone else I know."

Oh, God. That was just it. She *wasn't* the woman he knew. Not anymore. Hell, she wasn't even a woman anymore.

Not in the way that mattered.

She closed her eyes against the passion, the pleading, she could see in his eyes.

"Aren't you going to ask why I didn't get mad? Why I didn't drive over to your place last night and vent my frustration the way I would have years ago."

She kept her eyes shut. "Because you've changed."

She felt him shake his head.

Though she knew better, she opened her eyes. She had to seal her lower back into the car and arch her shoulders to focus on Griff's face. He'd moved in that close. "Why?"

"Because you won't be marrying him."

She opened her mouth to argue, but didn't get the chance. He'd brought his hand up before she could blink and pressed his fingers to her lips.

"May I finish?"

She nodded mutely.

"Thank you. Now, I have two questions for you. If you can answer both and explain the discrepancy between them in your own heart, I'll not only step aside, I'll host the reception. You ready?"

No.

"When was the first time Alibek asked you to marry him?"

She couldn't help it, she flinched. How did he know? Dimitri would never have confided—

"Well?"

"L-Last year."

Griff nodded. She knew why. Just as she already knew the second question. "And when did you accept?"

"Griff, please don't—"

"When?"

She closed her eyes again. "Monday night."

"Hmmm. Monday night. As in, five nights ago? As in, what, a whole hour after I showed up at your house and laid all my sins out on the proverbial altar and you found it in your heart to forgive me? That Monday night?"

"Yes." She refused to open her eyes. Even when he trailed his fingers up the curve of her jaw before slipping them beneath the weight of her hair to slowly caress the side of her neck. Directly beneath her ear. Right where he knew it melted her resolve. "Please don't do that."

"Then open your eyes."

She had no choice. She complied.

He dropped his hand to her shoulder, but his gaze filled her now. The silent accusation. He knew she was running from him. She'd all but confessed it. But he was right. He hadn't yelled. Hadn't demanded she explain herself as he would have all those years ago. She almost wished he had.

It would have made this easier.

"Griff, I—"

He shook his head. "I'm not done."

She waited. Breathed. Prayed.

"I've changed, honey. I think I've proven that to you by now, yes?"

"Yes."

"Eleven years will do that to a man. Especially when he's forced to spend those years without the woman he'd planned on spending them with. But in case you haven't noticed, I need to make sure you understand that in some ways—the important ways—I haven't changed. And I never will. I still love you. I always have. Always will. I couldn't kill it when I thought you'd slept with Chet, and I sure as hell won't be able to kill it even if you do marry Alibek. But I know you won't. Just like I know you're running from something."

She sucked in her breath and tried to pull away.

He wouldn't let her.

"Shhh. Easy. Let me finish, okay?" He cupped both his hands to her face and stared deep into her eyes. "I don't know what that something is, but I will find out. And, no, I'm not going to dog you and harass you until I figure it out, either. I'm going to wait. Right here. Across town. Across base. Day in and day out. Grounded or not, I'm not going anywhere. Not this time. I'm going to stick around until you finally realize that whatever you think I can't handle, I can. And then we're going to deal with it…*together*."

Maybe the hormones were getting to her. Because the tears were trickling again and she couldn't get them to stop. Not even when he smoothed the first wave from her cheeks. She opened her mouth, but nothing came out—so she sucked in a lungful of air and tried again. "Griff, I don't…" Oh, God. How did she say this? She tried again. "It's just—"

"—complicated?"

She nodded. Definitely.

"Then let me remind you of something that isn't. *This*." He dipped his head before she could draw her next breath, and captured her lips. Her gasp. He swallowed it immediately and came back for more, slanting his head and delving deep within her mouth to find it. A split second later, she found it, too, with him. The passion, the need, the absolute craving that only Griff had ever been able to fan and stoke inside her, that only Griff had ever been able to completely sate.

But right now, he wasn't interested in sating her, not yet anyway. No, his intent was to tease and to torment.

And torment her, he did.

Right there in that darkened, deserted parking lot, as he had in so many other shadowy places in their past. He took his sweet time too, slowly and thoroughly ravaging her mouth, feeding the fire between them, stoking it until it raged, until she was wrapping her arms around him and tiptoeing up for more. He tore his lips from hers and dipped his head, nipping the curve of her jaw before he dragged his mouth beneath the curtain of her hair to suckle the tender spot beneath her ear.

It had been so damned long since this man had kissed her there and it felt so damned good. *He* felt good.

She whimpered in protest as he pulled his lips away, until he scraped his jaw down and slowly rasped his evening shadow into the sensitive curve at the base of her neck. Her legs buckled just as they always had whenever he'd done that. Time hadn't faded Griff's memory either because he was ready. He simply caught her and sealed the length of her body to his as he pressed them both into the car for support. And then he sought out her mouth once more and began to plunder at will. Within seconds, she couldn't tell where the steel frame of the car left off and the iron muscles of Griff's body began.

It didn't matter.

Her body had melted into both.

Another few seconds and she was begging him, pleading with him to quench this insatiable fire that was coursing through her body, torching each and every one of the barriers she'd spent the past four years erecting. She finally gave in to the overpowering temptation and slipped her hands down to tug his T-shirt from his jeans. And then her fingers were gliding beneath, up the thick, sinewy planes of his chest, fitting themselves in the deep crevice at the center, swirling around his smooth, masculine areolas and savoring Griff's dark growl as she raked her nails over his nipples. But before she could latch on and rub, he tore his mouth from hers, leaving them both gasping for air as he stood taut and towering over her, pure hunger and absolute male satisfaction raging within those dark gray pools. It took several moments, and several more ragged breaths before she realized why.

There was a car approaching from behind. She couldn't see the headlights, but she could hear the engine. Several more moments passed and, then, so did the car.

Still, she didn't move.

She couldn't.

Her legs were still quivering with unspent passion, barely able to support her and definitely unable to support motion.

Fortunately, Griff remembered that response too, though she wondered if he knew she'd discovered since that it was unique to him. Not that she'd have confessed it. She still could barely put two slow, deep breaths together. She was grateful when he took over, opening the driver's door that had closed during their kiss. He held on to her arms as he guided her wobbly legs around and then her into the car. He even leaned in and slipped the correct key into her ignition. Then he straightened. She was dimly aware of him reaching into the pocket of his jeans for something, then leaning back through the door to tuck it inside her hand. She stared at the card, trying to place it. He helped out there too, filling her ear with his dark, smoky breath and even smokier promise.

"My cell number. Call me when you're ready to talk. Day or night. I'll be there."

And then he closed the door.

She was pretty sure she imagined hearing the sound of his boots scuffing quietly around the rear of her Bug and across the darkened parking lot until he reached his rental. She did hear the Jeep's door open and close, heard it start up, too. Given the way her heart was still pounding in her chest, it was a miracle. And then, the Jeep was gone and so was Griff. A good minute passed before she realized she was still clutching his card. She flicked on the overhead light and skimmed the front, automatically memorizing his cell phone number. It wasn't until she flipped the card over that she realized that despite everything that had happened that day, Griff had been thinking about her and planning to leave her his card and his promise, his simple, heart-wrenching plea:

Still lost without you, Griff.

"Dad?"

Griff swallowed his curse as he turned back from the door to Vince's guestroom in time to watch Christy rub her eyes and sit up. "Sorry, honey. I thought you were sleeping."

"I was. But I felt you kiss me."

Despite his day, he chuckled. God willing, his daughter wasn't the only female in his life he'd managed to rouse with his kiss tonight. He sat down on the bed as she scooted to make room. "Thanks. Your old man could use a seat."

"What's wrong?"

He managed a smile. "Did I say something was wrong?"

"*Dad.*" The inflection came as only a ten year old could deliver it.

This time, his smile was real. "You should probably go back to sleep. We can talk in the morning." He hadn't planned on telling her until then anyway. Why ruin her night, too? Something in his tone must have given him away because she frowned. Either that or she just plain knew him too well.

Like someone else he loved.

She shook her head and hugged the shuttle that had succeeded in taking Penny Pony's prized place close. "If you leave, I won't get to sleep. And Mrs. Schultz is already gone so you'll be stuck making my milk."

She had a point. Alma had been almost as thrilled as he when his revised orders for Kirtland had come through. The transfer had also sealed the woman's decision to move to the States with them. Alma had a sister in Oklahoma City she hadn't seen in fifteen years. Two days ago, he'd suggested she fly out on his dime over the three-day Memorial weekend for a surprise visit. If he'd know today would turn out like this, however, he'd have waited for a better time.

"Well? Are you going to tell me?"

Griff pushed his daughter's sleep-snarled ponytail over her shoulder. "I have to, don't I? The new *all the truth, and nothing but the truth* rules, right?"

"Right." She nodded firmly, looking too damned grown up for his peace of mind as she did it. He sighed. For the little girl he was slowly losing to maturity and the harsher facts of life, and for himself. That he just couldn't seem to keep those facts from his daughter no matter how much he tried.

"You remember the almost accident yesterday?"

She nodded. "You said you just bumped the tail."

"I did. But it's still a big deal. The safety board has to know what went wrong so they can make sure it doesn't happen again."

"Oh. Okay. So…why are you so sad?"

Just say it. He tucked a straight tangle behind her ear. "Well, babe, someone on the board thinks I made a mistake."

She scrambled to her knees. "No way!"

"I'm afraid so."

"But…you *didn't*. You're the best chopper pilot there is, Dad."

He pinched her sleep-reddened nose. "Thanks for the support, kiddo. But you are right, I didn't make a mistake. But now I have to prove it."

She nodded solemnly. "Is that why Uncle Vince has been in his room on the phone all night?"

"Yeah. He's looking into some stuff for me."

"Oh." She pulled the stuffed shuttle closer, but she'd also taken the time to snag Penny Pony and add it to the hug. Not a good sign. She might be on the verge of her preteen years, but she was still a little girl. His little girl.

And she was scared.

He scooted closer and wrapped his arms around her, her stuffed friends—equine and machine—and hugged them all. He kissed the rumpled silk on the top of her head. At least that still smelled like the little girl he remembered. "Hey, easy now. Don't you worry. Your old man's the best, remember?"

She nodded.

When she didn't pull away, he snuggled her closer and waited. Eventually she'd had enough, as she did all too often of late. She squirmed away. "I'm okay, Dad. You should probably go see Uncle Vince."

He should. He'd come in here first.

He tipped her chin and stared into her heart-shaped face, studied it closely. She did seem okay now. But then, she'd learned to mask her moods. too. How else had she managed to keep that letter from him? "Need a tuck?"

She grinned. "Yup."

He grinned back. "Good. Me, too. You gonna come in my room later and give me one?"

"Dad!"

He laughed—and tickled her down to her pillow, waiting until she was all but screaming uncle—and not for Vince—before he relented and tucked her in. "Goodnight, pumpkin." He figured after his news she'd let him get away with it.

She did.

She waited until he was at the door before she spoke. But it wasn't to wish him goodnight. "Is Dr. Hall going to help?"

He froze.

Other than his admitting last night that, yes, Dr. Hall was the Samantha in that letter and that yes, he once loved her and still did despite her fiancé, they hadn't discussed Sam. He was tempted to fib. If only for his daughter's peace of mind. But then, he was the one who'd suggested the new *all the truth, and nothing but the truth* pact to try and repair their easy trust. It was up to him to uphold it.

"Yes, Dr. Hall is helping."

"Good."

She must have seen his shock despite the dark because she hugged her shuttle closer. "You're right. She is smart. And funny. Kinda weird, too. But she keeps her promises."

That was it. It was all Christy was going to give him.

He knew better than to press it. After the way he'd handled things since Ramstein, it was a hell of a lot. Especially since his daughter was bright enough to know that helping him save his professional hide would take more effort and more contact with him than getting her into summer camp had. In effect, Christy had given him permission to see Sam—but only to a point. It was all his daughter was ready for right now. He took the gift. He also went back to steal a third kiss and then he got the heck out of the room before the tears Sam had shed in that hangar started pouring out of him.

To his relief, but not his surprise, Vince was waiting for him in the kitchen, a mug of steaming coffee waiting, too.

"She take the news, okay?"

"As well as can be expected. Probably better." He shook his head, still stunned with his daughter's capacity for love and forgiveness as he sat. He retrieved the mug of coffee meant for him and blew off the steam. "She actually wants Sam in on this."

Vince nodded. "After the space camp miracle, it's understandable. But, ah, you might not want Samantha involved."

Something in his buddy's voice made him set the mug down, untouched. They'd known this might get ugly. It appeared he was about to find out just how ugly. "What happened?"

"I got a call back from Bailey."

He'd called his ex? Damn. He didn't think they were that desperate. Then again, it made sense. Bailey had been born in Russia, not to mention the woman was an agent with the Air Force's Office of Special Investigations. Still, Griff chose his words with care. Vince's breakup with the woman four years back had left a raw spot that had never quite healed. A lot like the one he'd nursed in himself over Sam. "I take it Bailey had something for you about Russia."

Vince nodded. "Yep. You remember the loadmaster telling us about the fire in the cargo hold?"

"Of course. The halon system crapped out on them." With the plane's built in fire-extinguishing system malfunctioning, the fire had eventually spread, forcing Sloane and Deavers to try and land the plane.

"Yeah, well, turns out there's a reason why the halon never deployed. The O-rings in the nozzles were sabotaged."

He cursed.

Vince nodded. "Yep."

"What about the fire? Was it deliberately set?"

"Bailey doesn't know yet. She's still looking into it. But there's more. Seems OSI has locked on to an interesting side connection regarding the C130 crash. One that may end up taking center stage real soon. That boss of Sam's—he was supposed to be on that flight, right?"

His stomach fisted. "Yeah, Phil Haskell. Why?"

"'Cause after the halon sabotage surfaced, OSI decided they ought to exhume the man's body, just in case. Turns out it was a damned good idea. Something came up on the man's autopsy that no one—and I mean no one—is talking about."

Griff shoved the mug away and stood. He paced into the open kitchen and stopped. Vince was still staring at him as he swung around and he knew why. Vince was right. He did *not* want Samantha involved. Nor did this appear to be about him and either of his crashes anymore. "You're telling me Dr. Haskell didn't die of a heart attack, aren't you?" His gut fisted tighter as Vince shook his head.

"'Afraid so. Man was poisoned."

Chapter 9

"How the mighty have fallen."

Sam bit down on her tongue as she twirled around in the plush ergonomic chair she'd forced on Phil two Christmases before. True to his frugal nature, Phil had been furious at first. He'd assumed she'd snuck the chair into the lab's budget without his approval. Upon learning she'd footed the bill herself, Phil had been forced to sit down and enjoy the relief the chair brought to his increasingly arthritic spine. Now if she could just get the darn thing to work the same wonders on the preening ape determined to ride *her* back.

Fat chance.

She mustered a politeness she didn't feel and nodded. "Good morning, Valentin."

He glanced down, his smile as smooth and phony as the finish on the faux Rolex strapped to his wrist as he snapped his gaze to hers. "It's nearly afternoon, Samantha, *Saturday* afternoon. If the job is too much, you have but to say so."

"Touché. But then, you're here, too." She reached out and

tapped the time stamp at the lower left corner of the computer monitor. "At ten-fifty-eight a.m., no less." She tapped her chin next. "I gather that means your latest conquest ended up crawling out of bed after experiencing your dubious prowess and escaped before you woke."

"Wrong." His pristine tennis shoes squealed for him as he strode all the way into Phil's office. "I simply thought that in the interests of the lab's reputation, I ought to stop by and assist you out of your—" He drummed his fingers over the upper edge of the oversized monitor. "—disgrace."

The temptation ripped through her.

Don't give in. She would pay.

Too late. She could feel her sweetest smile already sliding into place. "Gee, thanks, Valentin. I'm sure General Luft would love to know I got help from the man whose last design blew up on the launch pad." As expected, his lips thinned. Too bad. She wasn't done. The jerk deserved the rest, if only as retribution for all the grief he'd given Phil. "And—wait— weren't you the lead on the previous design, too? You know, the one that took out the entire observation tower?" She knew damned well he had been. According to Phil, Valentin had dived out of the tower seconds before the rocket hit.

Valentin responded by thumping his soda on her desk.

Diet Coke.

Figures. The machine in the break room had coughed up the last one for her hours ago. This time her smile was fueled by true jealousy. "I see your taste is improving."

He frowned. "The machine is malfunctioning again. I asked for bottled water and got this." He glanced at the cracked seal. "I was going to drink it, but changed my mind. I *had* decided to see if you wanted it instead."

Damn.

She knew she shouldn't have insulted him today. Sure, he was only sucking up to her. But the mood she was in, she could use it. Her belly had been hurting like the dickens this morning despite the set of pills she'd swallowed and the forgiving sweatpants and matching peach T-shirt she'd donned. But to top it off, she'd already run two complete diagnostics on the experiment and gotten precisely nowhere. And then there were the memories that kept streaking through her brain despite her restless efforts to banish them.

Her, Griff. Last night.

That kiss.

The new decision she faced. The one that affected more than her health. It affected her job, her home—everything. She sighed. Why not? Someone had to take the promotion. Might as well be someone willing to grovel for it. A month from now, Luft would be thrilled with his very own lapdog. "You know what, Valentin? I don't think I'll be able to make the planning meeting this Thursday. I don't supposed you're free?"

Well, what do you know. She stunned the man into silence.

Unfortunately, the unexpected peace confirmed her suspicions. Valentin had probably heard her whacking the soda machine in frustration and gone out and bought the Coke deliberately. A cracked seal added for effect, and the man had a readymade excuse to see if he could persuade her into moving his latest project requisition to the top of the stack. She didn't have the heart to tell him she didn't review his forms at work anymore. She had to save something to read in place of the Sunday funnies. Doonesbury had been on a seriously dark roll lately. Frankly, the strip needed livening up.

"Well?"

His frown bit in. "Why would you do this?"

Because she was going to be at Los Alamos interviewing at the time. But she wasn't telling him that. Nor did she have time for his tantrums or his suspicions. "You want the meeting or not?" They both knew with the way Luft felt about him, he needed all the face time he could get. And she was tired of Luft's incessant bullying. She hadn't wanted Phil's job before Griff showed up. She wanted it even less now. For her sanity's sake if nothing else. She mimicked Valentin's earlier motion, feigning a glance at her Timex. "Going once…going twice—"

"Yes."

"Sold to the muscle-bound Russian in black jeans and that hideous striped shirt." She snatched the Coke off the desk before he could change his mind. "Say, 'Thank you, Samantha.'"

Valentin scowled. "Thank you, Samantha."

She nodded. "Good. Now leave. I'll fill you in Wednesday. I've got work to do."

"Don't strain your—"

"Soda or not, I *wouldn't* finish that if I were you."

She had the satisfaction of watching the knot in his throat bob as he choked on the rest, just before he turned and left. She saluted the air and her success with the bottle of Diet Coke before washing it down with a welcomed, though stronger than usual carbonated burn. She would have forgone her longer, second, third and fourth swigs but for the fact that the burning sensation succeeded where the ibuprofen hadn't. Namely, in briefly overriding the ache in her side. The day was definitely picking up. Best of all, for better or worse, she'd made her decision. Taken the first step. All she had to do now was take the remaining ones.

Away from Dimitri...and Griff.

Just like that, the burning returned—this time in her heart.

She was bound to hurt them both. Dimitri, at least, would bounce back soon enough. And he would definitely be better off without her. She'd known from the beginning she'd never be able to return Dimitri's deeper feelings. Though she'd told him that a year ago, six months ago, and again three months ago, she should have insisted. Probably even cut off contact between them outside work. The man deserved someone who felt for him what she unfortunately felt for Griff. God willing, without her around as a crutch, Dimitri would go out and find it with someone who could act on those feelings, too.

As for Griff?

The burn increased, nearly incinerating her heart.

Last night had proven two things. One, she might not be able to take what they'd started beside her car to its natural conclusion anymore with anyone, but the desire she felt for Griff, the fiery passion they'd always shared, was definitely still there. Stronger than ever. But that passion had also sealed her fate. As soon as she proved Griff had not screwed up in that chopper, she was going to have a professional talk with General Luft. Not only did she plan on turning down the promotion, she was going to file her papers and resign her commission. The job she'd been offered at Los Alamos was for a civilian, government service employee. She wasn't crazy about giving up the uniform that'd given so much back to her, but she couldn't stay at Kirtland now. Los Alamos might be a mere hundred miles away, but it was far enough that she wouldn't have to risk running into Griff anymore.

That, she couldn't handle.

She lifted the Diet Coke, this time saluting her decision, and downed the final third.

"Now there's the breakfast of champions."

Sam spewed her remaining swallow—on herself, on the idling computer screen and worse, all over the handwritten equations she'd spent the entire morning scrawling out. She wiped her chin and the front of her T-shirt as best she could, waited a beat in hopes that her flush would fade, then swung around in Phil's chair. Griff's half-smile managed to hook her heart all the way from the doorway fifteen feet away.

"Morning, Captain."

It took her a moment to realize why he'd used her rank— until she spotted the security guard loitering in the hallway behind. She nodded in return, wishing she could kill her body's lingering response to that half-smile. "Colonel." The sight of the second, shorter form beside the guard succeeded in squelching it. "Hi, Christy."

The girl actually grinned, though shyly.

She smiled back. "I guess you've heard."

Her head bobbed. "Yes, thank you!"

"I didn't do anything, honey. You'll have to thank—"

And low and behold, there he was.

"—Dimitri."

Her still-current fiancé nodded to Christy, the security guard and the ex-lover she'd been kissing the night before. One more body and the growing crush in the corridor would rival Grand Central Station's. Fortunately, Dimitri's unflappable nature had kicked in, coloring his smile with amusement and bemusement equally as he stepped into Phil's office. "I stopped by to see if you had time for lunch, but I see you have guests already."

Two minutes ago she'd have been thrilled to see Dimitri. She'd even been contemplating calling and inviting him to lunch. Even before her run in with Valentin this morning, she knew she was going to have to tell Dimitri the wedding was off. The conversation would have to wait. Griff's smile might have been wreathed in warmth when she'd turned, but his stare had been chillingly serious. He had something to tell her. Something about the crash. And he needed to do it soon.

"Dimitri, have you met Christy?"

He turned and faced the girl, basking in Christy's effusive gratitude as Griff re-introduced Dimitri as the man who'd gotten her into camp. Fortunately, Dimitri had picked up on her own unspoken request as well. He dismissed the guard before formally extending his arm, offering the girl a guided tour of the lab while her father discussed the failed experimental flight with Dr. Hall. She, Christy and Griff thanked Dimitri in turn. Griff waited until the pair departed down the hall before stepping into Phil's office.

"Good friend you've got there."

She noticed he'd left off fiancé. He couldn't know she'd already changed her mind.

Could he?

She ignored the stab in her chest and waved him toward a spare chair. "Have a seat and tell me what's wrong."

He stepped closer instead, closer than she was comfortable with given last night's activity beside her car. He hooked his thighs on the desk barely twelve inches from her shoulders and leaned down to trail a finger across her cheek before rubbing the pads of his finger and thumb together.

Great. She'd missed some of the splattered Coke.

She sighed. And not because he was playing Mop-Up Sam again. Because he was stalling. "Well?"

He tipped his forehead toward the computer screen. "You working on it now?"

She nodded.

"You get anywhere?"

"No."

This time, he sighed.

"Griff…you're scaring me. What's wrong?"

"I didn't say any—"

"Dammit, Griff. We've been through this. I'm not an immature kid anymore and you've changed your overbearing, tightlipped ways. So let's prove it. We both know you wouldn't have brought your daughter with you to a high-security facility, much less on a Saturday, if something wasn't seriously wrong."

He finally nodded. "You're right. And I am sorry for the tag-a-long. Couldn't be helped. Mrs. Schultz is out of town and Vince is…tied up for the moment."

"Tied up?"

Another nod, this one more solemn. But he didn't elaborate. He kicked out his boots and reached beneath his dark blue T-shirt to withdraw a sheet of folded paper from his pocket. He held it out. She took it, but she didn't open it. The memory of the last two times she'd scanned papers from this man sliced in. She tucked her hand over her belly, instinctively pressing in as the throbbing she'd been unsuccessful in ignoring all morning ratcheted to piercing.

"Are you okay?"

She lied. "Yes. What is this?"

"I thought you'd need proof, so I waited for it before coming here." He flicked his stare toward the sheet. "It's a fax. Take a look."

She unfolded the sheet cautiously.

No, not sheet. Sheets.

There were several pages to the grainy plain-paper fax. Together they detailed part of an OSI report on her crash. She flipped though what appeared to be a post-crash analysis on the C130's halon fire-fighting system. She flipped to the last page and skimmed the summary. The words were legible enough, but she couldn't quite get the meaning to sink in. Until she reached the final one-word assessment that'd been underlined.

Sabotage.

She sucked in her breath as the throbbing in her abdomen suddenly snapped into agonizing. She blinked back the swift sting of tears that came with it as she gaped up at Griff, struggling to ignore what was happening inside her body long enough to make sense of what he was trying to tell her about the C-130. "I don't understand. Who? *Why?*"

"I don't know yet. But OSI thinks it's connected to this lab. To your late boss. When the sabotage came to light, they exhumed Phil Haskell's body. The man was—" He broke off, then started again. "Honey, I don't know how to tell you this except to just say it. Phil was murdered."

The blow slammed in deep, for a second, surpassing the ever-increasing ache in her belly. "Murder? That's impossible! I was there, so was half the staff, including General Luft. One minute Phil was standing where you are, finishing his morning coffee and wrapping up last minute details for an inspection so he could get ready for Moscow—and the next, he grabbed his chest and collapsed. It was definitely a heart attack. The paramedics confirmed it. Heck, it wasn't even Phil's first. The man had open heart surgery six years ago."

"I'm sure it looked like a heart attack. At the time. But a forensic coroner ran another autopsy on Phil's remains. She found evidence of a lethal dose of nicotine."

"Nicotine?" Phil didn't even smoke.

Good God. He *was* murdered.

She slumped back as the shock reverberated throughout her entire body—only to gasp as her side hit the arm of the chair. She lurched forward but that caused the pain to spike again. She tried pushing in on her side. Only this time, the counter pressure drove the pain off the chart.

She cursed.

"Sam? What is it? What's wrong?"

The pain spiked again. Harder. She closed her eyes as she tried to absorb it. "I'm sorry. I just— *Sweet mercy*." The ache was spreading, intensifying. Unable to suffer the next spike sitting down, she shot to her feet—and promptly doubled over. Griff caught her just before she hit the floor.

"*Oh, Jesus.* Samantha, talk to me! What's wrong?"

She couldn't talk. All she could do was curl into him and hold on for life. She had never felt this bad. Not even when she'd headed to the hospital to have her left ovary removed. The pain was everywhere now, ripping through her entire belly. The blood was roaring so loudly, she could barely make out Griff's shouts for Dimitri, the guard, anyone and everyone. When he demanded to know what, if anything, she'd consumed besides the soda, she knew what he was thinking. That she'd been poisoned, too. She tried to correct him, even managed to open her mouth, but all that came out was a mewling whimper—until he hefted her in his arms. In that instant, her entire world mutated into absolute, excruciating agony.

She screamed.

A split second later, everything went black.

For the first time in months, she awoke pain-free—and it terrified her. Worse, Sam turned her head and found the one man she dreaded more than any other staring down at her. From the way his dark-brown eyes narrowed behind those equally imposing wire-framed glasses, Dr. Stanley Burrows did not look happy to see her either. She accepted the straw he offered and sipped the water, then waited for him to replace the foam cup beside what she recognized as one of Kirtland's emergency room beds before she risked speech. "Hi, Stan."

He continued to glower down at her as he retrieved her medical chart. He snapped the chart open and scrawled something inside. "Hi, yourself."

"What—ah—happened?"

Stan's glower deepened as he dumped the chart beside the cup of water before running his hands through prematurely salt-and-pepper hair he'd sworn months before was due to patients just like her. "Do you really need to ask?"

No. But just in case, she took the time to probe her abdominal muscles through her sweatpants, searching for undue tenderness, bandages, stitches. Anything that would clue her in as to which parts were still there—and which weren't. All she found were her old scars and an otherwise slightly swollen belly. Her cyst had ruptured; that was it. From the way she'd passed out, it had probably happened when Griff had lifted her into his arms at her office—

Griff.

She stiffened as the reason for his impromptu visit flooded her brain, sweeping away the remaining, Demerol-induced cobwebs. *Phil had been murdered.* Grief and shock stung her eyes, just as they had in her office. It didn't make sense. Who would want to kill Phil? Steal his idea and his work, sure. Half the world's militaries had probably thought about it, if not taken steps to make it happen. He'd even been the near victim of a kidnapping attempt once. But again, the plan had been to hold the man ransom. But murder?

"Are you okay?"

She shook her head mutely. She also remembered Griff showing her part of an OSI report. If OSI was investigating, she shouldn't be talking about it. She probably wasn't even supposed to know. But she was darned sure going to be searching for answers. Sam stared at the IV someone had inserted into one of the veins on the back of her left hand. Just as soon as she got out of here. But first, she had her doctor to contend with. His understandable anger.

She sighed. "I'm sorry, Stan."

"You know if you'd look at me when you grovel, I might believe you."

She did—and forced herself not to bow beneath his lingering fury and worse, his disappointment. "I mean it. I am sorry for causing trouble. I just—" Blast it. The stinging was back. She had to press her lips together to keep them from quivering. Lord, she hated those hormones. She'd been an over-active tear factory since Stan had started her on them.

But at least they got him off her back.

His sigh filled the room. "I shouldn't have come down so hard. But dammit, woman, for a scientist you can be—"

"Determined?"

"*Pigheaded.* Foolishly so."

She decided not to argue. She punched controls at the side of the hospital bed until she'd raised her head up to his still scowling level, holding up her hand when she finished. Stan's frown deepened as he caught her unspoken request. But he complied, turning to retrieve several squares of sterile gauze from the tray table. He folded two of the squares over as he snagged her hand, pressing the gauze into the IV site as he removed the needle from her vein. Silence crackled between them as he continued to press down for several more moments before sealing a Band-Aid over the puncture site.

"Can I go now?"

He shook his head. "I'd rather you waited another couple hours at least. You've slept off the bulk of the Demerol, but I'd like to give the rest a chance to work through your system. See if you still have any pain when it does."

She nodded. That much she could give him after everything he'd tried to give her. "Okay."

Besides, it might be easier telling Griff here.

Who was she kidding? It wasn't going to be easy for either of them, no matter where she said it. Or when. Unfortunately, she couldn't afford to wait for the chopper investigation's conclusion. Today's rupture had sealed the time and place. Griff was right, she had been running away. Part of her prayed Stan had already told him…so she could keep on running. She wet her lips. "Is he still waiting?"

To her surprise, Stan rolled the IV stand out of the way and shrugged. "Now which *he* would you be referring to? The one who claimed he's your fiancé…or the one acting like it?"

Dimitri. She flushed. Most of what had transpired since she'd passed out was still lost in a fog, but she should have remembered him. "Doctor Alibek's here?"

Stan shook his head. "He was. He left about thirty minutes ago, after I assured him you were fine. He said to tell you he needed to make sure your office was secure. He seemed to think you might be concerned about someone going through your papers?"

Valentin.

As far as she knew, he was still in the lab when she'd passed out. The man might not be responsible for Phil's death or her health, but neither was Valentin above taking advantage of either one to further his personal scientific and career objectives. And Phil's office was wide open, computer password already plugged in, inbox overflowing. Ripe for snooping. Even now, Dimitri was trying to help her pick up the pieces of her life. It made what she had to tell him all the harder.

But Stan had mentioned two *he's*. "Is—ah—Colonel Towers still waiting?"

This time, Stan nodded. "Along with a Captain Racey, a little girl around nine or ten and a pair of OSI agents to boot. Though I understand they had to leave too, to arrange lodging." Stan shoved his glasses higher as he shook his head. "I gotta hand it to you. When you finally decide to show, you bring half the base with you. I'm surprised you didn't bring General Luft along. But then, that would've spared me a call."

Yeah, Stan was still ticked.

And evidently still determined to see this through on his terms. But after today she had to grant him at least one of his points. An internal look wouldn't hurt. Might even help her let go. "Come on, Stan, we both know you won't call Luft. If you were going to file an official medical profile against me you'd have done it by now." Besides, now that the cyst had ruptured, she'd actually garnered a reprieve and they both knew it. "But if you promise to get off my case, I'll set up another appointment for the laparoscopy before I leave."

He snorted. "And what guarantee do I have that you'll actually keep this one?"

Given her track record, she supposed she deserved that. "You have my word." She just hoped to heck with everything going on she'd be able to keep it.

Stan seemed to read her mind as he stared down at her. He finally nodded. "All right. But if you even think about skipping out again, I won't bother calling Luft. I'll call that colonel out there instead. Something tells me your tush will be in my office within *seconds*."

She forgave him that threat, too. For all his bluster, Stan wouldn't violate doctor-patient privilege. She ought to know. It was the only thing that had kept her hobbling along these past few months. However, she also knew Griff well enough to know he'd gotten something out of Stan. She needed to know how much. She retrieved the cup of water from the tray table beside her bed and took a sip, hoping to wash the lingering cotton from her mouth and buoy her courage at the same time. "So…what did you tell Colonel Towers?"

Stan's brow arched at her second attempt to avoid Griff's first name and the validation of his suspicions that came with it. Stan must have decided she'd suffered enough though, because he let it go. "I told him the truth—that you had a cyst and it ruptured. I left the rest for you. I wouldn't have told him that much, except the man was flat-out frantic when he carried you in. He kept shouting something about nicotine poisoning. I have no idea why. Once I assured him I was your doctor and that I knew exactly what was wrong, he wouldn't explain himself, either. You have any idea what he meant?"

She shook her head, hoping the shame didn't give her away. Stan was right. She should have dealt with this a long time ago. At the very least, the night Griff had shown up at her house. It would have saved him the horror of today.

Stan retrieved her chart. "Well, you two can swap stories, then. You ready for me to send him in?"

She nodded, but it was just another lie.

She'd never be ready to tell Griff what she was about to. Unfortunately, she had no choice. Her body had made it for her years before she and Griff found their way back to each other and there was no changing it. She ought to know.

She'd already tried.

"Colonel? You can go in now."

Griff jackknifed to his feet before the nurse finished. He was halfway across the waiting room before he realized what he'd done. Who he'd left. He forced himself to stop, to turn back to the half-filled row of chairs. Christy was still sitting between his now vacant seat and Vince's occupied one. The unease simmering within him was mirrored in her eyes. From the way Christy had been gripping his hand for the past hour, she'd been as terrified as he that, despite Dr. Burrows assurances, Sam wasn't really okay. In fact, Christy might've even been more afraid than he, given her age, the confusion of it all—and the answer he'd never been able to give to that all important question regarding her mother's death.

I don't know, pumpkin. These things just happen.

They did.

But why the hell did they have to keep happening to them?

He stretched out his hand. "You want to come, too? Just for a minute?"

Her smile lit up the waiting room as she bobbed her head. Her ponytail whipped behind her as she shot across the room, locking onto his fingers before he could change his mind. He held onto hers just as tightly as they turned to follow the nurse out of the waiting room and down the corridor.

He clutched his hope even tighter.

The same hope he'd been clinging to from the moment that gut-wrenching scream of Sam's had pierced straight through his heart back in her office. God as his witness, the past hour-and-a-half had lasted longer than the past eleven years. They followed the nurse until she stopped at the door he'd spent the first half hour pacing outside. Until Vince had arrived and dragged him into that waiting room.

To his daughter.

The daughter who squeezed his hand now as the nurse nodded and left. "It's gonna be okay, Dad."

He bent down and hugged her quick. Before she got any older or any smarter. Or worse, any less forgiving. She gave his hand another squeeze, holding on tight as he straightened. But the moment he rapped his knuckles on the door and pushed it open, he felt her bravado flee. That was okay, though. Samantha's smile welcomed them both. He hung back by the door, determined to wait his turn as she waved Christy closer.

"Hi, there. I bet you didn't expect a tour of the emergency room today, too, huh?"

"A-Are you okay, Dr. Hall?"

Her smiled deepened. "Call me Sam. I'm fine, I promise. In fact, I'll be heading home soon. Tomorrow, I'll be good as new."

"I was so scared you wouldn't wake up."

His heart damned near broke as the woman he loved more than the wings they were about to rip from his chest, reached out to tuck a strand of hair behind the ear of the little girl who'd squalled her way into his heart all those years ago. "I know, hon. I'm sorry you had to see that. But it hurt a lot. My body just shut down. Kind of like when you're in the car late at night and you get so sleepy you can't stay awake anymore. See, I had something called a cyst right about here." Sam pointed to her right lower abdomen. "This cyst was sort of like a balloon that got bigger and bigger until it broke. And now that it has, I'm okay." She waited for his daughter's nod of understanding, then added, "Well, I do have to wait for my insides to clean up the yucky stuff that spilled out."

"And then…that's it?"

"Uh-huh. That's it." That gorgeous, whiskey gaze met his over his daughter's head. She was lying. He could see the guilt slipping through the shadows from here.

Fortunately, Christy couldn't.

He waited as Sam accepted his daughter's genuine relief along with a quick, impulsive hug, then cleared his throat. "Pumpkin—"

Christy grimaced. "I know, I know. You said, just for a minute." He swore his daughter had aged ten years as she turned a solemn gaze on Sam. "You guys need to talk."

They sure did.

"I'll go wait with Uncle Vince."

He tugged her ponytail as she trudged past to let her know how much he appreciated her, then nodded to Vince, discreetly marking time at the end of the hall. He closed the door. He turned to face Sam, only to discover he'd suddenly, inexplicably, lost his bravado just as Christy had. The fear had locked back in, too. Without his daughter standing next to her, she looked so damned lost in that bed, just as she had when they'd finally let him in her room at Ramstein. Somehow, her own clothes made it worse. She managed a smile.

He couldn't return it. Not until he knew.

"You're not okay, are you?"

Her smile fled. "I'm sorry you thought I'd been poisoned. I'll never forgive myself for not having been upfront with you from the beginning. If I had, you wouldn't have had to go through what I did when your chopper nearly—" She broke off, wrapped her arms over her chest and hugged herself tight. When her eyes began to glisten, he lost it. He stepped forward.

Her hands snapped up. "Don't."

He couldn't help himself, he took another step. "Sam—"

"*Please*. If you touch me, I'll never get this out."

Dammit, if he didn't touch her, he was going to die. Somehow, he managed to force his boots to turn to the right and pace a path to the stainless steel counter that ran the length of the opposite side of the room. There, he anchored his fingers beneath the lip of the counter as he leaned against the cabinets. He forced himself to wait. Even when her gaze dropped down and settled on his chest.

A good half a minute passed before she spoke. "I know Stan told you I had a cyst and that it ruptured. What he didn't tell you was that it wasn't just any cyst. This type of cyst was formed when some of the cells that make up the lining inside my uterus traveled outside it and began to grow somewhere else. Somewhere, they weren't supposed to be."

He shook his head. "I'm not sure I understand."

Her gaze snuck up, then dropped again. "You know what happens to a woman every month?"

Huh? "You're talking about your period?"

Pink stained her cheeks just as it had whenever he'd brought up her body's menstrual cycle. Evidently the topic still embarrassed her. He never had understood how someone so bright could get so self-conscious over something so natural. Nothing about her body had ever bothered him—other than the fact that it had been so damned young. Fortunately, that had passed. But her embarrassment hadn't.

"Sam?"

"Yes, I'm talking about my period." She dragged her breath in deep and met his stare. "Specifically, the cells that cause the bleeding. These endometrial cells, they continue to bleed every month. If that bleeding—that shedding of the endometrial lining—occurs inside the uterus, a woman gets her period. But if those patches of cells aren't inside the uterus, they still bleed. They also leave adhesions and scarring in their wake. The condition is called endometriosis. It's chronic and I have it. I was diagnosed four years ago. In some women, those cells have also been known to attach themselves to ovaries. When that happens, the bleeding is encased in a cyst which builds up or…grows every month. The result is called a chocolate cyst or an endometrioma."

He was no expert, but none of this sounded good, especially that last part. She had her period every month. "Are you saying that this cyst—*your* cyst—is coming back?"

"Yes."

Terror shot through him. "Is it…terminal?" He tightened his grip on the counter at his hips, damned near crushing it.

"No."

The relief seared in, so hard, so fast and so deep he had to close his eyes and slump back into the cabinet to absorb it. She was still staring at him when he recovered. He dragged his numbing fingers from the counter and shoved them through his hair. "You need an operation, don't you?"

"It's not that simple. If Stan operates, I lose my ovary…the only ovary I have left."

"That's *it?*"

The moment the words came out, he regretted them. He vaulted across the room before she could finish flinching and hauled her in close. "Honey, I'm sorry. I didn't mean that the way it sounded." God as his witness, it'd been the relief talking, though he was wise enough not to add that. "If you lose your ovaries, it's a hell of a lot. I know that. But it's not everything." It wasn't her *life*. He raised his fingers, not even caring that they shook as he smoothed the tangled tresses from her face. "Sweetheart, I know we always talked about kids. But we can always adopt. Or not. It's up to you."

It truly didn't matter. All he cared about was her.

If he'd had any doubts his love had faded through the years, today had murdered them. Completely. He would hear that scream until the day he died. And love her longer. His stomach fisted as her eyes filled with tears—because they weren't the good kind. He smoothed the drops from her lower lashes before they could fall. "Shhh. Don't do that. It'll be okay, I promise. I know you need time to get to know Christy. But you will. Just like she'll get to know you." Dammit, he'd just seen them take another step closer to each other. "Once Christy's had a chance to adjust, we can get married and—"

"Griff, please. *Stop*. Let me finish, okay?" She covered his hands with hers and pulled them down between them. She stared at their fingers as he knotted his into hers.

She didn't resist, but she did sigh.

"If this was about babies and forgiveness, we'd be halfway there by now. Probably farther. But it's not. I can't marry you. Hell, I can't marry anyone. I thought I could, but it wouldn't be fair to Dimitri, either. You wanted to know what I was running from? I'm running from *me*. And if you understood the extent of my condition, you'd be running too."

He shook his head. "You're not making sense. You just told me this wasn't terminal. You're not dying."

She shook her slowly, sadly. "I don't have to. I'm already dead. Inside. I already told you, I've got the scars to prove it. You might not be able to see them, but they're there, spreading through my belly, connecting organs to the inside of my abdominal wall, to each other and everything in between. Believe me, I'm reminded of their progress daily. Sometimes minute-by-minute. They pull at me constantly. And times, more painfully than at others. The pills I take, help. Sometimes a lot. Sometimes not at all. But if I'm having my period, forget it. Which, by the way, lasts a lot longer than you remember. But that's not the worst part."

He swallowed his shock and his horror as she paused.

His grief.

He had trouble forced the words past the lump of tears in his own throat. "What— What's the worst part?"

She slipped her fingers from his and smoothed them down his jaw, her embarrassment finally and completely seared away by cold, stark desolation. "I can't have sex, Griff. Not with you or anyone else. Ever. And I mean that in the most literal, penetrating, sense. It's simply too painful. That's why I agreed to marry Dimitri...and why I can never marry you."

Chapter 10

They'd argued for over an hour.

Par for the past for them—though the calm, rational form their words had taken was not.

Sam stared at the computer screen in her old office as the program codes blurred for the countless time since she'd arrived at Jarco that morning. She still couldn't believe she and Griff had had a subdued discussion over something so intense. Granted, Griff hadn't once lost faith that it was a discussion he wouldn't win. If Stan hadn't interrupted, Griff would still be trying to convince her to change her mind.

How could she?

It didn't matter how much Griff swore they could get around her condition. She knew the truth. She'd lived it. Desperate to get him to accept her decision and stop hurting them both, she'd even discussed her last relationship, finally admitting she'd had sex with Shawn, though not often because of the increasing tenderness. But eventually, they'd stopped trying. The laparoscopic surgery that was supposed to have excised the worse of her adhesions two years before, hadn't. In fact, it had made the scarring worse. The pain during intercourse, insurmountable. And her humiliation at having to discuss her failed relationship with another man with Griff?

That had been utterly complete.

Fortunately, that was when Stan interrupted. Griff had finally ceded to her doctor's pronouncement that she needed rest and left. But not before pointedly waiting for Stan to leave the room first so he could deliver his sultry, parting kiss in private. A kiss that nineteen hours later, still simmered deep within her core. Worse, she could still hear the husky vow that accompanied it. *I'm not giving up.*

That was what she was afraid of.

Probably because *she* wanted so damned bad to give in.

"Well now, Captain. This explains why you're not still tucked in bed, waiting for your promised visitor."

She jumped. Prayed. Turned.

It hadn't been her imagination. Griff was standing directly behind her chair, completely unconcerned that the lab's roving security guard had also heard the deliberate, double-entendre that thrummed through his voice. That was still thrumming in his stare and his stance—despite the fact that Griff was in Dress Blue uniform. No doubt about it. Griff Towers was staking his claim and he didn't care who knew it.

Worse, he wanted everyone to know it.

She was in trouble. Big trouble.

She pulled her stare from the imposing rack of ribbons on Griff's chest—and the even more imposing breadth of muscles beneath—and nodded to the guard in the hall.

"Thanks, Joe."

Amusement wreathed the man's weathered features as he waved her off. "No, problem, Doc. You need anything, you just give me a call." She nodded as he left. She needn't have bothered. The man had been in to check up on her three times during the morning already. Given the scene she'd put the man through yesterday and his relief at seeing her walk in under

her own power today, she probably had a year of father-hen-
ning to go. Too bad she couldn't get him to stick around and
buffer her conversation with Griff.

She finally faced him. Spoke. "Hi."

He inclined his head, but he didn't respond. His frown settled in, instead. She had a pretty good idea why.

She'd deliberately let Griff assume she'd be staying at the
hospital overnight. He'd have shown up at her house otherwise. She hadn't been up to it. Not after listening to his
impassioned pleas, however calm they'd been. The
heartache had been compounded five minutes later when
Dimitri arrived. She'd managed to hurt him, too. So much
so that Dimitri had decided on the spot to accept a rain
check from his friend at the space museum in Alamogordo.
His unspoken request had been clear. Please allow him the
courtesy of licking his wounds in private. It was the least
she could do.

Griff, on the other hand, had no intention of doing the
same. Especially now. "I'm sorry I mislead you last night. I
just…needed time by myself."

To her surprise, his frown faded. He even nodded
Shrugged. "It's okay. I think we both needed time to ourselve
last night. To think, among other things."

She'd told him she'd planned on telling Dimitri it was over
as soon as possible. She didn't ask what those other things had
been for him. Nor did he offer. He did surprise her again, however, as he tipped his head past her shoulder.

"Did you get anywhere?"

The computer.

She'd completely forgotten about her latest program review. With half a dozen, tight-lipped OSI agents crawling
through Phil's office down the hall and around the rest of the
lab, she'd had no choice but to invade Valentin's new turf and
resume her old desk. Valentin would be pissed when he found
out. She didn't care. So long as her efforts paid off and she
found something to exonerate Griff before his wings were re-

voked. Despite everything else that had surfaced about Phil, the board intended to issue its initial decision.

In *two* days.

She sighed. "I was just sitting here double-checking information, looking for errors…for the thousandth time. I still can't find anything wrong."

"Can you show me how it was supposed to work?"

"Sure."

Since he and Vince had come in at the last minute, neither of them had had a chance to see it in action. Or as he'd just said, it was *supposed* to have happened. She waited as he removed the coat to his Blues and tossed it over the back of the spare swivel chair. He loosened his tie next and sat. Given his attire, the hour and the day, she could only assume he'd been called in for an emergency meeting at headquarters in lieu of church. Not that she expected him to discuss that meeting. They both had their jobs and their professional secrets. She only wished she could ignore the man himself. Unfortunately, the familiar whisper of Griff's aftershave filled her lungs as he scooted his chair directly beside hers, bringing too many heady memories with it and him. She shoved each one from her brain and nudged her fingers over the keyboard, tapping several interconnected files closed. That done, she opened the experiment's demo and leaned back in her chair, still amazed the motion didn't cause her to automatically shift—because the pain wasn't there. For now.

But as she'd told Griff, it would return.

Soon.

She shoved the self-pity aside and dragged her attention back to the present. Specifically, to Griff's face as he watched the demo. She could feel his professional interest pick up as the computerized chopper and the voice-over she'd added took them through Phil's initial work, summarizing his progress on shortening the time needed for the chopper's existing radar to detect and acquire an enemy target's range, azimuth, elevation and velocity—thereby reducing the time needed for the onboard computer to calculate an enemy's future position before a defensive weapon could be deployed. Griff's excitement all but radiated off him as the voice-over moved into stage two, detailing her plans for a new defensive weapon. Because that weapon wasn't just another missile, but a smaller, tactical version of the pure laser/directed energy weapon she'd designed for the nation's Star Wars program.

The demo finished. Griff continued to stare at the screen for several long moments. Then he turned and faced her.

"Have I ever told you how bloody brilliant you are?"

Fire singed her cheeks. "Griff—"

He shook his head. "Don't deny it. You can't. But there's something else you can't deny, either." When he paused, waited a beat, appeared to be searching for the right words to finish, she knew. He *knew*.

Oh, boy.

His slow nod confirmed it. "The first time I heard about this experiment, it didn't make sense. Not the idea, mind you. That makes a lot of sense. Hell, what you've just shown me is a pilot's fantasy come true and we both know it. No, what confused me was why you were even working on it. Let's face it, Sam, choppers aren't your area of expertise, much less your interest. Are they?"

So General Luft was fond of reminding her.

She offered him the same fib she'd given Luft. "I saw an area of application and then I figured out how to make the modifications so we could transfer the technology. That's it. Well…*maybe*. I still haven't figured out why the first experiment failed."

Unlike Luft, she could tell he didn't buy it.

But he did shrug. "You'll figure it out—and then you'll fix it. Meanwhile." His smile dipped deep as he leaned close. His voice dipped deeper. "Forgive me if I take a moment to bask in the proof that my screw-up over that Russian lake affected you so deeply that it inspired a technological leap years ahead of its time."

She licked her lips as she struggled to ignore the warmth that had enveloped her. His warmth. That haunting aftershave didn't help. "Griff, you didn't screw up over that lake."

He nodded. "I know."

She shivered as he moved in closer, all but touching her.

"But it did affect you, didn't it? *I* affected you." His quiet confidence seduced her, even after all these years. And he knew it. Heck, he was using it. "I still do." Damned if she couldn't feel his self-assurance deepen as his lips caressed the curve of her ear. "Not bad work for a man you won't marry, huh? A man who plans on sticking around until you change your mind. Calling you, stopping by. Inviting you to lunch, dinner. Concerts, museums, the movies, anything he can think of. Shamelessly using everything he remembers about you—and he remembers a lot—to keep on affecting you whenever, wherever and however he can, until you finally realize that man meant what he said in that hospital room. He not only still loves you, he'll take you *any way he can get you.*"

Oh, Lordy. She turned her head.

Big mistake. Those swirling gray pools filled her view. Filled her. Invading her mind and her heart. Her soul. Filling her as deeply as Griff now knew he'd filled her every moment these past three months, whether sleeping or awake. Only now, his dark, seductive heat was filling her, too, and then his very breath as his mouth moved in even closer...

"Griff, please don't do this—"

"—Doctor Hall?"

They sprang apart.

Griff stood as one of the OSI agents she'd seen heading into Phil's office earlier entered. He crossed the room and extended his hand in what Sam knew was a conscious effort to give her a chance to recover. She appreciated it. Her legs were shaking and she wasn't even standing. She dug her fingers into her thighs in an attempt to quell the tremors.

"Bailey! Good to see you again."

"You too, Griff. It's been what, all of ten hours?" The

woman's impish wink told them the maneuver hadn't fooled her for a second. But the dimpled grin that followed also told them she was willing to let them off the hook. For now. Good thing, because Griff had actually flushed. Or maybe he was simply still flushed from that near-kiss.

She sure was.

Sam could feel her color darkening as the woman stepped deeper into the office, shamelessly assessing the cream T-shirt and jeans she'd donned that morning. Though her stomach was still slightly swollen today, she hadn't cared. It had been far too long since she'd been able to wear the faded hip-huggers. "Wow. I have to say, doctor, you look fantastic for a woman who spent yesterday in the emergency room."

She gave up hope the fire in her face would cool and stood. "Please, just call me Sam." At twenty-two the title had thrilled her. At thirty, with her biological clock all but clanging, it made her feel that much older. "You must be Agent Smirnoff. I'm sorry I missed you yesterday." Griff had confirmed Stan's report that the woman had left to secure lodging with the rest of her OSI team. Griff had added that either Smirnoff or the woman's partner would track her down sometime today. Agent Blackwell had already done so, catching her on her way into the lab earlier that morning. The man had grilled her regarding the details surrounding Phil's death over coffee, Diet Coke and package of dry vending machine donuts in the lab's lounge for a good hour.

Not that she'd had anything helpful to offer.

She was still trying to get used to the fact that someone had deliberately set out to murder Phil.

The woman leaned over the desk and extended her hand. "If you're Sam, then I'm Bailey." Humor flashed amid the woman's dark eyes and exotic Russian features as she straightened. "I know, I know. *Bailey Smirnoff*. My parents must have been drunk, right? What can I say? They were new to the country when I was born."

"Hey, Smirnoff! She still there or not?"

The woman stepped up to the doorway and stuck her head out into the hall. "Keep that lighter in your pocket, Blackwell. We're on our way!" Her smiled shifted to professional as she glanced back. "You got a minute?" Before Sam could answer, the woman stepped all the way out of the room and headed down the hall toward Phil's office.

"Ah, sure."

Griff's brow shot up as they stepped into the hall. "What's up?"

Sam shrugged. "I have no idea. Her team has been huddled inside Phil's office since before I arrived—and they closed the door when I passed." It had been a bit unnerving. Before they'd parted that morning, Blackwell informed her that an OSI computer contingent would be plowing through Phil's office. Until the technicians finished, she was not to go back inside—for anything. At least her empty soda bottles, notes and God only knew what else she'd left splayed out when she'd passed out weren't still scattered around. She had Valentin to thank for the ten-second tidy, though she knew full well the man had simply been sucking up again.

Unfortunately, those notes, tidied or not, were still inside Phil's office. While she sincerely hoped the team would uncover something that would help them solve Phil's murder, without access to her own notes and files, she'd been forced to work on the failed chopper experiment from scratch.

Griff stopped as they reached Phil's office and waited for her to enter first. Both OSI agents as well as a pair of lanky, barely post-pubescent computer techs were crowded around Phil's computer station. Valentin had done a decent job. The soda bottles had been dumped in the garbage three feet to the left, her briefcase—no doubt with everything else crammed haphazardly inside—had been tucked down beside it. Blackwell waved her closer. She held her breath as she stepped forward. Even if she hadn't been trapped in the staff lounge with the man that morning watching him puff cigarette after cigarette, the smoke clinging to his dark-blue civilian suit would have given his multi-pack-a-day habit away.

"What do you make of this, doc?"

Sam resigned herself to the stench and stepped all the way up beside him to scan the screen. "It's an internal security report." She tapped the timestamp column running down the left side of the screen. "Each time someone accesses the computer it's logged here." She reached down and slipped her hand over the computer's mouse to move the cursor. "When you highlight this column, you receive a brief, coded summary of what that particular person did at that time. See?"

The shorter, dark-haired tech nodded.

But the young, blonde bean on the far right did not. He moved in. Sam caught the flash of white stitching above the chest pocket on his dark blue coveralls. *Stringer*. The name fit. "Yeah, we caught that part—'cept we can't decipher the codes yet. What we don't get is why all the entries have verifiable initials against Jarco's staff except these two?" The tech trailed a skinny finger halfway down the screen. "Here." He kept going until he reached the bottom. "And here."

Huh?

She pointed to the chair still tucked up into the console. "May I…?"

Stringer shifted several paces to the right along with everyone else to give her room to pull the chair out and sit. She tapped her way through the series of data files. Sure enough, UNK was the only set of initials that popped for those two entries. UNK…unknown?

Impossible.

But it wasn't. Worse, it would have to be deliberate. Each time a person signed on to the system, they had to swipe their security card. The computer did the rest, automatically entering the user's corresponding initials into the column the techs had noted. Sure, the initials could be changed. But who would want to? The numerical code read off the user's security card remained the same no matter what. So unless—

She stiffened.

All five bodies surrounding her followed suit.

It was Griff who spoke. "What is it?"

"A hunch." One her stomach rolled at the mere suspicion of. She moved the mouse, clicking on the two "unknown" entries in succession. The user identification numbers matched. Even before she shifted the cursor again to access the logs from a good four months back and clicked on a prominent set of initials, she knew she had another match. Names might stick with her about as long as the files in her laptop's testy temp cache, but numbers had always managed to burn their way into her brain. Especially, the important ones. And that particular number was a *very* important one. She swallowed hard, hoping to quell the acid that was now roiling freely through her stomach. It didn't help. The acid darned near ate through as she checked the summary data on the two "unknown" timestamps against her memory. "Agent Blackwell?"

"Yes?"

She no longer cared that he'd brought the stench of stale smoke with him. She was too busy trying to absorb the significance of the timestamps screaming through her brain. "Do you remember my telling you this morning that Phil's briefcase disappeared the day he died?"

"Yup. You said no one knew for sure what was inside."

She nodded. "I know now. One item, at least. His security card." The card that had been recovered off Phil's body at the hospital and promptly destroyed had to have been counterfeit. This proved it. Sam glanced up as Blackwell touched her arm.

"Doc, are you saying what I think you're saying?"

Unless Phil Haskell's ghost has been haunting the lab these past few months, she sure was. "Someone has been accessing the lab's computer. Someone who is actively working to keep his activities far removed from his true identity."

Smirnoff nudged Blackwell out of the way. "Who's supposed to check this log? And how often?"

Well, *she* was. "With Phil dead and his position still technically unfilled, I'm ultimately responsible. I have been since my return from Moscow. According to Jarco's computer security directives, I'm to review this report as well as several others no later than the thirtieth of each month."

"Five days from now."

Sam nodded. "And before you ask, no, I haven't conducted this month's review yet." Though she would shortly.

"But it's a monthly review. Surely someone looks at it more often? Someone who also knows how often you review it?"

The implication behind that second, cooler question caused the acid in Sam's stomach to churn faster. She nodded despite it. She had to. It was true. "It's also reviewed weekly." And it was Sunday. Two full days past when that one should have taken place. "I can't believe Valentin would—"

"Valentin? As in, Dr. Valentin Novosti?"

The acid whipped into a frenzy at the chill in that one. "This is ridiculous." The man was a self-absorbed, skirt-chasing, career-obsessed jerk. But he was not a *murderer*...was he? Valentin had been at the meeting when Phil was most likely poisoned. But then, so had she. Hell, so had half the lab's staff. Except, now that Phil was gone, his temporary replacement—her—couldn't even keep an experiment off the ground. Literally. "Surely you guys don't think Valentin would murder Phil for his position here at the lab, do you?"

Or worse, was this about espionage?

"Thank you, Dr. Hall. That's all we need for the moment."

Polite, firm. Clipped. She'd definitely been dismissed. The woman's dimples had disappeared, too. As had the laughter that had lurked within the woman's gaze after she'd all but caught that near-kiss down the hall in her old office. The effect wasn't so much unfriendly as completely focused. *Bailey* was gone. *Agent Smirnoff* had assumed her place. Sam could all but hear the woman's brain clicking through facts she had no intention of sharing, not with her. Fine. But before she left, she needed to check one more thing—

"I said, *thank you*."

Griff's hand closed over hers. He guided it away from the keyboard, then her entire body up out of the chair.

"Agent Smirnoff, you don't understand. I—"

"*Samantha.*"

She caught the unspoken warning Griff had issued with her name. She knew that warning. Years before, toward the end of their relationship, it had set her on edge almost daily. But this was the first time she'd heard it issued professionally. And for the first time, she obeyed it without question. For the moment. She included both techs as well as Smirnoff and Blackwell in her smile then turned to follow Griff out of Phil's old office and down the hall, right into her old office and up to her old computer. There, she disobeyed it.

Why not? She was still logged on.

Griff frowned as she sat. "What are you doing?"

She ignored him and reached for the keyboard she'd used an eternity ago to access the demo. This time she used it to access the log she'd just been denied.

"Samantha—"

"Hush. This concerns you, too. This might be about Phil and possibly about me, too, but you got caught in the cross-fire." She tapped the screen. Specifically, the two timestamps that corresponded to the questionable entries. "Look. Do you notice anything interesting?"

He leaned over her shoulder. Stared.

Cursed. "They occur before and after my last flight."

She nodded. "Exactly." She tapped the first timestamp in question. "In fact, this access occurred not only the day before the flight, it occurred minutes after I finished some last minute tweaking and a mere two hours before I downloaded everything into the core modules." Modules she'd then taken directly to the hangar across base where she and the pilot originally scheduled to fly the experiment had installed them into the Pave Hawk. Sam slid her finger down the screen and tapped the second timestamp. "But this access is even more interesting, don't you think? It occurred while you and I were in that exam room waiting for your post-crash checkup."

Griff had evidently gotten over her disobedience—because he pulled up the spare chair and joined her at the computer. "Didn't you say there was an activity summary?"

She nodded. "Yeah. That's what I wanted to check."

"And?"

"It's been wiped clean, see?" She highlighted the applicable entries in succession again. She then checked at least a dozen timestamps surrounding them, some relating to her work, some not. Each display had an activity summary, all but ruling out a software virus or other random glitch. She clicked the report closed and spun around in her chair. "What really gets my goat is that whoever tampered with the files didn't get everything. I make backups during all phases of my work." Though that was confusing, too. Everyone at the lab knew she was fanatical about backups. Including Valentin. Either way, "Griff, I *have* a copy of the master program as it existed during that window of time. I made it minutes after I downloaded the information into those modules."

"Let me guess."

"Yep, the disc is in Phil's office. I was working on it when you showed up yesterday, comparing it to an earlier version. I'd hoped to locate a last minute change that ended up altering more than I'd originally thought." Sure she could go in and let the techs know what she'd just discovered—and she would. But she could also all but guarantee they wouldn't let her touch that disc now. Not after the way Smirnoff had just shut her down. But that didn't make sense either.

What did they know that she didn't?

And why wouldn't they share it?

Unable to contain her frustration, she stood and paced over to the row of gray filing cabinets. She kicked the base of the first set. Childish, yes. She didn't care. "Dammit, this isn't right. Phil's dead, Valentin's name stopped them cold and your career's all but—"

She froze. Stared.

Huh?

"What's wrong?"

"Nothing." Or something. "I don't know." She studied the bottom drawer of the filing cabinet. The one that'd slid open by roughly three inches after she'd kicked it. Why hadn't the cabinet been locked? It didn't make sense. Valentin was as fanatical about security as she was.

Or not.

At the very least, he'd missed a weekly COMPSEC check. The reminder was enough to make her bend down, slide the drawer open all the way and suck in her breath as she spotted the distinctive scarlet Jarco rocket emblem. Now that was definitely weird. In three years, she'd never once known Valentin to store his briefcase in his filing cabinet. Or was that really Valentin's briefcase...or Phil's.

"Sam? You okay?"

She shook her head. "I don't know."

She definitely felt sick to her stomach even suspecting what she was suspecting. But it was possible and she knew it. It even made sense. If Valentin had stolen Phil's case, he couldn't just walk the contents out of the lab. Security would have noticed. They opened everyone's briefcase and or bags, each time one was brought into or out of the lab. Secretary and scientist alike. Even General Lufts' gear was checked.

She heard Griff stand as she plucked the case from the drawer. By the time she stood, he was at her side. He stared down at it with her. "You think it's Phil's, don't you?"

"I hope not."

"Well, open it and see."

She tried. "It's locked." She laid the case on its side as Griff reached for his ever-present pocket knife—and cursed.

"What is it?"

Not what, whose. "This is *my* briefcase."

He glanced down. "How can you tell? I've seen half a dozen of those things since I arrived at Kirtland."

She tapped the brass latches. The ones that had been wrenched askew. "See this? I did this the day you arrived. When we ran into each other in the hospital."

"Open it."

She did and, this time, they cursed together.

"That's the backup disc, isn't it?"

She nodded. "Yup." Along with a ton of paperwork and other classified files Valentin had no bloody business having in his possession. "Oh, my God. He killed Phil."

Griff snagged the case with one hand, her right elbow with his other. He guided her back to the computer and down into the chair she'd vacated earlier. He laid the case in her lap. She was grateful. It gave her something to clutch.

"I don't understand. Why would he do it?"

"Espionage."

She jerked her head up. That was when it hit her.

Why Griff was in his Blues on a Sunday morning. Where he'd been. Griff had been at HQ as she'd suspected, but he hadn't been getting a grilling. He'd been given a briefing.

He nodded slowly, confirming her worst fears. "I can't tell you what they found—mainly because they're not even telling me. Not the bulk of it. All I know is that several seemingly unrelated security breeches have come to light this week, now that OSI has been looking. And the more they dig, the more breeches they're finding—and the more they seem to fit together. But, honey?"

"Yeah?"

"I need to ask you a favor. A big one."

Her head was still spinning from the shock of it all, so she settled lifting her palm. "Shoot."

"Let me spend the night."

"*What?*" She wasn't foolish enough to think it was a clever ploy. She almost wished it was. No, this was not about them— or sex. He was worried about something. Her. "Griff, what the heck is going on? Valentin set out to kill Phil, not me. For some reason, he's happy with just discrediting me."

But Griff was shaking his head calmly. Steadily. But his gaze was anything but. Those dark gray pools were filled with shadows, tortured. He was tortured.

"You've been ordered to keep your mouth shut about whatever it is you've learned—*or else*. Haven't you?"

He nodded. But then he spoke. "When's the last time you had tech in for preventative maintenance on that machine?"

"Huh?"

He reached over and tapped the computer screen. "This thing. When was the last time someone serviced it?" He was trying to tell her something...*without* telling her.

Preventative maintenance? Machine?

Computers?

She shook her head. "I'm sorry, I'm not get—"

"You'd better have someone work on that machine soon." He hiked a distinctly pointed brow. "It could crash on you."

Crash? Machine?

Holy sh— "The halon system." Just before she'd passed out yesterday, he'd shown her the OSI report stating that her C130's fire-extinguishing system had been tampered with. Someone had taken a look at the maintenance schedule in the meantime and had been able to pin-point when the sabotage had occurred. And like those timestamps, the information had turned out to be significant.

To her.

Griff nodded.

She licked her lips. "When—ah—do you recommend I get someone in to look at it?"

He didn't miss a beat. "The morning before you plan on firing it up, at least. Especially if you want your email to wing its way to Russia."

The sabotage had occurred the day before her flight?

But Phil had been dead by then. She and Dimitri had already been tapped to replace him. Valentin knew that...and he'd been ticked. "Oh, my God. Valentin tried to kill me. Dimitri, too."

Griff reached out. His fingers shook as he smoothed his thumb down her cheek. His throat worked as he nodded. He slipped his hand beneath the bulk of her hair and around the back of her neck, pulling her close as he settled his lips against her ear. A moment later, his plea filled her. "May I stay over? Just until tomorrow." His voice broke. "*Please?*"

Her heart broke.

Valentin had to be under surveillance. Her, too. Or Griff wouldn't have even tried to follow his orders to keep his mouth shut. But he didn't really trust OSI. She couldn't blame him. If their positions were reversed, she'd be begging for the same thing. Besides, as if she'd be able to sleep now.

"Sure, you can stay. I've got a spare room."

He pulled away. Nodded. "Understood."

She stiffened. *Dimitri*. Valentin had tried to kill him, too. As much as Valentin had been loathe to accept reality, if she didn't agree to assume Phil's job, the position could easily pass to Dimitri. "What about Dimitri?"

Again, Griff shook his head. But this time, it was reassuring. "I took care of it. Him." Meaning he made sure someone would be watching Dimitri's back all the way in Alamogordo. She knew the whole situation with Dimitri still got to Griff. He truly had changed since college. He'd never been comfortable with her having close male friends. But he also understood that Dimitri wasn't Chet.

And he was trying.

She smoothed her fingers down his face, savoring the slight rasp that had already formed on Griff's jaw though it was barely noon. "Thank you for looking out for him, too."

He shrugged.

"What about Christy?"

"Vince is watching her. She thinks it's so you and I can work some stuff out."

She tugged her hand back and held on to the briefcase. Tight. "Griff—"

"I know. But I couldn't bring myself to worry her, too."

Unfortunately, she could argue with his logic. But even more unfortunate was her own burning curiosity. "Is she…okay with the idea?" Of them seeing each other?

"Well, now, I did suggest she might be able to talk her Uncle Vince into visiting that carnival they set up a couple blocks down the street from our neighborhood."

Our neighborhood. The phrase had a dangerously seductive ring to it. He darn well knew it, too.

I'm going to keep on affecting you.

She still smiled. "That's sneaky."

He caught the double-entendre and flat-out grinned. "Hey, her grandmomma didn't raise no fool." His grin faded as he retrieved her briefcase and stood. He held out his hand. "So how 'bout it? You ready to toss this sucker to those vultures squatting in Phil's office and let them prove your brilliance for you so you can head home with me?" *Home*. Despite the teasing in his tone, he was stone-cold serious. She knew better than to take his hand. But she did it. She couldn't help herself. Griff's warmth seeped into her palm as he led her from the room. She was powerless to prevent that too.

Much less the dream that seeped in with it…

Chapter 11

He was trapped on the cusp between heaven and hell.

Heaven, because he was here in Samantha's house—*invited*—about to spend the night. And hell, because of why that invitation had been necessary.

Griff shot off his last emailed "thanks" and leaned forward to set his laptop on the coffee table. He eased back in the armchair as he had so often during the past hour and stared at the woman he loved more than flying itself, snuggled atop a slate blue couch he'd helped re-upholster years before, snoring none-to-softly. She was the only thing about this day, about this entire blessed week, that made sense. And after what he'd seen that morning, he also knew she was the key. The knowledge came from deep within him, harvested from every screaming instinct he'd spent nearly twenty years cultivating. But the most frightening of all was that those instincts that screamed loudest were also those that had been honed in combat.

He didn't give a damned what that gaggle of generals and

fellow colonels at HQ thought. This Valentin Novosti might have killed Phil Haskell first, but Samantha had been the bastard's true goal all along. That demo proved it.

Three hours later, he was still trying to absorb the implications of what she'd shown him—what she'd *created*. The chopper applications simply blew him away. But if she was even close to getting what he saw today to integrate with the country's space-based intercontinental ballistic missile defenses, they'd be damned near untouchable.

Oh, yeah, she was the key all right. Unfortunately, even he had to admit General Luft was right.

It didn't make sense.

Scratch that. The attempt on her life did. Every nation outside NATO and three-quarters of the ones in would be willing to murder to halt the progression of technology he'd seen that morning—that, or steal it for themselves. But why go to all that trouble to try to kill her and then be willing to settle for merely discrediting her? Was screwing with her work simply an attempt at stopping it at all costs? And, if so, why didn't that explanation set well in his gut?

It was enough to give Buddha himself a raging ulcer.

Griff stood and stretched his legs, grateful Sam had insisted he take the time to stop and ditch his uniform in favor of a pair of worn jeans and a white T-shirt. He'd doffed the cowboy boots she'd bought him for his thirtieth birthday at the door upon entering the house. Mainly because they were visible from here—and, heck, he figured she needed the reminder that he wasn't going anywhere anytime soon. Ever, if he had his way. And he would.

Eventually.

For now he settled for one last gaze at those sleep-flushed lips and softly fanned lashes before savoring the luxury of crossing this woman's living room in his bare feet for the first time in over a decade. His contentment ended at the fireplace as he studied the photograph of Sam and her fellow Sisters that had been taken on commissioning day. The camera had captured then Second Lieutenant Hall's stunning beauty and newfound professional poise perfectly—but the camera had also captured something else. Her underlying pain.

No, not from the endometriosis he now knew she lived with daily, but the ache in her heart. He wondered if anyone else, even Anna or Meg had seen it. He did know he could. Just as he knew why it had been there, simmering just beneath that perfect, silken mask. Sam had been hurting because he hadn't been there that day as promised. She'd been incomplete. She'd felt it then; he felt it now. And he'd give anything to help her see that she was *still* incomplete…and so was he.

Dammit, it didn't have to be this way.

Granted, he'd been thrown for a loop in that emergency room yesterday. And even while he'd spent the next hour trying to persuade her to change her mind right then and there, he had to admit, he'd had his doubts. It wasn't that he didn't care about her. He'd fallen for the woman still snoring steadily behind him the moment she slammed into him in that elevator, shattering the casing on his very first laptop. Darn thing had still been under its ninety-day warranty. He could have gotten a new one, no questions asked. But if he had, she never would have come over to his apartment that night to fix it. And he would have missed out on staring at that amazing face and listening to that husky voice, stealing a whiff of her intoxicating scent every now and then for two whole hours. For a man who'd measured the past eleven years against the span of the previous one—with the greater duration always coming up short, those two hours were a lifetime.

His lifetime. He wouldn't trade them for the world. Or any of the other memories he'd hoarded from that year.

He had to find his way back to her.

He didn't know how it would happen or when—or even where. He only knew why. He loved her. Plain and simple. Always had, always would. If this chronic condition she suffered from meant they had to find new ways to express that love, never once returning to the old ones his memories still cherished so damned much, so be it. He'd already taken the first steps. Through the glory of an Internet search engine, he'd even located a bunch of new friends who were ready, willing and able to help him find a few shortcuts. He wasn't proud. He'd take all the help he could get.

She was worth it. *They* were worth it.

He just had to find a way to convince her to let up off herself long enough to give them a shot. From the advice he'd gotten last night and this past hour, he knew the real problem wasn't that the endometriosis wouldn't let her be a woman. It was that with the endo she didn't feel like she was a woman. Not a whole woman.

Well, she *was*. She was just…different now.

Hell, so was he.

He glanced down, studying the respectable muscle definition beneath his T-shirt and jeans. Yeah, he was still holding onto his body, but he'd also bucked right past forty last year. Maintaining his grip took a lot more energy than it used to and eventually, he'd lose it. That was reality, too. No matter how much he might treasure those lines that had started in around her eyes—because they let him pretend she was catching up—he'd always be eleven years older. And he'd always look it. The passage of time was nothing, if not relative.

Well, so was sex.

She was turning him down because she thought they couldn't have it. Not in a way that would truly satisfy him over the long haul. Damned ironic when he thought about it. For a man who conceived a child with a total stranger—a stranger he hadn't even recognized when she'd shown up to give him the news—"normal" sex had definitely become a relative term. Especially when that man—namely him—wasn't anxious to repeat any part of that particular scenario. Hell, he hadn't had an orgasm in so long, he doubted Sam would believe the timeframe if he told her. Well, not one with anyone else around. He had taken to dealing with his self-imposed drought the way most men did. But then, his solo activities

hadn't really been solo, had they? Samantha had been in his
mind and in his heart even then—and, yeah, in his fantasy of
the moment, she was right there, wrapped around his flesh.

Whoa.

Best to nip that recurring daydream in the bud. Lest she
wake and read his thoughts along with something else. Something there'd be no mistaking or misinterpreting. He was
about to turn and head back to his armchair to close up his
laptop when he spotted the tiny teak box tucked behind her
commissioning photo. He reached up instinctively, out, only
to freeze. It had been years. Surely that wasn't—

"Yeah, it's in there."

He dropped his hand, turned. Absorbed.

She was sitting up on the couch. Her knees tucked beneath
her chin. Her rumpled hair spilling down around her as she
held on tight, those dark gold eyes still adjusting to the late-
afternoon light. "I guess I should return—"

"No." He injected a lightness he sure as hell didn't feel into
his shrug. "I told you eleven years ago, it was yours no matter what. I meant it."

Her nod was guarded.

He was okay with that. As long as he didn't have to take
that box back. What was still inside it. "Are you hungry?"

"Yeah. Are you?"

He nodded. He'd missed lunch. Vince was right, he'd gotten soft with Alma Schultz around to cook. He'd made do with
a couple breakfast burritos from a drive-through that never had
quite hit the spot, much less filled it. But he'd wanted to wait
until she woke. "I saw a couple of those gourmet pizzas in
your freezer. I can toss one in."

She dropped her feet to the floor. "That's okay, I'll—"

"—stay right there and rest. I seem to remember carrying
you into a hospital yesterday."

She shook her head, clearly exasperated. "And I seem to
remember hearing my doctor tell you fourteen separate times
that I'm better off now than I've been in months."

He grinned. "Fifteen, but who's counting?"

It worked, she laughed.

And he crossed the room before she could remember what had set her off. "I'll go turn on the oven. Back in a few."

He watched that whiskey gaze stray to the laptop as he passed, noticed the last message he'd answered was still open and decided to leave it that way. If he was lucky, her innate curiosity would get the best of her while he was gone—and she'd be ready to talk by the time he got back. He rounded the corner and headed through the dining room into the kitchen. He stood there in front of the oven for a good fifteen minutes—and never once touched the thing.

They had better things to do than eat.

When he couldn't take it anymore, he headed back into the living room—and found his reward. She didn't even glance up as he slipped between the coffee table and sank down onto the couch beside her. She just closed one of his responses and opened up the next "already read" message still sitting in his email mailbox. He'd left every one of them there and the laptop out and powered up on purpose. She knew it, too.

Because her tears were trickling down.

She finally looked up. "How…? Why…?"

He reached out and smoothed the tangles from her right cheek, tucked them behind her ear. "Because I love you."

"Oh, Griff—"

He pressed a finger to her lips. "Shhhh. Don't talk. Read. Read them all. Then we'll talk."

She lowered her watery stare to the computer in her lap and opened the next message. He glanced at the sender and header. Dave Andrews. Yeah, he liked that guy.

The man had had some pretty sound advice, too.

By the time he'd arrived at Vince's from the hospital yesterday he'd been desperate for it. Must have shown in his initial message to the *Men and Endo* electronic listserv he'd stumbled across the night before, because no less than thirty guys had responded by this morning. Vince had taken Christy

to Chuck E. Cheese pizza for the evening to give him some
space. In his fury and his grief, he'd hit the 'Net, searching
for instant answers to quite a few questions. Some self-serv-
ing, and some not. Like what the devil was endometriosis and
why had the goddamned disease planted itself in *his* woman?
Screwing up her life and theirs?

Fortunately the moderator had been on-line when he'd re-
quested access to the listserv for men-only. He'd never been
one for support groups, but last night had changed his mind.

And his outlook.

Guys he didn't even know, from all walks of life had written him back. Told him, yeah, it sucked. Big time. But he'd
survive. They had. There were days when their wives and girl-
friends wanted to make love, but couldn't. And there were
days when they could. Either way, you just went with the flow.
Some of the men had even gone so far as to suggest positions
known to reduce the depth of penetration—or remove it from
the equation altogether. He hadn't really needed that advice.
He and Samantha had explored damned near all the suggestions during their time together in Austin. No, what he'd
needed more than sex tips, was the knowledge and reassur-
ance that while he and Sam might not be able to overcome
this thing the guys had called endo, they would be able to live
around it. Love around it. He'd discovered that couples all
over the country and the world did it every single day—and
they not only survived, they were better off.

Because they still had each other.

He slid his hand up Samantha's back and threaded his fingers into her hair, stroking the silky length as she closed the
last e-mail message and severed the wireless Internet connection. She closed the laptop and laid it on the coffee table.
And then, to his profound relief and absolute joy, she grabbed
the box of Kleenex from the coffee table and turned into his
arms, laid her head against his chest and cried. He had no idea
how long he held her. He only knew that even as each and
every one of her shuddering sobs tore through him—at the

same time, those sobs were also helping her to heal. He also knew it was the first time she'd ever really let go of it. Ever truly shared the pain and disappointment.

The battered and bruised hope.

Yes, her sorority sisters knew of her condition. She'd confessed that in the hospital yesterday. Though Anna and Meg knew the most, since it turned out Anna had lost an ovary to a conventional cyst herself the year after he'd left Austin— and Meg had been able to take time off to fly to Kirtland for Sam's first ovarian surgery three years ago. Turned out Meg also knew why she'd been considering Alibek's offer of a marriage based in friendship. She'd even been open with him about that too. And about why she was so determined to hold on to that remaining ovary of hers as long as possible. She might not be able to have conventional sex, but ironically, it seemed there was a decent chance she could undergo artificial insemination and carry to term.

She wanted a baby. It seemed having Alibek's baby had appealed to her more than having some stranger's.

Well, he was back in her life, thank you.

Griff snagged the wad of soiled Kleenex from her hand as he kissed her hair and tossed the tissue to the end table so she could grab a fresh one. Far as he was concerned, fathering this woman's potential children was his job. All she had to do was say the word. If it didn't work, well he'd meant what he'd said about that too. They could always adopt. As for Christy, the way she'd been affected at that hospital right along with him yesterday and even outright okay with him coming here today, God willing, she might be ready to become a big sister sooner than he'd hoped. Now there was a dream worth working for. The two women in his life, together. With him.

And okay with each other.

He continued to stroke Samantha's hair until the tears dried out. She laid in his arms afterward, contemplative, quiet. He knew this mood. It wasn't a bad one. More importantly, it gave him more hope than he'd had since Ramstein. She was on her way to accepting. Yeah, there'd be fits and starts for awhile. Hell, in him too. But hope had been renewed inside her. He could feel it spreading out. Growing. Not for something better. For something different.

And then, she moved.

The years fell away as he automatically shifted her until she was sitting in his lap with her legs tucked up on the sofa, just as she had so many times before. Her eyes were more red than gold, her nose scarlet and puffy from all the Kleenex, her smooth skin was blotchy and hot—and he had never seen her look more beautiful. Her smile quirked.

"You didn't turn on the oven, did you?"

"Nope."

She slid her arms around his neck and pulled him close. "Good, because I'm *starving*." And then she pressed those soft, swollen lips to his and kissed him.

To Sam's absolute shock, Griff pulled away.

She blinked up at him. Had she shifted in his lap without realizing it? Elbowed him accidentally? Pinched his tender parts before they had a chance to become nowhere near tender? It wouldn't be the first time her limbs and her desires had collided within her, or with him. "Did I bump—"

"I'm fine. More than fine. I just need to make certain you are." He tipped her chin until she was bathing in those gray, healing pools. "Samantha, are you sure? We don't have to try right now. We can wait. I swear to God, all I need tonight is to hold you in my arms. To feel you sleeping beside me again. I just wanted you to read those letters so you'd know I wasn't going anywhere. That we *could* do this."

Oh, Lordy, she was crying again.

Only this time, like that huge sob-fest she'd just indulged in, she knew it wasn't the hormones in those dang birth control pills. It was Griff. It had always been Griff. She reached up and rubbed the back of her hand against his jaw, savored the texture and the warmth she'd been missing in her life and in her heart for so very long. She strove for lightness, a dash of humor, desperately trying not to kill the hope that had begun to blossom in both of them. "It's been eleven years. How many more do you think we need to wait?"

He didn't smile. "I'm scared, honey."

She nodded. "I know. Me, too."

"If I hurt you—" He closed his eyes.

She smoothed her hand across his brow, gently erasing his frown. "You won't." She had to believe that. She wanted this to work. She needed it to.

She needed him.

He trailed his fingers down her jaw. "I don't want to come inside you, not for a second." He stopped. Smiled. "Let me rephrase that. I do want to come inside you. Very, *very* badly."

She shifted in his lap, slowly. Deliberately. "Yeah, I can feel that."

He chuckled. But then he cupped his hands to her face and his smile faded into sober. His voice turned quiet. "I need you to understand something. If in the coming months, we find out that none of those positions they suggested work for us and that I'm never, ever, going to able to enter you again…I will mourn the loss until the day I die. But I will also be okay, satisfied, content—with however we learn to make love. Just so long as it's you in my arms."

Oh, heavens. She dragged her breath in deep. "You're going to make me cry again. Stan has me on the pill. Heck, you've probably already read that it helps some women. But you also know how dang moody they make me."

He tucked her hair behind her ear. "S'okay. I can be pretty moody, too. Or so someone used to tell me."

"True…but can you still perform?"

His brow shot up.

She shrugged. Teased. "It's been long time. Maybe you've lost your touch. It happens. Or so I've been told—"

He hauled her in and kissed her. Hard. Long.

Wet.

Before she could come up for air, he shifted her so her neck was cradled in the crook of his arm and then he came right back for more. He swallowed her gasp and swirled his tongue deep inside her mouth, running it down the length of hers, around and back up, tasting, teasing and caressing her mouth as she'd teased him, just before he pulled away slightly to tug her bottom lip into his mouth and leisurely suck. She moaned and he shifted again, taking the kiss deeper once more, until he was savoring her very essence and sharing his own.

Mercy, he tasted good. As dark and as heady as he had out in that parking lot by her car two nights ago.

But even more dangerous.

His confidence whenever he'd touched her in the past had always turned her on instantly, but today it nearly drove her insane. But he managed to surprise her, gradually slowing the kiss down once again instead of quickening it. But then, just when she'd adjusted, he tipped her head slightly so he could delve further inside her mouth, more deeply than she'd thought possible. She was also dimly aware of his lifting her bottom so he could unsnap her jeans and drag the zip down as he continued to kiss. Suddenly, her jeans were gone.

He pitched them to the floor then slipped his fingers beneath the edge of her panties, sliding the pink silk down next. He tossed her panties aside, not even breaking their kiss as he lifted her upright to settle her astride his thighs. His jeans were soft and worn next to her quivering flesh, the muscles beneath, hard and bunched. The contrasting sensations were incredibly erotic. But they got even better as he tucked his hand beneath her T-shirt and scraped his fingertips down her spine with aching tenderness, then around her still slightly swollen belly. He didn't seem to mind, and she shivered as he smoothed his callused palms over the scars she hadn't had years before, every second, every inch of his slow caress assuring her she was still beautiful to him and, more importantly, that he'd missed her as profoundly as she'd missed him. She tipped her head to the side, finally breaking their kiss, silently begging him to move to her neck.

He did.

She closed her eyes and gave herself up to the suckling beneath her ear. To him.

His breath had begun rasping in and out, scorching her neck. But it wasn't enough. She wanted him hotter, she wanted him to burn for her touch as she burned for him.

She broke away from the seductive suckling to tug his T-shirt off, and then hers. He groaned as she bent low to graze her lips over the base of that awful, but healing bruise marring his chest. She was grateful the swelling had gone down. Still, she soothed the entire length of purple all the way up to his shoulder with her lips. There, she nuzzled her face in his neck and inhaled his musky scent. He allowed her to savor his fragrance for a single, breathless heartbeat and then he tunneled his fingers into her hair, using the length to arch her neck so he could bury his face in her throat and do the same. He nipped the hollow at the base as his nimble fingers zeroed in on her bra, on the front clasp he'd loved so much, deeming it quicker and so much more practical—for *him*.

A quick twist of his wrist and the pink cups fell away.

He grinned up at her as he claimed his prize, stealing her breath as he palmed significantly more breast than she'd carried at nineteen. He dropped his gaze and devoted his undivided attention to her nipples for several long glorious moments as he plundered and played and explored…before tasting. Unable to withstand the torment a moment longer, she slipped her hands down between them, unhooking the brass stud on his jeans and unzipping them, so very ready to move this—them—further.

But his hands shot down, locking about her wrists as she peeled the edges to his pants open.

"Sweetheart—"

She shook her head. "It's okay. I just—"

Oh, boy. This had always been the hard part for her.

Talking about it. Actually voicing the specifics. Before, during or after—none of it had been easy. But she was on fire now. For him. "Griff, I want—"

Just say it.

She sucked in her air and her courage. "I need to feel you…down…there."

He groaned.

Damn. "It's okay. If it's too much—"

He shook his head. His gaze seared to molten. "It's not too much. It's perfect." With a single, powerful thrust of his hips, he lifted them several inches off the couch. Somehow, he managed to shuck his jeans and his underwear without unseating her. And then he was pulling her close, settling her blond curls right up against the base of his dark, rigid erection.

She gasped. Sharply.

He stiffened. "Are you—"

"I'm fine. Just fine. *Perfect.*" Like coming home.

She rose slightly, dragging herself up the underside of his shaft inch-by-hardened-inch until she'd reacquainted herself with every glorious one. She reached the top and paused, then slid back down, zealously maintaining contact until she'd sealed her aching flesh all the way down against his base. The sensation was so incredible, she did it again.

And then again, feeling Griff grow stiffer and thicker with each successive pass.

He groaned. "Oh, yeah. *Absolutely perfect.*"

He sealed his palms to her bottom and dug in his fingers into her cheeks, kneading them as he took up the rhythm she'd initiated. He captured her stare as he lowered her and refused to release it. "You have to help me out here, honey. You have to keep talking to me. Tell me what's good. What's not. Okay?"

"Hmmm." It was all she could manage—because he'd lifted her again.

He dragged her down.

"*Yes*, slow. Just like…that."

Oh, was he hard. And so *hot*. He was growing hotter with each successive slide. She dug her fingertips into his shoulders and held on, anchoring her hands as he drove her straight up again, pushing her higher and higher until she'd reached his throbbing tip, he held her there for a single agonizingly taunting moment, intimate flesh against bare, aching intimate flesh, never once breaking contact…with their bodies or his fierce, stormy stare. This time, she left a trail of moisture in her wake as he brought her down. The moisture increased with the next pass, spread.

And the next.

He growled his appreciation. "So wet." Dark gray turned to flint on the next pass. His growl darkened, rumbling from deep within his chest. "Oh, baby, you feel so damned *good*."

"*Yes*."

She felt his arms begin to tremble, then quiver, then outright quake. She was so very close to the edge. And that strained, smoky stare pushed her even closer.

"Sam, I can't…hold this pace much…longer."

She pressed her forehead to his and drowned herself in an endless reservoir of love she'd never been able to find since this man had walked out of her life. She dragged her lips to his ear and whispered the words she should never have left unsaid eleven years ago, the words she'd regretted leaving unsaid every single day of her life since. "Don't leave me, Griff. Take me with you. *Now*."

He snapped, jerking her bottom in hard, grinding their bodies together, all but fusing their flesh as he rubbed her up and down his shaft furiously. Within seconds, she was ablaze. Still, he rubbed on. How he kept up the frenzied pace she'd never know, but he did. Over and over, until his harsh panting drove him headlong into the blistering inferno along with her. A moment later, his sharp curse filled the room as he stiffened—the very reason for it, ripping her own release from her. She locked her arms about his neck and held on as her entire world imploded in a teeming fusion of the past, the present and the promise of their future.

And then it was over.

Her limbs were still shaking as she collapsed into him,

completely spent as Griff gathered her closer and finished pulsing between them. She laid there in his arms, against his solid chest, sated and at peace for the first time in eleven years, basking in the warmth of Griff's boundless love. She never wanted to leave it, or him, again. She sighed.

"You okay? Nothing hurting?"

She lifted her head. Stared into his love and concern and best of all, his purely sexual satisfaction. She smoothed her hands across his jaw and smiled softly. Spoke.

"I've missed you."

She watched, amazed as his eyes began to shimmer, then fill with tears. She caught the first one as it spilled over, then smoothed the next and the next as they trickled down his whiskered cheeks. He finally tipped his head against the sofa and wiped the rest of them himself. His smiled was sheepish as he came back. He shrugged. "Must be the hormones."

She laughed, teased. "Thank God. For a moment there, I was afraid it was the sex."

He sobered. Instantly. "*Hell, no.* Honey, don't you dare worry about that, don't ever worry about it. Sure, making love was different just now. And it'll continue to be different. But that was bound to be, anyway, because we're different now. *Both* of us." He tipped her chin, smoothed her hair from her face. "But the best part hasn't changed and it never will. How I feel about you, how I know you feel about me. That's our foundation, our core. Whatever you want to call it, it's what makes us work. It's what's always made us work, even back in Austin when everything else was screwed up."

Something tickled at her brain. She ignored it.

She nodded instead. He was right. The most important part of them hadn't changed and never would.

Their love *was* their foundation.

It tickled again. But this time, it was more like a thought or an impression had ghosted through her brain. Not quite enough substance for her to get a clear look at it. She lost it as Griff shifted her slightly.

His brow quirked as he glanced between them. "Besides, I'd say some of the evidence of my satisfaction is—ah—hard to miss right about now."

She laughed. Stood. There was no sense getting embarrassed. Not when that evidence would become commonplace.

The ghost was back, getting stronger.

The evidence is hard to miss. How? She'd been looking for it nonstop for days. She scooped her T-shirt off the coffee table. Hard to miss…or was it just hard to see?

"Sam?"

She turned to the couch. To him. "Huh?"

"You've got that look."

She blinked. "What look?"

She wiped her stomach with her shirt.

"The one you get when your brain is working overtime. Right about the time an idea would lock in and take shape." His lips twisted wryly. "And right before you'd shoot out of the apartment, dumping me, dinner and whatever else we had planned that night for a love-session with your computer so you could test that new idea."

"I did *not*. I am not." About to dump him, that is.

His brow shot up. "Oh, really?" He tipped his chin to her hands. "Then why did you clean yourself up with my shirt?" His gorgeous half-smile dipped in. "Not that I mind. It was my mess. But it's also the only clean shirt I've got with me."

She stared at the T-shirt. It was white.

It was his.

She glanced down at the table. Her cream T-shirt was still pooled beside his computer. The CD tray was open. The catch must have popped when she'd set the laptop on the table before her cry. The Norah Jones CD she'd given Griff gleamed up at her. Taunting her. Why? She dropped Griff's shirt. She was about to close the tray when the ghost crystallized.

"That's it!"

He shook his head. "That's what?"

Oh, God. "The program. The sabotage. Where Valentin put

it. It's so basic, it's ingenious. I kept thinking I'd screwed up. I mean, I must have because I knew you didn't. So I was looking at my improvements. *My* work. Not the core, the foundation. The work that was already there. It's probably something so simple as a transposed digit in a matrix."

Griff frowned. "You're losing me, darlin'."

"The turret you clipped. The tank it was attached to. You see that tank as a shape. I see it as a shape. So we *saw* it. The computer controlling the autopilot doesn't. It only sees numbers. The visual input—shapes—from your optical radar is converted into a matrix."

"Numbers."

She nodded. "Exactly. Numbers. Lots of them. But if even one of those digits is out of place—"

"It doesn't see the right shape."

"Worse. It probably didn't see any shape. Not that one. According to the computer, the tank wasn't there. Hence, the chopper's autopilot didn't have to worry about a collision. There was nothing to collide with."

"Well, I sure saw the damned thing." He rubbed the bruise on his shoulder ruefully. "Felt it, too."

She grabbed her panties and tugged them on, then grabbed her bra and latched it. "It could be something else, but my money's on this. It's so simple it would've been written off as a keystroke error if the security breaches hadn't come to light. Worse, because that data was part of the existing portion of the program—not an improvement—I never even looked. Valentin would know that, too. He also knew how Luft felt about this program. Luft thinks the cost is prohibitive. I don't. Not for the return we'll eventually get. But I also made an agreement with Luft that if this first flight failed, I'd let it go. Valentin probably figured I'd be so ticked I'd take the job offer at Los Alamos."

Griff stiffened. Sat up straighter. "What job offer?"

She waved him off. "Don't worry about it. I'm not taking it." She grabbed their shirts and tossed Griff's to him. "Here, throw it in the laundry basket in my bedroom and grab a clean one from the bottom drawer of my dresser." She kept her baggy, *I feel like a swollen mess today* shirts in there. One of them was bound to fit him. "I've got to get to the lab and take another look at that disc."

She tugged on her top as Griff cleaned himself up, donned his jeans, zipping them as he stood.

"You can't go."

"Griff, now is not the time—"

He shook his head. "Not because I say so. Sam, they are not going to let you at that disc. You saw Bailey's face. You'll never convince her to let you look at it until she's ready. She's not going to care how much you need to see it. You don't believe me, ask Vince. That woman is ruthless."

"Well, I can be ruthless too."

Griff grinned as he snagged her jeans off the floor. "You're a pushover, honey, and we both know it. You certainly never left me spread eagle on my own bed, flex-cuffed to all four posts…while you got on a plane to somewhere else."

"*What?*"

"Yup."

Spread eagle? Bailey might be a special agent with OSI, but Vince Racey was twice as tall as her. A combat vet. An in-shape combat vet. How the devil had a woman that tiny managed to get Vince to drop his guard? "Was he…"

"Naked?" Griff tucked her jeans in her hands as she nodded. "As the day he was born."

"Good Lord, why?"

Griff tossed off a shrug as he crossed the room. "I didn't ask. I just cut him down." He grabbed the receiver to her cordless phone and waited until he was two feet from her before he tossed it to her. "Give the lab a call. It's just after five. Maybe Blackwell and Bailey are still there. If not, try the techs. Tell them what you've got. Maybe they can verify it." He retrieved the jeans she managed to drop in favor of the phone. "But do me a favor and put your pants on first. You may end up with Blackwell and, darlin' I have to confess, I don't like the idea of you talking to another man in your panties—whether or not the man knows it."

He tucked her jeans over her arm, kissed her hard on the mouth and turned and left, whistling to himself as he scooped up his dirty shirt and headed down the hall to her bedroom.

The rat.

She should make the call nude just to spite him.

Blackwell's face floated through her mind. She donned the jeans and made the call.

Neither Bailey nor Blackwell were there, but Stringer was. Five seconds into their conversation she realized he was also as obsessed with finding the tampering as she was. The kid was sharp too, immediately latching onto her suggestions and running with them. If she was smart, she'd steal him from OSI. Griff whistled his way back into the living room wearing the dark-blue *I'm too sexy for this shirt* concert tee Meg had left behind a couple years back.

He was definitely too sexy for it.

She snapped her attention back to Stringer's barrage of counter suggestions as Griff headed for the hearth.

Wow, the kid was really, really good.

That settled it. She'd get Luft to steal him in exchange for taking Phil's spot. She'd told Griff the truth. She was staying at Kirtland and not because of her career. Because of the man reaching for the teak box she'd kept tucked behind her copy of the Sisters' commissioning photo. She wrapped up the call as quickly as she could, hoping she hadn't been rude as she hung up. Her heart began pounding against her ribs as Griff crossed the room. They both knew what he was going to ask her. She knew what answer she wanted to give him, too.

But what about—

She jumped as the phone shrilled.

Griff nodded to the receiver still in her hand. "Go ahead. I'm not going anywhere."

Her heart still pounding, she lifted the phone. Ten seconds

into the call, her heart was slamming so hard it damned near shattered her ribs. She dropped the phone without even hanging up. The pain barely registered as it slammed into her foot. She was dimly aware of Griff tucking the box in his pocket as he vaulted forward to grab her as she swayed.

"Honey, what is it? What's wrong?"

She stared up at him. "That was Vince. He took Christy to the carnival. She's *gone*, Griff. Vince can't find her anywhere."

Chapter 12

He couldn't have missed Vince if he'd tried.

Griff swerved his Jeep to the right and killed the engine directly behind the half-dozen flashing cop cars crammed into no man's land between the carnival's temporary concrete barricade and the rest of the strip mall's over-crowded parking lot. He didn't bother closing the door as he bailed out of the rental. He was too busy shoving his way through the flock of salivating human vultures already racked and packed in and around the cars, craning their necks to catch a glimpse of the city's latest batch of emotional carrion. And there was the first course—Vince—head and shoulders above the milling crowd, grief and guilt carved into his face and all but pacing in place as he and a uniformed cop scanned each patron who passed. A split second later, his buddy saw him.

Vince shot across the lot, leaving the cop yakking to air as they linked at the base of the Ferris wheel.

"What the *hell* happened?"

"I don't know. I swear to God, I was watching her every freaking second."

"Well, you bloody *missed* one!"

Ah, Christ, what was he doing?

Griff sucked in his air and tried slamming the panic down, staunching the raging fury and absolute blinding terror that kept ripping through his heart. His own massive case of guilt. None of which were helping anyone. Least of all, his daughter. He dragged his hands through his hair. "I'm sorry, Vince. Look, I didn't mean—"

"It's okay, man. I deserve it."

"No, you don't. Just tell me what we got? *Please* tell me we've got something."

"Well, we stopped for a snack right over there." Vince pointed over a passing throng of kids to the concession stand where the uniformed cop was still standing, searching. "I'd just bought her a soda and handed it off. I turned back to grab the hotdogs, but the guy behind the counter had a radio on. A news report caught my interest so I stood there and listened for twenty seconds, maybe thirty and when I turned back, she was gone. It's like she just walked off."

Oh, Lord. This didn't sound good. As he did so often when they flew together, Vince read his mind.

Part of if, anyway.

"Where's Samantha?"

He shook his head. "She's back at her place. Don't worry, I ordered the security detail inside the house, just in case." Sam hadn't been happy about the man's change of post, much less his request that she remain behind, but she'd understood his need to focus, had even anticipated it, telling him he had enough to worry about with finding Christy as she snatched his cell phone off the coffee table, shoving it in his hands as she shoved *him* out the door—her frantic order ringing in his ears: Get out of there and *go bring Christy home.*

He'd obeyed.

But he could still see her face. Her eyes. Her own guilt. Had

Christy taken off because of her? He'd mentioned that Sam lived nearby. Was she searching for him? The worst part was, they both actually hoped so. Prayed. It was better than the alternative. But what if she wasn't?

He refused to think that scenario through.

This was a stunt. Please God, a stunt.

Christy was in the fun house, hiding. In a bumper car screaming her head off with a friend she'd just met, or by some stroke of luck, had known in Ramstein. She was rocking in a seat at the top of that Ferris wheel fifty feet away or stuck inside one of those port-a-potties by the exit. She was *anywhere* but trapped in the horror he could see all too clearly in his heart.

"Vince, Griff!"

They spun around in time to catch Bailey of all people and her chain-smoking OSI sidekick vaulting the concrete barricades and barreling headlong into a horde of teenagers. They met the pair by the concession stand Vince had pointed out. The uniformed cop had headed down to the end of the counter, stopping at a cotton candy dispenser to meet up with a fellow officer.

Bailey bypassed Vince and gave him a hug. She was wiping her eyes as she pulled away. "Griff, I'm so sorry. We caught the call on the civilian scanner on base. Any word?"

"No. What about—"

She shook her head. "That's the first thing I thought of. Blackwell called on the way over. Doctor Novosti's still under surveillance in his house. He didn't take her."

"Hey, we got something!"

All four of them took off together toward the end of the concession stand. Griff didn't bother blaming his rolling stomach on the overpowering stench of spun sugar. He knew damned well it was pure, nauseating fear. The cop Vince had been talking to when he drove up waved his buddy closer.

"Captain Racey, we—"

Vince jerked his chin over to him. "This is Colonel Griff Towers, Christy's father."

The cop faced him, stuck out his hand. "Officer Banning. Sorry to meet you like this, sir."

Not as sorry as he was.

And, Jesus, this close up, the guy didn't look old enough to shave. This *kid* was going to find his baby girl?

Griff forced himself to guard his tongue until he had cause to loosen it. "You said you had something?"

"Yes, sir. We have a witness who claims he saw your daughter talking to a mature man with a heavy accent—like German or Russian. He couldn't place it. The witness says she seemed fine, too. Didn't look like she was under duress."

Alibek.

But that was impossible…or was it? Griff swung around to face Bailey. "Where's Alibek?"

"He's two hours south in Alamogordo, staying with that space museum buddy Samantha mentioned. They put a local FBI team on the house until we're ready to take down Novosti. I thought you were briefed. Hell, you're the one who demanded the protection be extended."

"Call the team. Make sure someone sees Alibek's face." Christy might know a hundred folks at least who spoke German, but something in his gut just wasn't buying that scenario. For one thing, as far as he knew, they were all still in Germany. On the other hand, aside from Vince and Bailey, Alibek was the only other person on the planet his daughter knew who spoke Russian. If she went willingly, that had to be significant. Vince caught his gaze as he turned back. The knot in his gut tightened as his buddy motioned him aside.

Away from the others.

He glanced at Bailey. He couldn't be sure if she'd seen the subtle gesture. "God dammit, Smirnoff, you gonna—"

"I'm on it!"

They spun apart in unison. She headed for Blackwell and he headed for Vince, careful to keep his voice well below the canned carnival music blaring down around them.

"What have you got?"

"It ain't good." It was more than Vince's tone. It was the look in his eyes. He'd seen it only three times before. The first, over the skies of Iraq while dodging half that country's arsenal as they roared in for that SF team, the second just before they'd slammed into that Russian lake and the third, while they were screaming towards that tank.

Griff braced himself.

"That news that I stopped to listen to?"

He nodded.

"It was breaking coverage of the discovery of a mass grave of Chechen terrorists located in the woods about a mile from that cabin we were holed up in. The area's had a deluge of rain this spring. Some local hunter stumbled across what was left. I had to concentrate because they had some Bambi reporter yakking in the foreground trampling over the hunter's Russian in the back. But I swear to God the man said there were only seven bodies in that grave."

"Yeah? What the—" Griff stiffened.

Seven bodies? The news conference he and Sam had caught in that hospital room in Ramstein claimed that seven Russian soldiers and *two more* Chechens terrorists had died in that firefight after they'd abandoned the cabin. So, where were the two extra Chechen bodies? But he knew.

And Vince was already nodding. "There were no Chechens at that cabin at all that day. Not while we were there. We killed a squad of Russian soldiers." Russian soldiers who'd been looking for them. They'd killed their own blessed rescue squad. Because Dimitri Alibek told them to.

Son of a bitch. "Someone lied."

Vince nodded. "Alibek."

Griff shook his head. "Someone else, too. Someone in a critical spot at the Kremlin. The conference came from them, straight from the Minister of Information. They must have made up the report to cover the deaths of those soldiers."

Russian soldiers who have wives, parents and children who'd eventually go looking for them otherwise.

Vince cursed.

Griff nodded again, even as the ice-cold dread slid right down into his belly. The Chechen separatists had been fighting for decades, looking for a bargaining chip they could toss Russia's way in exchange for Chechnya's self-determination.

"You don't think—"

"Griff!"

Unfortunately, he *did* think it. In fact, he knew it. It was in the sheer terror cracking into Bailey's face as she sprinted around a crush of teenagers and a pair of couples pushing strollers. She was panting and holding her side as Griff caught her.

"Alibek's not there, is he?"

"How did you—" She cut herself off. "Never mind. No, he's not. He fed his friend some sob story about having his heart broken and needing space. Asked the guy to cover for him if anyone calls. Which the guy did. But Griff…there's more."

Just like that, the dread slammed back.

But this time, it was colder than that first Anchorage winter without Samantha and every other winter he'd endured without her since. How he got her name past the iceberg in his throat, he'd never know. It must have seared its way through on the blisteringly fervent prayer that came with it. Even still, all he could manage was the first syllable.

"*Sam?*"

Bailey shook her head. "I'm so sorry. Samantha took a call after you left. After she hung up, she told the security detail she needed a shower. When I discovered Alibek was gone I called her house. The detail just checked. The shower was running, but the window was open, too. She's gone, Griff."

Sweet Jesus, *no!*

He was right. This hadn't been about Phil Haskell. Sam had been the key all along. Her boss had simply been murdered to get her on that plane. He'd bet he also knew who set that fire in that C130 three months before—the one type of airframe someone would dare set a fire to due to its survivability. Just as he knew the Chechen separatists and at least one minister at the Kremlin had finally settled on their bargaining chip— the only woman he'd ever loved. They'd kidnapped his daughter to lure Samantha into the middle of their deadly game.

But where the devil was the board?

Where were *they*?

"Bailey, see if—"

Griff froze—hell, they all did—as his cell phone shrilled, displacing the cacophony surrounding them for a brief, piercing moment. He ripped his cell phone from the small of his back and stared at the caller ID in disbelief. He stabbed the connection open and jerked the phone to his ear.

It was her.

But it *wasn't*.

Samantha's voice was distant, muffled. As if her own phone was nowhere near her mouth. He caught half a dozen words, tops. Unfortunately, together they made no sense at all. His gut fisted as he caught the sound of crying, too. Christy? But it was the distinctive mechanical resonance he heard reverberating in the background that ratcheted his terror in until his nerves were all but screaming. A split second later, Sam's voice grew fainter, the muffling worse.

And then the phone went dead.

He knew then, if he didn't act now, he'd never see Samantha or his daughter again.

She couldn't see.

Sam struggled to focus on the limousine seat beneath her cheek. She couldn't. Her vision was still too blurred and she was completely furious—with herself. She'd blown it. She'd jumped the gun in her panic and punched Griff's cell number into her phone too soon. Dimitri's thug had been too close. And now her phone had been seized and she'd been left holding her battered, throbbing skull instead. If Dimitri hadn't interceded, that bastard would have killed her. She'd seen it in the man's deep black eyes—just before she'd seen nothing at all. Dimitri must have pulled the thug off her.

Dimitri. Some friend. Some fiancé.

She'd been a commodity to him all along. She still was. Or rather, her brain was. It was the only thing he'd been protecting. But for now, she'd take it. Use it. At the very least to get Dimitri and his armed thug to let Christy go.

Think.

God, she was trying. But her head was still throbbing. Her ears still ringing. She raised her hand to shove her hair out of her eyes. To her surprise, both wrists came up. She blinked at the same type of zip cuffs Griff told her Bailey had used on Vince. No wonder Griff had had to cut him down. The more she twisted, the more the narrow plastic simply sliced into her wrists. She gave up and used both hands to probe the gash on her temple. It was still bleeding. She tried lifting her head from the blood washing the leather seat and blinked. She wasn't in the limo anymore. She was in the plane. She could make out the vague shapes of the King Air 350's plush interior. Or was it just wishful thinking?

"*Christy?*"

"I-I'm here, Dr. Hall—uh...S-Sam."

Relief seared in as she turned her head toward the girl's tremulous whisper. Dimitri's cohort had kept the girl in the front seat of the darkened limo when they'd forced her in the back blocks from her house. She couldn't quite see Christy, in part due to her fuzzy vision, the rest from the awkward bend to her neck. She tried propping herself up on her elbows, but with her wrists cuffed, the hem of her T-shirt tripped her up— the baggy one she'd dragged on just before crawling out her bathroom window into that thug's waiting arms. The ploy had worked, too. At first. The excess fabric had kept her cell phone concealed long enough to use it. Unfortunately, the thug had caught the faint sound of carnival music.

So much for Griff's belief in her brilliance.

She forced her thoughts into motion again anyway. She was pretty sure they weren't airborne, but with her ears still ringing and her stomach still churning, she didn't completely trust her senses. Not to mention all but one of the pleated shades on the King Air's row of windows were drawn. While that *one* was the closest to the door at the rear of the executive plane…it was the farthest from her. From the angle of her head, it was also impossible to view out. "Honey, I can't see very well. Are we still in the hangar?"

"Y-yes."

Thank God. Though…that didn't make sense. That Dimitri had obviously planned on keeping them in the hangar as long as possible did, but she'd heard the men discussing their imminent flight in the limo. That's why she'd called Griff. So why hadn't they taxied the plane out to the airstrip the base shared with Kirtland's International airport yet?

Griff. Had he heard enough after all?

She could only pray he had. Until then, they needed a weapon. Something to even the odds. For a moment, if nothing else. Something she could use to help the two of them, or at least allow Christy to get away. Unfortunately, she had no earthly clue as to what she could use. But her vision was clearing. Strengthening. She could make out those innocent features that reminded her so much of Griff. "Where are they? Dimitri and the other one?"

"In the cockpit. They're mad because the tower told them there was a delay."

Relief seared in again. "Can you help me up?"

Christy snuck out of her seat and crept towards her. Despite their respective bound wrists, they managed to get her upright in her seat. Sam forced a smile as Christy's face sharpened into focus, praying it was encouraging as the girl slipped back into her seat. They were in the middle of the cabin, on the same side, facing each other, but she was still facing the rear of the plane. Christy, the cockpit. She scanned the cabin slowly, looking for anything she could use as a weapon. The cabin was spotless.

Damn.

"They want you because you're smart, don't they?"

Sam swung her stare to Christy's. She'd have given anything to be able to calm the terror she'd heard threaded within that soft quaver, that she could still see in the girl's gaze. "Oh, honey, I'm so sorry you got caught up in this. But don't you worry. Your dad will find us in time. If he doesn't, we'll figure this out together, okay?"

Christy's nod was shaky. Her voice even shakier. "You love him, don't you? My dad?" Her gaze snuck past Sam's seat, toward the cockpit. "Mr. Alibek said that's why he had to kidnap you. Because you loved my dad and you wouldn't marry him like you were supposed to."

"Oh, baby." She couldn't lie to this little girl any more now than she could the night Christy had shown her the letter. "Yes, I love your dad. I've loved him for a long time."

"Then why did you tell him and me that you didn't want to marry him?"

Wow. This girl could pick the time and the place, not to mention the doozeys, couldn't she? Sam dragged her air in. So did Christy. Her gray eyes had watered, too. The ones that reminded Sam so much of someone else who filled her heart.

"It's…because of me, isn't it?"

Sam lurched forward, and not because of the whack she'd taken to her head, but the one she'd just taken to her heart. "Oh, no, sweetheart. I swear, what your dad and I have to work through has nothing to do with you. *Nothing.* It's grownup stuff, that's all. You're part of everything that's right about us. Everything that's good. I promise."

"Then, what's so bad?"

Even if the girl could understand, this wasn't the place. "Honey, I can't really explain it here. I wish I could, but it's very complicated." Hopefully, she'd forgive her.

To her surprise, Christy nodded. Solemnly. "He's coming."

She nodded, holding fast to the hope as well. "I know. I think I managed to call him—"

"Not my dad." The girl jerked her slender index finger toward the cockpit. "*Him.*"

"I see you've woken, Samantha."

Sam scowled as her ex-fiancé rounded the seat and knelt in front of her. "Dimitri."

He exchanged the 9 mm pistol in his hand with a small flashlight. He shined the light into her eyes and studied her pupils. "You don't appear to have lasting damage from Misha's enthusiasm. Excellent. How does your head feel?"

"Better than you will soon."

He smiled. "I doubt that. We've been given clearance. We shall be taxiing to the runway within minutes, my dear."

"*Don't* call me that."

Another of those damned smiles she'd once thought were so benign but now knew were anything but.

Dimitri Alibek—or whoever he really was—was a consummate actor. The man was a sleeper. A spy who spent years waiting for the right moment, the perfect mark, the most profitable reward. Then he was activated. The right moment it seemed, had been three months ago. The ideal mark, her. And the reward? Her life's work. The work Dimitri expected her to spend the rest of her life duplicating…in Russia. For Russia. And because of this phony bastard kneeling two feet away, pretending concern for her health, Phil Haskell was dead. Murdered. By a man she'd not only called a friend, she'd actually considered marrying. Griff was right. When it came to people, she was as gullible as they came. And no, it didn't help to know that no one else appeared to have seen through the man. Except Valentin of all people. That's why Dimitri had been setting him up and screwing up his experiments, too. To set up a fall guy if needed, but also to distract Valentin.

One more reason to hate Dimitri.

She was going to have to apologize to Valentin when Griff arrived. And Griff would arrive. He might not have shown up eleven years ago, but she knew in her soul he would be here today. In time. But until then, "Dimitri, let Christy go. Please, she's just a little girl."

"I cannot. I need her to keep you in line."

"He'll kill you if you take her. Either of us."

Who was she kidding? The man was a walking corpse now. Dimitri patted her cheek as he rose. "Believe it if you must." He smiled as she jerked her face from his fingers—and she realized why. Someone was opening the hangar doors. The King Air's twin propellers had kicked in too. They really had gotten clearance. Oh, God. If Griff waited much longer, it would be too late. She might not be able to see the cockpit, but she could feel the airframe shudder as the plane began moving. Taxiing. Out of the hangar and onto a runway.

A moment later, something caught her gaze beyond Dimitri's head and she stiffened.

Griff?

She blinked, prayed her vision wasn't acting up again. Stared. There, in the last window. The one directly forward of the King Air's locked door. It was definitely Griff!

He pressed a finger to his lips.

Then he was gone.

She snapped her gaze back to Dimitri before she could give Griff's presence away. Griff had warned her for a reason. He had a plan. What it was, she had no idea. All she knew was that all hell was about to break loose and he needed her ready. *Them* ready. She scanned the cabin as Dimitri returned to the cockpit, this time desperate for a weapon. Again, she spotted nothing she could use. She fused her attention on Christy, intent on warning the girl—and froze. Good Lord, was that really a…? It was. There was a Coke, tucked down at the side of her seat. It wasn't diet, but it would do. It wasn't bottled, either. It was canned.

Even better. And as yet, unopened.

Perfect.

Where the girl had gotten it, she didn't know. Right now, she didn't much care. But neither did she trust herself to stand. She was liable to fall flat on her face with her head still throbbing the way it was. "Christy, give me your soda."

The girl gaped at her.

"*Now.*"

Clearly confused, the girl complied, passing the lukewarm can from her bound hands to Sam's.

"Get back in your seat!"

Sam shook the soda up as rapidly and discreetly as she could, before he made his way around to her front, then tucked the unopened can beneath her baggy T-shirt as Dimitri bent down between them to secure Christy's seatbelt. He turned to secure hers. A split second later, all hell did break loose—*behind* her. Dimitri flinched as the approaching thunder reverberated through him, too. Not just any thunder. The same beautiful, rhythmically whopping noise they'd heard three months before beside that Russian lake. Now, like then, that thunder came from a set of composite main rotor blades powered by twin General Electric turboshafts. A UH-60G Pave Hawk.

Their new rescue chopper.

They might be on the civilian side of the Albuquerque airport, but that Pave Hawk was close. Very close.

Vince had to be flying it.

Bearing right down on the nose of the King Air.

She was sure when Dimitri cursed. A moment later, the plane's door blew off the bird. Smoke filled the compartment. She waited until Dimitri reached for the 9mm with his right hand and her with his left, then popped the top on the can and sprayed the soda directly into his eyes. He bellowed. And then

Griff was there, wrenching the man over the seats and dragging him down the center aisle toward the rear of the bird. Sam shot to her feet and scrambled forward to release Christy's buckle.

"Get down, Captain!"

She shoved the girl down to her seat and covered Christy's body as a bullet whizzed by her ear. Bailey and Blackwell barreled past next. She glanced up just in time to see Griff and Dimitri, fingers biting into each other's throats, tumble straight out the rear door of the plane.

She screamed.

A moment later, she heard the solid, unmistakable thwack of a skull on concrete. A skull that cracked, possibly open on that concrete. Unwilling to leave Christy behind, she hefted the girl's slight frame over her shoulder and raced down the aisle as fast as she could. Before she realized what had happened, she tripped over the mangled door, falling straight out of the plane, right down toward Griff's arms, with his daughter still in hers. Griff caught them both.

Dimitri lay at his feet, a scarlet stain spreading out beneath his skull.

Dead.

Almost an hour and a half passed before he was able to hold Samantha in his arms again.

An eternity.

But at least this eternity passed easier than the one he'd endured outside Samantha's hospital emergency room the afternoon before. For one thing, they'd let him remain inside the exam and x-ray rooms this time, almost directly beside her. And in between was his daughter, clinging not to him this time, but to both of them. He locked one of his hands to Christy's right while Samantha's slender fingers gripped his daughter's left. The best part was, he couldn't have said who was holding on tightest…of all three.

"You're free to go, Captain."

Griff glanced at the emergency room physician. "You're sure? She doesn't need to stay—"

"I'm fine, Griff. I just have a bit of a headache. Probably more from the stitches at this point than that whack."

Her doctor nodded. "She's right."

Relief swamped him. For a moment, Griff was afraid his knees had buckled. But then he realized it was his daughter, holding on so tight, she nearly pulled him down. He smiled down at his two ladies. Grinned. "Ready?"

Both beamed back. "Ready."

He helped Samantha down from the exam table while his daughter barreled out of the room and down the hall to where her Uncle Vince was still waiting. They followed at a more leisurely pace. To their surprise, Bailey was waiting as well. She stood as they approached. Vince scooped Christy up in his arms and kept going, out the emergency room's automatic doors and into the fading twilight. Griff knew then, they'd be getting a debrief.

Bailey nodded to him and extended her hand to Sam. "Excellent work today, Dr. Hall."

Sam flushed as she returned the agent's grip.

He knew why. She was still embarrassed she'd tumbled headlong out of the plane with Christy in her arms. He didn't have the heart to tell her his presence at the base wasn't chance. He knew damned well what would be happening next if he hadn't dusted himself off after Alibek's demise and planted himself beneath that door. He didn't have the heart to tease her. She'd had a rough enough day. Hell, a rough enough week.

So had he.

All he wanted to do now was figure out a way to curl up on the couch with his ladies on either side and relax. Breathe. Draft his remaining humble thanks to the good Lord up above. Until it was time to send Christy to bed, that is. Then, he had other plans. Hopes. Prayers. Ones that involved— He searched the front pocket of his jeans. It wasn't there. Had he left it at Samantha's house? In the Pave Hawk? Either hangar? He forced himself to stop looking, to cease panicking. At least for the moment as Bailey held up a slim file.

"This is all I can give you."

He waited as Sam opened the file. There was a single sheet inside. Part of an OSI initial debrief. At least half the page had been inked out. Bailey tapped the first line that was still legible. "We got most of this from Dimitri's Russian counterpart on the plane. A Misha Babin."

Sam's brow shot up. "*Russian* counterpart?"

Bailey nodded. "You were right. Dimitri was a sleeper. Chechen. He struck a deal with someone. Your knowledge and your work was the currency. Unfortunately, we don't know who that someone was. But we will. I will. Eventually." Griff didn't doubt the woman for a second.

From her expression, neither did Sam.

Bailey continued, "According to Misha, marriage had been Dimitri's goal all along—but only to get you to Russia for a purported honeymoon. It was the only way Dimitri believed someone with your background and security clearance would ever be allowed to cross the Russian boarder, except on official, full-out protected government business. But ultimately, kidnapping would have come into play, too, had those marriage plans been a success. However, failing marriage, Dimitri decided to ensure your presence aboard the C130 by murdering Phil Haskell. He also arranged to have the halon system sabotaged and, we think, set the fire to the cargo hold himself while he was out of your sight. That in turn forced the C130 down over Russian soil. Unfortunately, the pilot held the plane aloft longer than Dimitri anticipated. The Chechen separatists who shot down Colonel Tower's bird weren't able to track your group to the cabin in time to kidnap you. Like I said, that's as much as I can give you. I hope it's enough and, of course, I must ask you to keep it to yourself."

Sam tightened her grip on his hand. They both nodded. There wasn't much else they could do.

Bailey smiled. "I also have a message for you. You too, Colonel. Stringer found the program tampering right where you thought it would be. I'm to tell you, he's impressed. So, Colonel—Griff—you're off the hook for both incidents. I've already spoken to the board. They agree. In fact, I'm also authorized to tell you there was never any question as to your flight status or your abilities. The board simply agreed to help us smoke out whoever had killed Phil and sabotaged the bird." She shrugged. "I knew Vince would call me."

His grip tightened instinctively on Sam's hand. Griff forced himself to loosen it. Then, he just let it go—Bailey's statements, the information—not Samantha's hand. The anger wasn't worth it. A few days embarrassment around base was nothing compared to this woman's life.

He nodded. "Understood. But you owe me now."

Bailey nodded. "How about I subject myself to your friend's company for the night and offer to baby sit your daughter?"

"*No.*"

Bailey's brow shot up along with his. They both stared at Sam. She shook her head firmly. "I want her home with us tonight. If it's okay with you…and her."

"Why don't you ask her?" He nudged her toward the doors. His daughter and friend had returned. They'd both heard.

Christy was grinning. Beaming.

She was also holding on to something. "I…found this under the plane, Dad." He stared at his daughter as her smile eased into shyness he knew she rarely felt. She held up the teak box. From the glint in her eyes, she knew what was in it. Even more incredibly, she seemed okay with the knowledge.

Very okay with it. Approving.

Christy stepped forward as Bailey retrieved the folder she'd handed Sam and tucked it beneath her arm as she in turn headed toward Vince. To Griff's surprise, Christy placed the box in his hand, then reached for Sam's and laid it over the top. "But maybe I should have dinner with Uncle Vince first?"

"Sure." His voice was hoarse.

Couldn't have been from the lump in his throat. But when his daughter tugged on the tail to the T-shirt he'd donned in Samantha's bedroom hours before, so she could tiptoe up and reach his ear, he knew it was.

"Keep it simple, Dad. Okay?"

Her stage whisper was loud enough for the whole blessed ER to hear. Fortunately the waiting room was relatively empty.

"I will…pumpkin."

She glared, but she let it go. Mostly because she'd left. His ten-and-a-half, going on thirty-year-old daughter had already looped her arms through Bailey's and Vince's and lead them through the automatic doors.

Griff waited until the doors whooshed shut, then turned. He slowly opened the box and held it out. Then stared into those mesmerizing, glistening eyes and he began to lower himself to his knees. Again, just as he had all those years ago.

His heart fisted as she stopped him.

Several strands of silk caught over those awful stitches at her temple as she shook her head. Just like that, the horror of the night ripped through him once more—until she smiled. "She said to keep it simple, Colonel."

He followed that soft gold gaze to the double doors. To where his daughter stood with their friends, waiting.

Watching.

He straightened. Turned back to the love and desire he'd waited so long to see burn openly again. Then he removed from the velvet bed the ring he'd discovered at an estate sale outside Austin all those years ago and had somehow managed to purchase and get resized without this woman noticing. He held the pink antique diamond between them silently. But his heart was pounding louder than the blades atop every single one of the choppers under his command *together* as Samantha held out her slender hand and allowed him to slide the ring onto her finger for the very first time. Griff pulled her into his arms beneath his daughter's stare and lowered his head, slowly capturing the lips of the woman he loved and needed more than the blood coursing through his veins. He took his time, slowly but thoroughly, asking the question that had been burning in his heart and in his soul for the past eleven years. By the time he finished, her lips had long since answered.

Yes.

* * * * *

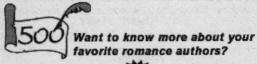

From *USA TODAY* bestselling author

MERLINE LOVELACE

Trained to put their lives on the line.
Their hearts were another matter....

A Question of Intent
(Silhouette Intimate Moments #1255,
November 2003)

Full Throttle
(Silhouette Desire #1556, January 2004)

The Right Stuff
(Silhouette Intimate Moments #1279, March 2004)

Available at your favorite retail outlet.

Where love comes alive™

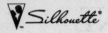

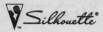

COMING NEXT MONTH